Legend of the Oracle Runes
1

NORNIEN ODYSSEY

A fantasy novel
by Debbie Stansfield

CONTENTS

Debbie Stansfield is the author of Legend of the Oracle runes and various other novels. When she is not lost in her next writing idea, she enjoys gardening, playing games and spending time with family. To learn more visit oraclerunes.wordpress.com

Legend of the Oracle Runes
1

NORNIEN ODYSSEY

A fantasy novel
by Debbie Stansfield

Chapter 1

The Beginning

In the village of McLeod's there lived a young girl with a big secret. If you were to look at her though, you would never say that she was in anyway special or different. In truth, she was a witch. If she were among a crowd, you would never think that she was any different from those around her.

And that was okay with her, although she was getting tired of having to always hide her powers from everyone. Sometimes her biggest wish was to walk around with everyone knowing her truth without having to worry that she would be stoned to death. For now, she had to accept that it would not change anytime soon.

At least she had the Fairies and other magical Creatures where she could be herself without having to worry that someone would notice. When her parents were murdered, she was sent to the Fairy Queen who raised her. At first, she had struggled to adapt, but everyone had been patient with her and willing to help.

Even though she kept mostly to herself, she got quite a bit

of unwanted attention because of her physical appearance. She had her mother's beautiful long brown hair and lips, as well as her father's piercing grey eyes and nose. Even though she did not agree, everyone always remarked about her good looks to her.

A number of young men in the village liked her but she only had feelings for Justin, the stable boy. Unfortunately, he was only interested in his work and did not notice her at all. She decided it was a good idea that she cleaned her house now, instead of having to do it when she got back. She stepped back after she had done what was necessary and smiled. It was worth it even if it wasn't always pleasurable.

As she stepped out of the front door she realised for not the first time that as much as she tried keeping to herself, everyone still knew her.

"Good day, Alexandria!" Luanda, the butcher's daughter, asked smiling. "How are you on this beautiful sunshine day?"

"I am well, thank you. I must say, you are absolutely glowing today! I assume that you are well?"

"I am fantastic. You will never in a million years guess what happened last night!"

"Do tell. You have me absolutely curious."

"Michael asked my parents for my hand in marriage and

they said yes! I have been in the clouds ever since."

"That is wonderful news and I am so happy for you, my friend."

"Thank you, I am very excited!"

Giving the girl a hug and congratulating her once more on her engagement, Alexandria continued walking. She had only walked a few steps when Eric stepped into her path.

Eric was known as one of the most enthusiastic young men in the village. The Mayor, or King as he proclaimed, had assigned him as the Court Jester. If he was not by the Mayor's side entertaining those around him, he was running around the village making everyone laugh.

"Good morrow miss," Eric greeted, grinning. "May I enquire as to where you are off to on such a wonderful morning? You seem to be in such a hurry that you are missing all that is going on around you."

"Yes, you may enquire good Sir. I'm just going for a long walk."

"It is *not* Sir, it is Sir Court Jester."

"Oh, how silly of me, of course. Sir Court Jester!" she replied, giggling before walking away.

She reached the market and walked through the stalls, humming softly while looking at all the villagers trying to sell their fares. She stopped at the bakers table and chose some freshly baked goods, handing over the money with a smile. At the next stall she picked up a bag filled with nuts and dates that she could hand to the bakers in the forest. She knew they always appreciated the effort she went through to bring them things from the village.

Out of the corner of her eye, she noticed that Justin was not far from her as she paid for the goods. He seemed to be arguing with another villager over something that was making him terribly upset. Shrugging, she continued on her way to the edge of the village, just out of sight of the people wandering around. Placing her things down on a rock she carefully looked around to make sure that she would not be caught.

When she was absolutely sure there was no one around she closed her eyes and concentrated hard. She felt the welcome shiver running down her spine as she transformed into an eagle, soaring into the sky. Diving down, she grabbed her things up in her claws, soaring higher so that she could stretch her wings and observe the village as she normally did.

She turned towards the forest and noticed Justin saddling up his horse, but quickly dismissed the scene. Her mind was already on the fresh water of the waterfall. Diving in and out between the trees, allowing nature to surround her, she cleared her mind of all her worries. This was no time for worries. She heard shouting from the scouts who spotted her arrival.

Grinning to herself as she flew straight through the waterfall, she landed gracefully and changed back into her human form.

"One of these days the scouts of Antithia will shoot you down!" a voice said from behind her. "Or perhaps one of the unicorns will stab you with their horns. Or maybe the fairies will even mistake you for a real eagle and capture you, and keep you as their pet. Be that as it may, welcome back my sister and friend."

"Oh Amethyst! You know very well that they would never do that. They like me too much! You also know that the unicorns never use their horns for violence, unless they have no other choice. As for the scouts, I think that after so many years they would not mistake me for an intruder."

"Darn it, and here I thought you would make an excellent pet," Amethyst replied with a wry smile.

"I missed you and your unique sense of humour."

"You were here yesterday, and the day before yesterday and the day before that!" Amethyst said grinning. "But I assure you that you were missed as well. Just as long as you remember that the fairies and I are always here for you."

"Thank you for that Am, it means the world to me. Truth be told I do not think the village will ever truly feel like home without my parents."

"I would tell you to move here if it was safe, but we both

know that if the villagers suspected that the magical Creatures had anything to do with your sudden disappearance, they may want to take revenge and come here, if not burn the entire forest down. You know that they are not very trusting."

"I know that all too well," she agreed. "Can you believe that the Mayor put out a notice that unicorns are evil and that they feed on human souls? If it wasn't so sad, I would have laughed until my stomach hurt."

"Oh, that old windbag does not know the difference between the smell of his own farts and roses," Amethyst said, causing her to giggle.

"Thank you for making me smile. I really get too serious at times."

"My pleasure! You are one of the few people that understand my humour at times. Rather humiliating when the fairies stare at me blankly and then laugh as though they actually get it."

"I get your sense of humour, because we basically grew up together," Alexandria said, her voice changing to a more serious undertone. "It was a terrible event that brought me to your mother's doorstep, but she invited me in with open arms. That means the world to me. I even appreciate you, even though you tried to kill me most of the time."

"I was not trying to kill you. I was determined to teach you a life lesson!"

"Right; when you figure out what that life lesson is please let me know," Alexandria replied, giggling and picking up a story book.

"That was my mom's favourite book. Do you remember how many times she read it to us? She always found a way to make it seem like a brand-new book each time."

"Oh, I remember alright, I also remember when we hid the book and she panicked because she could not find it."

"If my mother was still alive, I am sure that she would be completely grey by now. We gave her so much grief."

"I don't doubt that at all! Although she would have made it look like the best thing."

"I miss her a lot, you know," Amethyst confessed, bowing her head in thought. "I sometimes wake up screaming for her and I have to calm myself down before the guards come storming in. If only there was a way that I could turn back time and stop her murder from happening."

"What the Centaurs did was cold blooded and heartless. She did not deserve to die."

"That was one of the main reasons why I decided to ban them from the forest as well as the surrounding area. Not that I think they listened."

"They only listen to their leader," Alexandria reminded her.

"Is there any other news besides the silly leader thinking that unicorns are soul-sucking beasts?"

"Everything is quiet and I have not heard whispers of anything that might make us worry,"

"To tell you the truth, I did not expect whoever is attacking us and the other magical Creatures to attack the mortals as well. It would be rather stupid and cocky of them."

"They would then reveal who they are and it seems that is not what they want."

"It would be counterproductive in their eyes I am sure," Amethyst said thoughtfully. "How I wish that they would stop being cowards and just show themselves."

"It is easier for them right now to attack the Creatures when they are on their own and not in a group. They would consider it easy pickings."

"If I could stop it I would, but there is nothing I can do."

"We cannot perform miracles, Am. But I do agree that we need to put a stop to the attacks before they get out of hand."

"I think so too, Alex. But the problem is, how do we do to stop them?"

"I have been thinking that I should go looking for these beasts."

"There is no way that I will allow you to go looking for these Creatures on your own!" Amethyst shouted, startled by her comment. "They are way too dangerous and it would be like giving them a free kill."

"I'm not exactly defenseless and you know it," Alexandria said, winking at the fairy.

"I know that very well, but it does not mean that I wish to lose more friends or family to them. If anything gets done about this, we will do it smartly and with a definite plan of attack."

"What if we have no time for figuring out a plan?"

"Amethyst! Amethyst! Trolls are on their way here!" a fairy shouted as she burst through the water.

"Uh-oh," Amethyst said, flying through the waterfall to stand on a rock and look towards the forest.

Alexandria quickly ran after Amethyst and jumped out from the curtaining water and landed next to her friend, ready to fight if necessary. It seemed to take forever for the trolls to emerge from the forest. Alex gathered all her energy, ready to attack the trolls if they made a threatening move or if it looked as though they were there for any other reason besides to talk.

"WAIT!!!" the one troll shouted suddenly. "We will not attack you. We need the witch's help!"

"And why should we believe you?" one of the braver fairies asked.

"Sssh, Tagitha!" Amethyst soothed.

"We would have attacked you already if we wanted to hurt

you. We would not stand here like a bunch of cowards in front of a witch and fairies, begging for help," another troll grumbled.

"Let us hear them out," Alexandria said after swiftly looking at Amethyst.

"We will hear them out. If we do not like what they have to say, I am sure that they would leave peacefully," Amethyst said looking at the trolls.

"Of course we will," the same troll said. "I am the leader, my name Grograncha, or Grog if you prefer."

"Nice to... err... meet you Grog. I am the queen of the fairies, Amethyst," the fairy introduced before pointing to the human. "And this is Alexandria."

"Nice to meet Queen Amethyst. And of course, Alexandria. We have heard so much about you and your powers."

"Charmed, I'm sure," Alexandria said smiling slightly.

"So how can we help you and your pack, Grog?" Amethyst asked.

"Like we said, we need the witch's help," the troll answered. "Our cave got attacked by the menace that is roaming the land."

"Then you know what it is threatening our land and all of the Creatures?"

"Unfortunately, we do not. They used some kind of sleeping mist to ensure we could not defend ourselves or even stop them. But there are a lot of hoof prints near the cave that we do not recognize."

"That could be men on horses," Alexandria observed.

"We are not sure and that is why we came to ask for your help," Grog said imploringly. "Maybe if they are mortals, you could find out who exactly they are and talk to them and try to convince them to leave the forest. This fighting has gone far enough. It has caused so many unnecessary deaths. I am sure that if you talked to them, Alexandria, that they would listen to you."

"I doubt that it is mortals," Alexandria replied. "I would have heard it in the village if it was so and I have not heard anything that would make me suspicious. The whole town would be full of people talking about the attacks, as they would find it an accomplishment."

"We disagree with you on that remark. As you know the two communities have a truce not to meddle in the other's business. Maybe some of the mortals are tired of all the magical Creatures and are trying to rid the world of anything that is magical. The rebellion group could have a leader of their own."

"No, the village people stand together," Alexandria said. "All of them would know if someone had planned an attack on the magical Creatures. They would stick together and not let people go out there on their own."

"Alex is right," Amethyst confirmed. "The villagers are a close-knit group that would support each other if there were fighting involved."

"Very well, then we believe you. We thought that it was perhaps humans because of the hoof prints we saw," Grog said.

"There are other hoofed Creatures besides horses, you know," Alexandria said suddenly.

"Lexie, if you mean the Centaurs, you know as well as I do that they have been banished from the forest. They had to go find themselves another home."

"And that was not by choice Amethyst, you know it. They did not want to go. Perhaps they wanted to get revenge and decided the best way to do that, in their eyes, is to attack the magical Creatures. Besides... not so long ago you mentioned that you doubt they listened."

"I may have said it, but I still do not want to believe it."

"It was just an idea; maybe it isn't them. But would it not be for the best if we prepared for the worst?"

"There is no maybe about it," Amethyst replied. "And any battle that would result in war would be preparing for the worst."

"Okay if you say it is not centaurs, then I will go along with you very grudgingly. I have my personal opinions nevertheless."

"Now, if you do not mind," Grog said unexpectedly, "we would like to get back to us."

"Yes! Sorry about that," Amethyst replied, embarrassed. "We got a bit carried away on that topic."

"Will you help us, Alex?" Grog asked.

"Yes, I will help you," Alexandria answered not looking at Amethyst. "It will help not only you, but all the other magical Creatures. So, I will help you without a doubt."

"I told you earlier I that I will not let you go, Alex!" Amethyst burst out, incensed. "I will not allow you to go on your own it is too dangerous."

"I will be okay, Amethyst. I am a witch after all, and a powerful witch at that. Your mother said it herself."

"I am not denying that you are powerful, Alex, but you still cannot go on your own. It will still be a very dangerous trip." Amethyst looked at the trolls. "I am sorry if I offended you. But it is true."

"That is fine, your majesty. If you can come up with a solution so that she is not alone then we are willing to go along with it," Grog said.

"She will not be travelling alone!" a male voice called out from between the trees. "She will have a travel companion throughout the entire mission."

All the fairies, including Amethyst, flew into hiding places among the trees and flowers. They did not recognize the new voice and it was dangerous for them if it was someone that wished them harm. Alexandria turned toward the sound of the voice, noticing from the corner of her eye that the trolls also turned in that direction. The trolls grumbled and grunted angrily when they saw that it was a human man.

"Justin?" Alexandria asked in bewilderment.

"I never knew how interesting this part of the forest was until now," Justin said as he jumped off his horse. "I have been in Pecan forest before but not here. And I never knew that you would be hanging around in such a dangerous place miss..? I am sorry, what is your name again?"

"It is Alexandria," she said, pausing to look into his eyes for signs of malicious intent. "And what exactly do you know about me?"

"Just that you seem to love horses a lot. You walk by the stalls every morning and evening. Pausing for a few minutes before continuing on with your day."

"And you think you know me by observing my every move? You are so wrapped up in your work that I am surprised you even noticed that little detail."

"Oh, you would be surprised to know that I see quite a bit," Justin said, smiling slightly. "What I do not see, unfortunately, is how a young woman like yourself would walk around a magical forest on your own. Have your parents not taught you that this is a very dangerous place?"

"What do you mean '*a young woman like me*'?"

"I did not mean anything appalling. I am just stating a reality."

"Alex? Who is this handsome young man?" Amethyst asked cautiously, reappearing from her cave and landing next to Alexandria

"Amethyst, this is Justin, the guy I told you about a while ago. Justin this is Amethyst, the fairy queen and general ruler of the forest."

"Whoa! I did not know that there really were still any fairies left or any of these magnificent Creatures!" Justin said. "I thought it was just a myth concocted by parents to tell their children. I mean, there are unicorns right there!"

"We are quite real, we just prefer to keep to ourselves," Amethyst said "We strive to tell the tales of our adventures, but we do not interfere. The laws that my late grandmother and the mayor of your village agreed upon keep us from going into the village, and as a matter of a fact the humans from entering the forest."

"And what does the law say about hanging around with trolls?" Justin commented. "Well, I never thought that Creatures of light would hang around with the foulest

Creatures on the earth. Especially if the legends are true, then they are some of the most dangerous Creatures there are."

The trolls glared at Justin and stalked closer threateningly.

"Grog, stop right there," Alexandria said, stepping in front of them. "He is just a mortal after all. He cannot do a lot of damage to anyone. What does he know of any of the magical Creatures except of what he has heard or what he's read? We know that you are not foul. You standing right here and having a decent conversation with us is proof enough of that."

"I take that as an insult, I will have you know!" Justin said outraged.

"It is the truth, not an insult. I cannot help if humans are so ignorant towards what is right in front of them. And you are just a human."

"And what do you call yourself if not human? A magical creature maybe?"

"Of course, she is not saying anything like that," Amethyst interjected, looking meaningfully at Alexandria. "She is, of course, just a human, like yourself. She is just a bit more knowledgeable about the magical world than you."

"Yes, that is what I meant," Alexandria added.

"Okay, so then it is Alex and this young human who will help us to find out who has been attacking the Creatures?" Grog asked getting impatient. "we are getting strange vibes from them, so we aren't sure whether we feel completely safe with that."

"No, it will just be me who will help you," Alexandria said, receiving an elbow nudge from Amethyst. "And of course, Justin who will help you, as we seriously need to find out who is attacking the Creatures. And two heads are better than one, naturally."

"This will be interesting to say the least," Amethyst said smiling. "But it will of course help to save the forest and all the magical Creatures.".

Alexandria pulled Amethyst to the side.

"I would not be able to use my powers in front of him," Alexandria whispered to the fairy. "And that could put us in even more trouble than we already are. I may really like him, but I'm sure that you noticed how much we are fighting. We would not listen to each other at all if we bicker the whole time, and that could be just as dangerous as it would distract us from what we are supposed to be doing."

"You can try using your powers when he is not looking. And you are only fighting with him because you have strong feelings for him, that's all. It is quite understandable that you would quarrel a bit."

"And how does quarrelling help us exactly?"

"You will see as your journey progresses what I mean,"

Amethyst hinted. "It may turn out better than you think."

"Amethyst, that is not fair! How can anything work out if I am stuck with the man I love... Okay, maybe love is a strong word. And it would be great being on a trip together if he felt the same about me as I feel towards him."

"How do you know he does not feel the same way about you as you feel about him?" Amethyst asked, amused by the change in conversation. "Have you asked him how he feels?"

"I just know it. I just get a feeling that he does not like me in that way or at all for that matter!"

"Excuse me for interrupting your conversation," Justin said suddenly, causing Alexandria's heart to flutter in fright and embarrassment. "But we really do need to make plans for the trip."

"Yes, you are right of course, we do need to make plans for your trip," Amethyst said rubbing her head thinking.

"Now, do you have a horse that you can travel on Alex?" Justin asked. "It would make the journey go a lot faster and easier than if we were to travel on foot."

"No, I do not have a horse," Alex said, frowning. "The horse my family owned disappeared along with my family."

"I am sorry; I did not know that you have lost your family," Justin replied, looking down and feeling ashamed. "Also, sorry for my earlier comment. How exactly do you want to get to the trolls cave if you do not have a horse to travel on?"

"I was going to fl... I mean... walk there."

"That could be very dangerous, you know," Justin warned her.

"I know all the Creatures that live in the forest," Alexandria informed him haughtily. "I also know the whole forest like the back of my hand. I could get there quicker than you could, horse or not."

"I doubt that you could do that; not on foot."

"You can believe Alex, Justin," Amethyst defended her "She essentially grew up in the forest with all the fairies and other magical Creatures. And she does know the forest really well, having run through it as a child."

"If you say so. Not that I believe you, but ok."

"So, do you have any provisions that we can take with us?" Alexandria asked Amethyst.

"Everything you may need we can provide and most of the things are available in the forest," Amethyst replied.

"Thank you, that is really appreciated, your majesty," Justin added, smiling at them.

"It would only be a pleasure to help you on your mission as much as possible, Justin; it might just save the forest and the whole world for that matter."

"Sorry to interrupt, but can we get a word in please?" Grog

suddenly asked, startling Justin and Alexandria. "As you have seemed to have forgotten about us."

"Of course you can Grog," Alexandria replied.

"We do not think that it is a good idea for a mortal to wander into the forest alone. There are too many other magical Creatures that could cause trouble. We of course, would not make trouble as he will be helping us."

"But he will not be alone; he will be with Alex," Amethyst said, leaping to the defense again "And everyone knows her and they would not mess with her or start trouble."

"It is still risky. Are you sure you want to take that risk?"

"I will be fine," Justin commented, staring at them with a warning in his eyes. "I do not need some female who has a high opinion of herself to look after me."

"I am not just some female," Alex muttered.

"Okay, how about you two start this journey of yours tomorrow morning?" Amethyst suggested. "It is getting a bit late and it would not make sense if you started now as you would have to set up camp only a few hours into your journey."

"That is a good idea," Justin agreed "I really should get going for now. I have to tend to the other horses and stuff. I will see you again tomorrow, your majesty. Alexandria."

Justin said bowing slightly jumping on his horse's back.

"Bye Justin. See you tomorrow morning."

They watched as he rode off into the forest and back towards the village.

"I cannot believe this!" Alex exploded in rage, rising into the air a few inches off the ground. "I will not be able to go through with this journey with Justin. It is going to be a big mistake if we go through with this."

"Calm down Alex. He is just going to help you, and us for goodness sake."

"I wanted to do this alone, Am. Not get help from the man I like and who seems to hate me. And it is not that I think I am superior or anything."

"He does not hate you, Alex," the fairy said, trying to calm her down.

"He is definitely not showing that he likes me. He thinks I am... I am full of myself. And you know I am not."

"Yes, I know you are not Alex, and isn't that all that matters?"

"We also have to go," Grog said. Amethyst and Alex looked at them as they prepared to leave "We will see you at our cave when you get there, Alex."

"Okay, Grog, see you then," Alexandria said as she lowered her powers and settled back down onto the ground.

"Bye your majesty, enjoy the rest of your evening."

"Bye Grog. Travel safe," Amethyst greeted.

"Thanks, your majesty. We will do our best."

"Do you want to eat with us tonight, Alex?" Amethyst asked as the trolls walked into the forest "The fairies are making a special dinner which, in the craziness with the trolls and Justin, I completely forgot to tell you about."

"Yes, thank you Amethyst," Alex replied and they both returned to the cave.

Some of the fairies were already busy making food when they arrived. Tagitha bought the two of them something to drink with a distant smile on her face.

"Thank you, Tagitha."

"You are welcome, Amethyst," the fairy replied, with the honour of serving her queen shining on her face.

"Why do you think that Justin hates you, Alex?" Amethyst said, carefully approaching the topic. "You should be able to see if he hates you or not. Why do you not just look at his thoughts?"

"I tried doing that, Amethyst," she replied, "but for some reason I am not able to see what lies within his mind."

"That is very strange," Amethyst said with concern written over her expression. "He would have to be able to block his thoughts or be really powerful to prevent you from seeing his thoughts. I cannot see how he would be able to do either of those."

"Yeah it is very strange. I guess he is blocking his thoughts some way or another, otherwise I would be able to see it. The bigger question is, why is he doing it? What is he hiding?"

"Perhaps all humans have some kind of hidden ability that remains hidden to everyone but themselves," Amethyst said thoughtfully as the other fairies put the food in front of them.

"Yeah I guess they do," Alex said nodding. "Amethyst this looks delicious! I have not seen such a wonderful meal in quite a while."

"I am so used to all this luxury; I think I have gained some weight actually," Amethyst said sheepishly. "The fairy cooks are wonderful though, so I would not complain at all. As long as they do not mind an overweight Queen."

"Yes, I would be able to get used to it as well," Alexandria said giggling. "And there is no way that you could get fat, Am. And even if you were, they would still love you."

They spent the evening speaking until late into the night laughing and reminiscing about when they were younger. Alexandria was enjoying her fairy friend's company that she almost forgot that the night was getting away with them.

"Well I should better get home before it gets too late and before the people get suspicious," Alex said, hugging Amethyst.

"Have a wonderful night and I will see you tomorrow morning my friend," Amethyst replied.

"Bye Amethyst; you have a wonderful night too and see you in the morrow." Alex turned towards the entrance before running and jumping off the edge, and turning into an eagle.

She flew back over the forest looking down to the forest floor and wondering what kind of animals were running around. Suddenly without warning, she thought she saw a wolf running, but when she looked again it had disappeared between the trees.

She shook her head slightly and reminding herself that they had not seen any wolves in the forest for years. Looking up into the sky and at the stars she felt at peace with herself and everything around her, a song singing in her heart.

She loved flying during night time. She found it relaxing and it was as though the problems of the world faded away. Deciding she was a bit calmer than when Justin had appeared at the waterfall, she flew to a clear space near the village, once again making sure that no one was around before turning back into her human self.

While walking through the quiet village and towards her house everything seemed so peaceful, as if the events of earlier and the last few weeks could not really have happened. Unlocking her front door, she walked inside and closed the door behind her.

She sat down at the table and looked around her small place. It was nothing special, just a small living space that her parents had left for her when they had disappeared. It had two bedrooms, a small kitchen, living room, a small bathroom and then the smaller exterior room her father had turned into a work space.

Her mother had always told her that she had asked her father to convert the room into a space where she could work. Instead of listening to her, her father had made a space where *he* could work.

Alexandria stopped her observations as she got a sense of foreboding. Something was going to happen and she did not know what. There was no way that she could prevent it. It felt almost like a premonition, but not a proper one. It did not show her what was going to happen, just felt that it was going cause a lot of trouble for her, for them... humans and magical Creatures alike.

And there was no way for her to stop it from happening...

* * *

Justin watched Alexandria walking past the stables that night. He did not call to her. When he was sure that she could not see him, he walked to the back of the stall and towards the edge of the forest. There just out of the faint light the moon was casting on the area was one of the beings that were responsible for the attacks on the Creatures.

"Good work," the leader said to him. "I must say I am very impressed with what you did tonight. I never thought that you would ever succeed in gaining the witch's trust."

"It was easier to gain her trust that we thought, especially with the fairy queen's help," Justin said, very satisfied with himself "She is so trusting and pure, and she fell for my act without any problems or questions."

"I am happy that everything went well my son. You have not disappointed me... thus far."

"I try to be as good as you would want me to be father, and how you have trained me to be."

"Maybe one day you will be able to take over successfully and make me and your grandfather proud. And I would not have to worry about leaving my clan in the hands of an imbecile."

"I will try my best not to disappoint you father, and I promise, when I do take over the clan, that it will be as prosperous as though they were still in your or grandfather's hands."

"That is good to know. And you better not disappoint me,

Justin. Now what plans did you and the witch make?"

"We are scheduled to meet at the waterfall in the morning. From there we will start to travel and search for the 'evil' beings that are responsible for attacking the poor innocent Creatures. Eventually we will end up at the troll caves as they need our help."

"And you know what your job is. Until further notice you are to keep her from us, stall her for as long as possible."

"Yes father, I will keep her occupied as long as is possible. She will not know who is responsible for the attacks until it is too late for her to stop any of our plans."

"Good," his father said, pleased. "The centaurs will not be banished just like that and not be expected to get their revenge against those responsible for the banishment."

"That is true. Getting revenge and getting the forest back is the most important task at the moment. Once we have reached that objective, we can live better lives like we did before the banishment."

"The centaurs will rule the forest once again. I refuse to be shunted to one side like a worthless dog."

"We will not get shunted father; no one has the right to do that to us and get away with it. The last time we could not really defend ourselves as we were powerless, but this time is going to be very different."

"Okay, good," his father said, pride filling his eyes. "I am glad to know that you are taking an interest in our welfare. Be careful not to be discovered by the witch though. It could just cause a lot of unnecessary trouble for us. And we do not want that... not yet anyway. We will in our time decide when we will reveal ourselves to them."

"I will not be discovered father, I promise you that. I will pretend to be the helpful guy they think I am. Although I will always be on the side of evil. This is the best side to be on. By the time they find out that I am not on their side it will be too late for them to stop."

"Now go get some rest. You will need it for the journey ahead."

"Yes father, you are right, of course," Justin said as he watched his father retreat. Walking back to the stables and his *home*, he smiled an evil smile, already prepared for the next day...

Chapter 2

The Journey

The next morning, she woke up earlier than usual to make sure that she would be ready to start the journey with Justin. She was not very happy about the fact that they were being forced into working together to find those responsible for the attacks, but she had no argument against it. Amethyst did not want her to do this on her own and she would fight tooth and nail against it. They were after all determined stop the killings.

As she looked around her house, she wondered how she would be able to use her powers without Justin noticing. It would be problematic if he found out as she was sure that he would run to the villagers with the news. Perhaps if she believed really hard there would be no use for her to use her powers, it would make it easier.

She shook her head knowing that something would always happen which would force her to use her powers, but she vowed that she would only use it when and if there was no other choice. Biting her lip, she walked thoughtfully into the kitchen to pack a few things that they might need, filling her canvas bag with nuts and bread.

She knew that if she missed anything Amethyst would have it for them and, if push came to shove, they would be able to collect a few things from the forest. As she stepped into the early morning sun, she felt that same feeling of foreboding that she had the previous night. She shook it off as she closed the door to her home.

This was not the time for her to start doubting herself and what she was able to achieve. As she walked through the quiet village she glanced around, she thought about how times had changed from when she had lived here with her parents. Everything seemed to be the same, but she knew that underneath it all there was a dark secret brewing. She reached the edge of the village, turned into an eagle once again and flew into the sky, straight towards the waterfall.

As she transformed back into her human form she glanced around. It was clearly visible that the fairies had been busy. There was a bag in the corner that she was sure Amethyst had ordered them to pack. The room has also been completely rearranged, which she knew her friend did due to Alex being nervous and unsure about the future.

"Good morning Alex. I hope that you slept well?" Amethyst asked walking into the room.

"I am fantastic, thank you," Alexandria replied, smiling.

"Don't you dare fake a smile. I will hurt you and you know that is not just an empty threat. I have known you for way too long to be fooled by your 'oh, I'm so happy' face."

"Sorry Am, I should have known that you would see right through me," Alexandria said, lowering her head. "I am just worried about this trip with Justin. I would love to stop the evil beings attacking and killing the Creatures, but I am scared that something happens that requires my powers, and not being able to use it because I have to hide it from him."

"As far as you told me, you liked him? Why is it such a problem that he is offering to help you with this 'mission', for lack of a better word?"

"I do like him, but I am getting a bad feeling about all of this, as though I am going to turn my back and find a very large sword in my back. And he does not seem to like me very much, in case you forgot... we argued most of the time yesterday."

"That is not a surprise," Amethyst commented. "We were all surprised that he showed up here. How about we do it this way. Go on this journey with him. *If* you still feel the same at the end of the journey, then you know that your feelings for him are real. And *if* you don't feel the same, then you know that it was just a crush that meant nothing. You can then move on with your life and perhaps find a nice human to date, perhaps one that lives in the village."

"I'm not so sure how I feel about dating someone from the village, but very well... I will see how this journey goes and only then will I make up my mind about what to do about this. You are right, of course. I can't just think or believe one thing and then the next moment think something else."

"It would not be fair on you or on him," Amethyst added, "even if he doesn't even know that you have feelings for him."

"Am, not long after I got home last night, I had this really strong sense of foreboding. It was a very strong feeling that something bad is going to happen, and it was nothing good at all."

"Do you mean that you had a premonition?"

"No, it was not a premonition at all. It wasn't like normal where I see things happen. It was more a really strong feeling."

"Perhaps it is just your uncertainty about this whole trip that is making you worry. Maybe your subconscious is warning you to not just judge what you think might happen."

"I really hope so Am, as it made me really nervous."

"As I said, let us see how this journey goes before we decide whether we should panic or not."

"How was your evening after I left? Did anything interesting happen?" Alexandria asked, pointedly looking around the room.

"I did not get any sleep as I had to make sure that the fairies packed some things for you to take on your journey. I was looking at the room afterwards and decided that a change might be good, not just for me but for everyone. I have heard that a change is as good as a holiday and, as we are not able to go on a holiday, I have to make the best of things."

"I am sorry if I cannot reassure you that all of this will all work out for the best," Alexandria said. "If it was in my power, I would make you that promise right now."

"You do not have to promise me anything," Amethyst reassured her. "I already feel better knowing that you are going out there. If I were to doubt you and your abilities now, I would have to doubt my mother and her training. She also trained me, so that would be like blasphemy."

"Thank you for believing in me when I don't even always believe in myself. It is difficult to be positive when things seem to be going downhill more and more lately."

"It is always and forever a pleasure Alex; you are my sister and we need to stick together."

"Your majesty, the human from yesterday is here and he asked me to call you," Tagitha said as she flew into the room. "He is waiting down by the pool."

"Thank you so much my dear," Amethyst responded. "Would you please tell him that we will be down shortly?"

"Let this journey start and let us hope that nothing terrible will happen," Alexandria said while sighing.

"Do not be so negative," Amethyst said, providing some guidance and support. "Positivity will take you a lot further than negativity. Just think about how great you will feel once you succeed in stopping whoever has been attacking the poor Creatures."

"I know that all too well, Am. It is just that I am not used to depending on anyone but myself and you. How many times were we told that humans are dangerous and might hurt us if we aren't careful?"

"From everyone? Every day. But if you remember, my mom told us that we should not judge people by what we see or hear. Rather get to know them and then decide if they are good or bad. Only then would one be able to give an honest and true opinion."

"Oh, your mother and her wise, wise sayings. I am sure that we would be able to fill a book with all of the things she taught us."

"Let us go down and see to your handsome young man," Amethyst said teasingly, "and make sure that you have everything you need for the trip. It would be for the best to stop the evil beings sooner than later as there have been enough losses."

"Very true. I just have one question though."

"And what is that, Alex?"

"How am I supposed to get down from the waterfall without showing that I have magical powers?"

"I will carry you down," Amethyst informed her. "Like the good old days."

"That will just make me feel like a little girl again. But as there is no other way, we better get going."

Alexandria shook her head with a small smile, grabbing Amethysts hand and holding on tight as they flew down to where Justin was waiting for them.

"Good morning, your majesty. I hope that this morning finds you in good health?" Justin asked as they landed in front of them. "And a good morning to you, Alexandria."

"Good morrow Justin. I am well if not a little tired, but that is none of your worries. How are you today?" Amethyst asked smiling.

"I am doing very well, thank you," Justin responded with a smile of his own. "A good night's rest does one good. Are we ready to start the journey? I believe that the sooner we start the sooner we can stop the evil from striking again."

"I am all packed and ready to go," Alexandria said. "Amethyst just wanted to check with you whether we needed anything from them."

"No, I think that we are all set," Justin confirmed. "I have camped before so I have a very good idea on what we would be able to eat if needed. Unless the berries look different in the magical forest, but I am sure that Alexandria would be able to warn me before I poison myself."

"There is no difference in the berries and fruits," Amethyst said giggling. "But even if it was, you are right. Alex does know which ones are poisonous."

"I can't help but notice that you are here without a horse," Alexandria observed. "Have you realised that it would be too difficult for the animal in the forest?"

"That is not the reason why I made the decision. I thought that it would just be more courteous of me to be on foot as well. Then we do not have to worry about moving too fast for the other to keep up."

"It is time for us to get going Am," Alexandria said, the anxiety building up in her. "If we keep standing around talking it will be nightfall again and the trip will have to be put off till tomorrow."

"You are right," Amethyst sighed. "I wish that I was able to join you, but you know that I need to stay here and make sure that the magical Creatures stay safe and do not start panicking. It would have been a great experience though if I had been able to go with you."

"It would have been like old times, but I understand,"

Alexandria told her friend hugging her tightly. "I will send word to you as soon as we find out something more."

"Then we will see you again soon, Your Majesty," Justin said bowing and disappearing into the woods.

As she walked after Justin, she wondered when she would see Amethyst again. She was afraid that she would be only bringing back bad news. Even though her friend was so sure that it was not the Centaurs, Alexandria was almost a hundred percent sure that it was them and it would break her heart to see her friend be hurt.

She heard Justin stumble and sighed. It would have gone so much quicker if it had been only her, but she knew that it would have not helped at all to argue. Amethyst had made up her mind and she was rather stubborn once she put her mind to something.

For a second, she considered disappearing into a bush and allowing him to get lost, but knew instantly that it would cause only more trouble. With the amount of noise he was making, there was a very strong possibility that he would attract those Creatures that were on the loose.

"Alexandria, could you please slow down a little?" Justin asked, out of breath. "I cannot see properly, so my feet keep getting stuck in hidden roots. It would be counterproductive for one of us to get hurt so early on in the journey. And I am sure that you are used to the area, but please remember that I am but a stable boy. It is not in my job description to walk around the forest on a daily basis."

"You will have to pick up speed a little if you wish to get to the Troll's cave before nightfall," Alexandria informed him grumpily. "It might not seem like such a long journey, but if we keep delaying then we will not make it. And I am sure that you do not want to be around here in the middle of the night?"

"No, that is not what I wish, as I value my life," Justin replied, a slight tremor in his voice belying his fear. "Perhaps if we were to talk it might get easier for me? I am not used to so much silence."

"What do you wish to talk about?"

"I don't know," Justin said thoughtfully. "Perhaps you could tell me more about yourself? From what little I have seen from you, you like talking. But you have not said much since we entered the forest. How old were you when your parents died? Was it then that you moved to the fairies? What did your parents do for a living?"

"I will not speak of my parents," Alexandria said suddenly. "So if that is all you can come up with then the journey will continue in silence. I will however answer one of your other questions. I was sent to Valencia and Amethyst when my parents were murdered and, as they were like extended family, they took me in without question."

"Have you been in the forest a lot? Camping?"

"When Valencia got tired of us," Alexandria informed him, "and we got too much for her, she would send us into the forest for some 'quiet time'. Saying that it was so we could commune with nature. But in truth it was for her to just have a bit of a breather. We weren't always accepting of each other, but once we stopped fighting among ourselves we were quite a handful and not many people were able to handle us."

"So, would you still get lost if you did not pay attention to where you were going? Or do you know it so well that you would know exactly where you are no matter where you were in here?"

"Everyone would get lost in here," she said, smiling. "Everything grows so quickly that one week it could seem easy, but the next you will walk the exact same path only to find that it looks completely different. So, in short, yes, even I would get lost in here. That is why I am paying such close attention to where we are.

"In fact," she continued fondly, "there were a few times when we were young that we got so lost that Valencia had to send a guard looking for us. When they finally found us, we would be shivering and curled up next to a tree with no clue where we were."

"Okay," Justin said. "I chose that topic to make myself feel better, but I think that it just had the opposite effect."

"Don't worry, for right now we would not get lost as I know exactly how to get to their caves even though I've never been. But we were told where it is and I have wandered up there by mistake a time or two."

"That is good to know, I guess. Could I ask you when it is time to have a break? It feels as though we have been walking for hours."

"You are kind of right... We have been walking for about an hour and a half, which means that if we keep going through those trees you will find a fresh water spring. So, we can take a breather there."

He ran past her and through the trees throwing himself into the spring with a small 'whoop'. Shaking her head, she followed slower, sitting down and lightly dunking her feet into the stream. She always loved this spring; it was where she went when she needed to clear her head for a bit. It had always been her little place of solace and peace.

"Are you not going to get in?" he asked her, finally surfacing

"No, I am fine with just my feet cooling off. As you said before, I am used to walking in the forest, so I do not get as hot as you do."

"But the water is so great! How come no one knows about this place?!"

"Everyone knows about it, it is just not always the safest place to be. Especially in these turbulent days. But enjoy it for a few minutes more. We are still a distance away from the caves and the next part of the trip will not have any fresh water to cool off in."

"So, there is no fresh water on the way? What are we supposed to do when we are thirsty?!"

"Relax; Amethyst sent some jugs. With that we can fill up with water."

"And what about food? Are you expecting me to survive on berries and fruits until we arrive there?"

"If you remember clearly, *you* offered to help me with this. We didn't approach you for your help. What did you really expect, for me to carry a buffet lunch ready for when you get peckish?"

"That is just ludicrous!"

"No, you are being ludicrous. If you are such a big eater perhaps you should have ensured that you had food that was 'good enough' for you. I am not a maid, and neither are the fairies. We do not supply food on demand." She glared at him as she stood up. "Get your things and make sure that you have enough water. We need to get going so that we get there in time.

The forest is dangerous at night and I do not wish to still be here when the things crawl out of the dark."

* * * * *

A few hours later she stopped next to one of the trees and laid her hand on its trunk, closing her eyes and listening carefully. She was finally able to use some of her magic without it being too obvious and she smiled at the little tingle that ran across her spine.

"What are you doing?! Aren't you the one that insisted we keep moving because it will be dark soon?" Justin asked, stopping next to her.

"Oh hush; you were in no rush earlier," she replied irritatingly. "If you could just give me a minute or so to listen to nature, I would be able to give you a proper answer."

"How are you able to 'listen to nature' if you are not a creature of magic? Or is this something that can be taught to anyone magical or non-magical?"

She glared at him until he kept quiet before closing her eyes once more. Running her hand over the trunk and feeling its history, she flinched when she saw what had happened here not too long ago.

"This tree has seen the Creatures responsible for all of the attacks and deaths, but is refusing to say more than that."

"What does that mean?"

"That whoever is responsible for the attacks have threatened the forest," she replied, seeing the confusion on his face. "Before you ask, that means that they will burn the entire forest down. Or perhaps cut down some of the trees until they are happy, which might only be when there is nothing left. Or they may not want to talk because one of them is close by and might overhear. The latter being a little scary as we aren't exactly armed to fight."

"So, they know who and what has been causing the devastation, but they refuse to reveal who it is? That is just great; all this way to find out from a *tree* that it is afraid to talk."

"Stop blaming your impatience on nature. We did not come here to talk to trees; we are travelling to the *Troll caves* to speak with them and see what we can find out from them. I just thought that it wouldn't do any harm to ask if they have seen the Creatures responsible." Alexandria started to walk again.

"You never answered my question," Justin said quickly.

"And which question specifically are you talking about?" Alexandria replied. "You have asked quite a few."

"How is it that you are able to listen and speak to nature? You don't have wings, which means that you aren't a fairy. You aren't a unicorn, because as far as I can see you do not have a horn or four legs. You aren't a troll, as you aren't as big as them or smelly."

"Are those the only magical Creatures you believe are out there?"

"Well, at the moment they are the only Creatures I have seen so far and I do not want to make a fool of myself by saying there is a specific creature out there and it has been extinct or never existed at all."

"That is a fair enough point," Alexandria said, pausing for thought. "And I think that it is admirable of you to not want to put your foot in it."

"I do believe that is a compliment, and coming from you that means a lot."

"I've been taught that one needs patience, and in case you didn't notice... I don't have a lot of that."

"Is that why you have been so short and impatient with me? Because you do not have patience?"

"Kind of...," she replied. "Because I had to grow up without my parents, I was always convinced that I had to do things for myself, even though I had Valencia and Amethyst and the other Creatures. For me it is important to say that I was able to do something without someone's help. And I have seen how humans have treated magical Creatures and it is terrible.

"Which is why I was so against you suddenly appearing

out of nowhere to help us. What motive could you possibly have to, without warning, walk into the magical forest, find the waterfall and then offer, without blinking an eye, to go even deeper into the forest and travel to the caves of trolls? It feels like you have an ulterior motive. I have not seen very positive things from humans because when they are scared of something they will try and get rid of it. Most of the time that ends up in death or destruction."

"You do not have a very positive outlook on your own kind, do you?"

"It is getting dark and we are still nowhere near the caves," she replied, ignoring his question. "We will have to camp for the night."

"I thought that you said it is too dangerous to camp?"

"It is, but we do not have much of a choice," she said distractedly. "I will keep guard."

"You cannot stay awake the entire night. You will be exhausted!"

"Do not worry about..." she started, but stopped as a premonition fell over her.

"Alexandria? Is everything okay?"

She lifted her hand to make him keep quiet. Her glassy eyes staring into nothingness. It was the same as the night before; nothing clear, but a definite feeling of foreboding. She frowned, when suddenly she was staring at a picture from above. It was as though it was submerged in a pool of water. Try as hard as she could, she was not able to make out anything. Without warning she fell to her knees with a soft exclamation, her eyes shooting open just in time to see a shadow flit around the trees.

"Is everything okay?" Justin asked, sincere concern in his voice. You look kind of pale."

"It's nothing, I just thought I saw something hiding in the trees. But before I could see what it was, it disappeared."

"Do you think that it was one of the Creatures?"

"It could have been a rabbit for all I know," she said, attempting to clear her head. "It really did move too fast for me to know for sure."

"Very well then," he replied, walking onwards with Alexandria shaking a little and biting her lip.

She was not sure if being in the forest was a good idea at that moment, but there was no way she could force Justin to keep going. Taking a deep breath and promising herself that everything would be okay, she quickly followed in his footsteps...

Chapter 3

The Warning

When the sun went down, Alexandria convinced Justin that they had to rest for the night. Even though he was not happy about it, he accepted that they would get lost if they continued on during the evening. She knew that they were supposed to have been at the Caves a few hours before, but she had turned around when he suddenly 'got lost' and she had to go back to find him. He swore that it had been accidental, but she had told him over and over again to stick close to her so that he would not get lost but for some reason he had done exactly that.

"Are you seriously expecting me to just accept this as a meal? I am still hungry!" Justin muttered "I was not expecting to be treated like a child who barely eats anything!

"You are used to eating a lot if this does not fill you up, as this is what I have seen many humans eat," Alexandria said irritatingly

"Once again you go on as though you are not a human, as

though you are something different."

"It's a habit after so many years with the magical Creatures. To me it feels as though I'm more magical creature than human."

"That does not make sense at all, but I'm too hungry and tired to argue."

"Then go sleep," Alexandria instructed him. "Tomorrow we will get to the caves and they can feed you properly. I will make sure that they give you one of their single portions, which for you would be gigantic."

He stood up and walked to where he had made his bed. She heard him muttering the whole way and shook her head. How was it, that one person could be so unpleasant when they did not get what they wanted?

From what she had observed all humans had their good and bad days, but it was not as major as this. Even when they believed there was some kind of threat to their safety, they did not behave like they had not eaten in days.

Standing up, she walked to the stream nearby and rested her feet in the running water. She nibbled her lip as she wondered if she had perhaps imagined the shadow earlier in the day. After a few minutes of contemplation, she shook her head and looked around, swearing that she had heard something move.

Frowning, she placed her hands into the water, trying to ignore the feeling of being watched. Perhaps she was just overtired and it was starting to get to her. She considered it a possibility, as she had been struggling to sleep for a few days already. Nothing that she had tried had helped her get the proper rest.

She stood up and took a deep breath. She turned around and started walking towards the camp, but stifled a soft scream when something rushed past her. She put her hand across her chest and took a deep breath, glancing around her with her eyes wide open.

How was it possible that something or someone could move that fast? After a few minutes of looking around and trying to spot what had rushed at her, she decided that it must have been a small animal that had gotten spooked. It was time for her to get back to camp. She was worried that Justin would wake up and wonder where she was and then come looking for her. She would not be able to explain what she was doing there when she did not even really know.

She had only taken a few steps forward before she felt a light push against her shoulders causing her to stumble backwards and tripping over a hidden branch. She landed in the stream and became completely soaked.

"You have got to be kidding me," she muttered irritatingly.

"Justin? Was that you?"

When she got no answer, she quickly got up out of the stream looking down at her soaked clothing. She considered how she was going to explain this to him. She wished that bad things could just stop happening to her. It felt as though everything was going after her with full force.

She took a deep breath, removed her clothes and hung it on a tree branch. She quickly closed her eyes and summoned a slight wind to dry her clothes. It would be so embarrassing if someone stumbled on her right now. After some time, the wind died down and she touched her clothes to make sure that they were dry.

She smiled, safe in the knowledge that nature would never disappoint her. As she got dressed, she glanced around the darkened forest out of instinct rather than a warning and froze when she saw someone standing not that far from her.

"Justin, is that you?" she asked frowning, but got no reply. "I do not think that this is funny and if you, whoever you are, were in my position you would feel the same way."

A soft growl reached her ears and she suddenly shivered as though she was stuck in an icy wind. Swallowing hard, she tried saying something, but no words came out. She felt as if something was choking her. She took a deep breath and tried to get the cold fear away from her heart, but nothing worked.

Just as suddenly as the feeling of panic appeared, it seemed to drop away, leaving her heart fluttering wildly. A spell jumped to mind. It was as though she could see the spell happening without actually casting it.

"Calm down Lexie," a gentle voice said. "I promise that you are in no danger from me."

Alexandria looked at him surprised, wondering how he knew her name. She could not help but notice that he had the voice of an angel, and even though she knew that she should not get distracted by that fact, she could not help it study him intensely.

"My name is Shadick," he announced. "I am known by the magical Creatures as a wolfane."

"What exactly is a wolfane?" she whispered, licking her lips.

"It is a person that comes from a human and werewolf coupling. It basically makes me half wolf and half human."

"So you are part werewolf?"

"No, I am not a werewolf," he corrected her quickly. "A werewolf has no choice when he or she turns at the full moon; my mother was a werewolf when she became pregnant with me."

"Well, as far as my knowledge on this lore goes, you should then also be a werewolf."

"My father knew of my mother's curse," Shadick

continued, "but it did not matter to him at all as she was his true love. Every month they would go to a secluded cabin, so that she would not harm anyone. One night they became intimate and lost track of time.

"I was conceived as my mother was turning. She jumped out of the window and only returned the next morning, full of apologies about just taking off. He laughed it off, saying that they should do it again the next month. Three months later my father made her go to a doctor because she was sick for a few weeks already and it was not passing at all.

"It was then that she found out that she was expectant with me," he continued, looking down at the ground as if contemplating something. "They were shocked, but happy. Of course, they did not know what I would be as there had never been reports of such a birth. When I was born six months later, I appeared quite normal, and as I grew older, they noticed that even though I sometimes liked a bit of raw meat, there seemed to be nothing to show that I was a werewolf in anyway."

"I know that it is not my place to say," Alexandria commented, "but you still had some wolf in you. Does that not mean that your dad was in danger?"

"He was in quite a bit of danger, but we were his family so he did not care," Shadick replied, shaking his head clear of his thoughts. "But I did not come looking for you just to tell you about my history."

"You came looking for me?" she asked, shocked. "Whatever for?"

"I need to give you a warning, and I know that coming from a stranger it might seem kind of like a shot in the dark. But I need you to listen and listen carefully."

"Very well then, what kind of warning?" Alexandria asked, concerned by the ominous tone his voice took. "And on that point, how do I know that you aren't the one that is planning on hurting me? Or now that I think about it, how do I know that you aren't the one attacking the magical Creatures?"

"You have not been able to see me since I started following you. There is no way you could have stopped me if I had wanted to attack you."

"I am a witch and can cast a spell to stop you," she replied, with a mixture of confidence in her abilities and offense at him implying that she was magically impotent against him.

"Even with your powers, I would be able to have hurt or even kill you by now if I wanted to," he said carefully in an attempt not to scare her off.

"Fair enough," she said crossing her arms, a tiny flicker of defiance sparkling in her eyes. "You would probably still be able to hurt me, but I would put up a fair fight."

"You will just have to trust that it is not my plan to hurt

you," he said, stepping closer to her.

"I am not sure if I can believe you," she said, hesitating before stepping backwards. "It is not in my nature to just trust someone I've just met." She exclaimed softly as she bumped into a tree behind her.

"Is there no way for you to use your powers to help you figure out whether I am good or evil?"

"Do you not think that I have tried to do just that ever since you appeared from out of nowhere? All I get is a blackness that I cannot explain."

"I've seen you with some of the humans as well as the magical Creatures and you have been able to read them quite accurately," Shadick said, confusion littering his face. "I am not sure how you would not be able to read me. Perhaps you are the one that is not being truthful with me?"

"I assure you that if I was able to you read you, I would not be scared half to death of you," she informed him. "I would either be trying to get away from you or actually be able to relax. As you can see, I have not moved all that much neither have I relaxed at all, so that should be proof enough."

He shook his head and then stepped forward again.

"We have no time to argue the point that may or may not be invalid. I have a warning for you. I'm not here to have a discussion about how your powers work or why I am able to block you."

"About this warning. Why is it that you waited until I am alone to give it when you could have approached myself and Justin earlier today?"

"The enemy is closer than you think. You must be on your guard because the enemy can and will strike without any warning at all. You need to be careful about who you trust."

"That does not make sense at all, Shadick," Alexandria said, frowning. "What enemy is closer than I think? Do you mean the ones responsible for the attacks on the magical Creatures? Are they watching us right now? Or are you talking about the shadow I saw earlier today?"

"I am indeed talking about those Creatures. You will find out soon enough who they are. But they aren't watching at present, which is why I took the opportunity to speak with you. They are even closer than that. As for the shadow that you noticed..." he said grinning

"That shadow... it was you! I saw you last night and again earlier today!"

"Yes, that was me. I have been following you ever since before the beginning of your journey, watching your every move and making sure that you are in no jeopardy."

"Then I guess that I have to thank you. But about this enemy that is closer than I think, could you tell me more about that?"

"For now, I have told you all that I can," Shadick replied.

"But you didn't really tell me anything at all!" she said exasperated. "So how am I supposed to know what you mean?"

"I am sorry that I am not able to help you more than that."

"Is it some kind of rule?"

"No, it's not a rule," he said cautiously, "more along the lines of that I am still discovering the answers myself."

"Oh, so you do not even know what kind of Creatures they are or a name of the one that is closer than I thought?"

"No, unfortunately I have not worked that out yet, but I get a feeling that I am missing a simple clue, something right under my nose," Shadick said thoughtfully. "So you will just have to help me figure out whom or what it is that is threatening the magical world."

Shadick had stepped close to her, so close that their faces were a breath away from each other. She was about to reach up to touch him when all of a sudden, she froze, her eyes going glossy as a premonition slowly ran over her. A soft cry escaped her lips as the future rushed through her mind; she saw horse hooves along with the shape of a man's body, but there was not just one of these beasts.

As the picture got bigger, she saw an entire army of the Creatures. These Creatures were getting ready for a war, sharpening weapons and meeting with other kinds of

Creatures. It was then that she heard a cry of war and two groups of magical Creatures meeting in battle. It was difficult to watch the magic flying and hearing the swords clashing, but there was nothing that she was able to do.

"Lexie, is everything okay?" Shadick asked, shaking her lightly. "Could you please just answer me?"

But even though she tried she was unable to say anything, staring into nothingness without blinking. It was only when there was a powerful explosion that she screamed and fell to the floor, breathing heavily.

"Lexie, what happened?" he asked in a panic. "You just went quiet and didn't even blink."

"I had a premonition."

"And what happened in this premonition?"

"A war."

"What do you mean you saw a war? You are not making sense at all, so could you please explain exactly what you saw? What kind of war was it?"

"I am not even sure," she replied, still trying to regain control of her mind. "All I know is that it is the strongest premonition that I have had in quite a while. Which can only mean, that it will happen whether we want it to or not."

"You mean that you have seen this before? Had this 'vision' of the future before, I mean?"

"No, I have not seen this before" she said, understanding his need for clarity but becoming annoyed at the questioning. "All I received last time was a really cold feeling. Some kind of foreboding of what might be, but this time I actually saw what things happening."

"Were you able to see who started this war?" Shadick asked as he lightly picked Alexandria up by the arms, a small shriek of surprise escaping her lips as the ground disappeared from under her. She felt his strong arms around her as he lightly put her down on a rock. "Now take a deep breath and explain to me what it is you saw exactly."

"I apologize for the squeal," Alexandria said, feeling embarrassed. "I have not been picked up by anyone besides my father, and it has been years. As for calming down, I am not so sure that I would be able to. Not after what I saw."

"I can just imagine that it was not easy to see, but you need to talk about it before it disappears completely."

"What I saw was a war, yes," she informed him, closing her eyes as she tried to recollect the vision. "I saw men, but they were not humans. Not that I have ever seen anyway.

"How do you mean that they did not look like humans? What did they look like?"

"The premonitions can be very confusing and I cannot always make out what they mean exactly," she told him honestly, although unsure as to why she trusted him so much. "It is difficult to decipher and if done wrong it could be very dangerous."

"Very well," Shadick said, trying a different line of questioning. "Were you able to see any other Creatures that were part of this war?"

"Not really, just that it was the magical Creatures against these human-like Creatures. I remember seeing horses and bodies of men. I also saw them sharpening weapons and having meetings with other Creatures, but nothing besides that. "

"Then why did you scream? It sounded as though something happened to you in the premonition. We can discuss the bodies of humans and creatures a bit later."

"I screamed, because there was a big battle and the magical Creatures were outnumbered. I could only stand there and watch. The fighting started and there was some kind of big surge of power that went all over the battlefield."

"Then I apologize that you had to witness it, but I do believe that we could use this in our favour."

"I guess you are right," she said after considering his words for a moment. "It would help us bring more magical Creatures to our side so that it would not be such a great loss."

"There you go," he said, his smile revealing that he was pleased. "Already thinking how the premonition can be used in our favour."

Shadick stood up and took a step back. Alexandria watched him, wondering what he was about to do. She had enjoyed his company and feared that it was the end of their conversation.

"I gave you the warning and I hope that you will be able to figure out what it means before it is too late."

"You're already leaving? There has to be more than just telling me and then disappearing."

"I really have to go," he said with an undertone of comfort in his voice. "Unfortunately, the young man you are travelling with is looking for you and is on his way here. It is for the best that he does not know about me."

She watched him run off; frowning before shaking her head slightly. She believed for a moment that it all had to be a really bad dream and that she would wake up soon and everything will make sense. Why did these things always seem to happen to her?

"Alexandria! Is everything okay?" Justin asked, suddenly appearing from behind a tree. The sound of his voice caused her to flinch at how deafening his voice sounded after Shadick's.

"Yes, everything is fine. Thank you for your concern," she said, trying to even out her voice to sound as convincing as possible. "I thought that you were sleeping?"

"I was," Justin said, looking around for the presence of anyone else, "but when I awoke there was no sign of you and I started worrying. So I thought that I should come looking for you in case you were in danger. Did I hear you talking to someone?"

"No, you misheard," she said quickly, and then cleared her throat. "I was not talking to anyone. No one around to talk to besides the trees and they are asleep right now as well."

"Perhaps it was just my sleep addled mind then. What are you doing out here anyway?"

"I just wanted to get some fresh water, but my thoughts kind of ran away with me," she said, holding up the water that she had collected.

"I went to sleep over two hours ago Alexandria," Justin said, actual concern apparent in his voice. "And I really was worried about you because, as you have said yourself, there are dangers out here and we should not be alone."

"It's been two hours?!" she exclaimed louder than she intended, shocked at how quickly time has gone by. "Wow, I did not notice time passing so swiftly. And I apologize that you had to wake up and find yourself alone. I can just imagine the things that had run through your mind when I was not there."

"Nothing as scary as you seem to think," he said strangely, causing her to wonder what he meant. "Shall we get back to camp so that we can get some more rest?"

Nodding, she stood up and she followed Justin back to camp. Shadick's warning ran through her mind. To her it made no sense at all; it all seemed like a load of gibberish and, had it not been for the premonition, she might have just shaken it off.

It all happened within a few minutes of each other though, so it had to be true. Her mother and father had always told her that if her instincts were telling her to believe something and all signs pointed at it, she should believe it.

"Are you sure that everything is okay, Alexandria?" Justin asked after they had walked in silence for a while. "You seem to be a thousand miles away."

"Do not worry about me," she said, annoyed at the interruption. "I am just lost in thought, that's all."

"May I ask as to what you are thinking? Or is it too personal?"

"My thoughts aren't exactly personal, but I am not one to share unless it is of utmost importance or needs to be said," she said, her distrust of Justin rising to the fore again. "Right now, I am thinking about the attacks that have been occurring. I mean, who do you think is responsible for it?"

"I have no idea and I wish that I was able to give you a better answer than that. Wouldn't it be awesome if we were able to just turn around and know things? But I am sure that whoever is responsible for the attacks will make themselves known soon enough."

As they arrived at camp Justin insisted that she go sleep, but she did not go quietly. She tried arguing the fact that she was not tired and that someone had to guard camp; just in case whoever was responsible for the attacks decided to go for them. Alexandria believed that they looked like easy targets, even though she knew that Shadick would be watching and would make sure that they had enough warning if an attack was going to happen.

She laid down and thought again about the warning he had given her. Lately it had been feeling as though men had been acting very mysteriously and made no sense to anyone, not even themselves. A lot of the time it looked as though they went into something blindly with no thought as to what would happen or with no care at all. If only there was a way for her to shake them, to make them see that they were not always right.

* * *

As Shadick watched Alexandria and Justin argue about how necessary it was to keep guard, he smiled when he noticed her eyes flicking between the leaves in the darkened trees. She knew that he was watching. It was funny watching her natural instincts fighting over what, or rather whom, she was trying to trust.

It was as he was watching that he decided that he should move closer, but only once they were both asleep. It would not have been good for Justin to know that they were being watched and followed. He thought about Alexandria's reaction when he did not have more information for her, but truth be told he really did not know much more.

All he had gleaned from the villagers on the way there was that the information was mixed and not always trustworthy, but any information was better than nothing at all. What he did know was that something really bad was going to happen and nothing could be done about it or stopped.

The villagers also seemed to like Justin, but only up to a certain point. After that, everything seemed to turn towards negativity because he had showed up the one day in the village and no one knew who he was or where he was originally from. He spoke very little about himself, which made everyone suspicious of him.

He frowned when he heard noises coming from the other side. He wondered where they came from. Shadick followed the noises, ignoring the fact that his brain was telling him that he was being stupid since he had given Alexandria the exact warning that he was now breaking; to be careful within the forest because of the enemy being closer than she knew.

He shook his head, grinning at what she would say. As he got closer to the noises, he noticed that Justin was not acting as careful and scared as what he was letting on. Was he coming to meet someone? That seemed unlikely to Shadick, as Justin was just an ordinary human and had not known about the magical Creatures before this journey with Alexandria had started.

Glancing back at the camp he instinctively knew that Alexandria would be okay. He really wanted to find out what this human was up to that time of the night, so he followed behind him silently. Just as he was about to jump lower to follow closer, Justin stopped as he greeted someone.

Shadick quickly dropped lower, making sure that he was completely hidden as he watched the young human waiting for someone to appear. If anyone had to ask him about his evening so far, he would have smiled at what had happened. First, he had seen Alexandria naked and, although he felt guilty about it, he had to admit that she had a wonderful body, with curves in just the right places.

Something else he had noticed was that she seemed to be in two minds over Justin, sometimes she seemed to like him but then in the next breath as though she wished that he was nowhere near her. Then there was the fact that Justin, who looked like an ordinary human, was sneaking around in a forest that he was not familiar with to meet up with someone.

"Father, are you there?" Justin whispered.

Shadick frowned and peered closer through the leaves that he was hiding in.

"I am right here my son; did she see you come here? And more to the point, why did it take you so long to get here in the first place?" a centaur asked, stepping out between some of the trees.

"I would have been here earlier, but she disappeared into the forest," Justin replied, almost apologetically. "She pretended that she was just getting fresh water, but she did not return until two hours later when I went looking for her."

"What was she doing when you found her?"

"She was sitting on a rock looking pale and spooked, but that was it."

"You are here now, and that is all that counts. Does she seem suspicious of you?"

"Not at all father," Justin replied, with a hint of uncertainty in his voice. "She does not really talk all that much, truth be told, and she always has this distant look on her face. Her excuse is that she is thinking, but no normal human being thinks that much, surely."

"Just remember that she is not just a normal human being, she is a witch," his father reminded him. "One that has to be watched really close in case she tries to catch you out. Keep acting like the innocent human willing to help the magical Creatures until the time is right."

"As far as I can tell she still thinks that I am just a stable boy who had accidentally run across them. I don't believe that I would ever be able to forget the fact that she is a witch. I still remember the story you told me about how you murdered her parents."

It was difficult for Shadick not to jump out and snap both of their necks as he heard them talking about her as though she was a nothing, as if she did not matter at all.

"That is good. Remember the story, as it might help you one day. Remember that if it had not been for me, she would have been able to wipe us all out with a single spell. They would have taught her *so* much more than Valencia was able to.

"Her mother and father were able to cast strong spells and their powers grew quickly. So, I just knew when I heard that they had a child, that she would be five times stronger than them and it had to be stopped. If I think about how hard Valencia tried, I wanted to laugh because she was not able to teach her more than half of the things that she needs to know."

"I am sure that the fairy queen thought that she had done an excellent job, but in truth she did almost nothing to help."

"Keep stalling the girl for as long as possible," his father reminded him. "Our army grows stronger by the day."

"Whatever you wish father," Justin replied in an austere tone. "I will make sure that she is distracted and will not notice what is going on. When she finally realises that I am one of her enemies, it will be too late."

"Go back to camp in case she wakes up, but know that I am never far away and I am always watching."

Shadick watched them part ways and he growled, they were going on as though Alexandria was just some worthless being that was not able to protect herself or those she cared about. He wanted to run to her and pull her away from this monster before she got badly hurt.

Yet, he knew that he had to let it play out, as she might not believe him and it might just cause the opposite to happen. He decided to wait and just be there for her when the truth was revealed. And he silently made the promise that he would make sure that he was there for her when that happened…

Chapter 4

Lies And Deceit

When she woke up the next morning, she was happy that Justin had not even stirred yet. She felt a little irritated that he had not kept watch as he had promised, but she was glad that the trip was coming to an end.

Stretching, she smiled. She knew that being out in nature had given her fantastic night's sleep. Although most people would have complained about not having a pillow, she was happy and felt better than what she had been the last while. She felt more rejuvenated and fuller of life than she had been in quite a while.

As she rummaged around their small camp, Shadick's warning from the previous evening kept pounding around her head. She feared that it might just develop into a headache if she was not able to make her mind think of something, anything else. She smiled and sighed, remembering when she had first seen him and how handsome he had looked.

Suddenly she froze and glanced around, realising that she was thinking about him as though she had some kind of crush on him. They had only met a few hours before. What was important, she thought as she shook her head, was that she needed to figure out what exactly he had meant in his warning instead of daydreaming about something that would or could never happen.

She had immediately known that his warning would so much for the journey ahead and, if she wanted to get out of this thing, whatever it was, she might not make it out alive.

The enemy is closer than what you think. The portent could mean so much or so little depending on how one looked at it. But without any more help or at least running it past Amethyst, she was not sure whether she would be able to figure it out.

What if it meant everything ended in disaster? Still frowning and in thought, she glanced around and noticed that there were footprints around the camp that did not belong to either her or Justin. She instinctively knew that it belonged to Shadick. Knowing that he had been keeping watch over them made her heartbeat slow a little and brought a small smile appear on her lips.

"Shadick? I know that you're hiding out there somewhere," she whispered

"Has anyone ever told you that you are way too smart for your good?" his voice rose from somewhere in the trees

"I've heard that probably more throughout my life than

anything else. Is it so wrong of me wanting to know what is going on and if something happened while I was sleeping?"

"A lot of things happen when one thinks no one is looking, especially from those you may or may not trust."

"It would be so much nicer," she said, glancing around, "as well as *easier* if I could see whom I was talking to. This sneaking around and hiding from me is getting old really fast. And I think that you hiding from me even after *informing* me of your presence is a little pointless."

He suddenly appeared right in front of her, causing her to gasp in shock and step backwards. He grinned at her.

"This is a little closer than what I meant," she mumbled as she blushed. "Good morning Shadick. It's good to see you."

"Morning sunshine, it's good to see you too. Did you sleep well?"

"You ask that as if you don't already know the answer to it."

"I just thought that you would appreciate it if I were to look out for you," he replied, grinning down at her roguishly and winking. "And before you say anything, I really do *not* mind doing that for you."

"I can't for the life of me wonder why you would mind watching a person while they are sleeping, even though it is a little creepy," she said sighing softly, and then grinned when he looked surprised. "Would you like some breakfast before you start running after us through the woods?"

"That is very nice of you to ask but I have already eaten. Thank you for asking, though. And I should get back to the hiding part in my little plan before your boyfriend over there wakes up and spots me."

"He is *not* my boyfriend!" she shouted defensively, before lowering her tone. "I do not even like him, for goodness sake."

"Either way, I still have to go. I ask you again to please not tell him about me or that you noticed something in the trees lurking around," he said smiling before jumping back into a tree and disappearing.

"Oh, that's very nice, saying hello before disappearing again. As though I'm some kind of unwanted and ugly person," she muttered, walking towards the place where the fire from the previous night was just fading. "Well whether he finds me unattractive or not, at least I offered him breakfast."

Carefully putting fresh logs onto the fire and gathering a few things for breakfast, she got lost in her own thoughts wondering if what Shadick had meant when he had told her that they were being followed by an enemy? Or by saying that Justin was the enemy?

If it was indeed the latter it would just reaffirm the bad feeling that she had been getting from him since he had shown up at Antithia. But the more she thought about it the more it seemed unlikely that he was the enemy. How could he be when he was just a mortal with no special powers or abilities? Everyone knew that the Creatures or things that had been attacking and killing the magical Creatures were using some kind of magic. Sometimes they used swords and what seemed like their own strength, but mostly it seemed to be magic.

"Good morrow Alex," Justin whispered from behind her and making her jump. "I hope that you were able to get a good night's sleep."

"Good morrow Justin," Alexandria whispered, taking a deep breath and trying her best not to show her shock. "I did sleep well, thank you for asking. How about you?"

"Very much, so thank you! But I am sorry that I was not able to stay awake for look-out too long. I was sleepier than I thought and I was unable to keep my eyes open. But when I passed out everything was quiet and I felt quite safe."

"No worries. I think that we were both sleepier than we thought and I have no doubt in my mind that there was someone watching out for us and making sure that we would not get attacked."

"Someone? You sound as though you know that for sure. And what is for breakfast, because it is looking absolutely mouth-watering!"

"Do not get overly excited as it is nothing special," she replied. "Just a little recipe I learned from the fairies a few years ago. Fish along with a few selected berries."

"I must say that it looks as well as smells delicious! I must remember to ask you for the exact recipe."

"Thank you, I will take that as a compliment and pass it on to the fairies the next time I see them. But I have to admit that we may have something amazing to eat, but we only have water to drink."

"No worries! To get me going is easy in the mornings and usually only requires scraps or left-overs from the previous evening. And what is wrong with drinking water? It is healthy, after all."

"Good to know," she said before pointing past Justin. "May I ask you to please just grab a few of the flasks and refill them? We do not want to be caught in the middle of the forest without any water."

He nodded, grabbing the flasks and disappearing to the water's edge. She was just able to make out his silhouette as he refilled their flasks. He walked back up and put them down by their bags. She held out one of the fish that she had finished frying before taking the other one for herself. Silence ensued as they both ate their food.

"How far do we have to travel today?" he asked a few

minutes later, putting the fire out and looking around at all of their things

"Quite a bit, but I am hoping that we can get to the caves by midday, which means that there will be no stopping along the way unless it is absolutely necessary. If we are thirsty, we can drink while walking. We have eaten so it should last us until then. And more importantly I am keeping to the path that I know and not listening to your *advice* on shorter routes."

"I really thought that the other path would be quicker," Justin replied, confused. "I did not think that it would get us completely lost and turned around the way that it did."

"And I have accepted your apology, yesterday already, but I am just informing you that I will not be listening to you again. Humouring someone for the sake of not causing an unnecessary fight works only for so long. Just beyond those trees there is a pathway that will lead us straight to the caves and quickly at that... if we don't dawdle."

"You are absolutely sure that we will not be stopping along the way?"

"We have no time to waste, so I do not see why it would be necessary for us to stop along the way," Alexandria confirmed. "Besides, the faster we get to the caves the sooner we can find out who is responsible for the attacks. Once we figure that out, we can come up with a plan to get rid of them."

"I understand why you do not want to stop and I accept it," he said with a strange tone in his voice. "I just needed to make sure."

"Do you have any other questions or can we get started?"

"No, I do not have any other questions and we can get started as soon as you are ready."

Picking up the flasks that he had refilled, she glanced at Justin and noticed that he seemed rather unhappy and gloomy that they would not be stopping or that she would not listen to his *advice*. But at that moment she did not really care about his feelings as she just wanted to get to the caves and have all of this trouble sorted out.

She frowned when he kept coming up with reasons to delay them more and eventually just started walking away and leaving him right there. After a few seconds she heard his hurried steps following her and she set her sights on the path ahead.

* * *

Both were lost in their own thoughts as they travelled swiftly along the path. Justin was thinking of his family, or more importantly what he was doing for his father and how much it meant to the tribe. To him it was very important for his father to finally approve of him and not just glare down at him as though he was some kind of outcast.

Before this expedition, his father had never trusted him enough to assign him to anything. He was the one left out and glared at because he was just a *useless* part of the tribe. Then one evening he had overheard his father telling one of his lieutenants that he would rather do the big missions himself than send his son. He did not completely trust him or his unwanted *gift*, but at that time they needed him and his *gift*, whether he liked it or not.

His father was forced to give him a chance.

To anyone else it may have seemed like a stupid and useless mission, but to him it was huge: mislead the witch, lie to her about his true identity and gain her trust. But of course, the most important part was that he had to keep up with the illusion that he did not know anything about her being a witch. He was to pretend that he did not know or believe anything about witches or any of the magical Creatures and that he had simply *stumbled* upon them and offered to help her.

The unfavourable part of the mission was having to pretend that he was just a simple mortal with no special powers or any kind of ability that would make him stand out from the other humans. Even more important, that she was not to find out that his father, Balditha, and his mother, Diliante, were the Centaur leaders and that they are the ones responsible for the attacks on the magical Creatures.

As his father had drilled into his head numerous times, he would be in a lot of danger if she were to find out that he was a Centaur and helping the other Centaurs attack and kill some of the magical Creatures as well as humans. The useless little witch would most likely attack him and unfortunately, in his human form, he did not have any powers. He would get hurt really badly if not killed if she attacked him.

Transforming back into his Centaur form did not happen in seconds and was a rather painful experience. She would have him at death's door before he was even halfway through the transformation. He grimaced at the thought of his father's face if he were to be discovered by the witch and he knew that he would not be happy with him. And if she did not finish him, his father most definitely would.

It was with this resolve that he was being even more careful not to reveal his secret, as he knew that the consequences of that would be endangering not just only his life but that of his family. He could not see how this could be anything but dangerous. It would cause a lot more trouble than they needed at the moment.

If his father was right, like he usually was, then she would be able to take out the entire clan without thinking about it twice. Knowing how strong this witch could be was the reason his father had killed her parents all those years ago. He had considered it such a big task that he had done it himself to ensure that nothing would go wrong.

With her parents out of her life there was no way that she would be able to reach her true potential, as only they would have been able to teach her some of the things that would have made her stand out. And that meant that the Centaurs could survive as well as not having to have to worry about a child interfering in their plans.

If this mission was to be a success his father would look at him differently than before and it would ensure that he would for at least once in his life get some approval from him and not just the constant disapproval that he was used to. He hated that his father looked at him as a major failure and nothing more, but he was determined that from now on his father would only be positive when it came to him.

He was tired of always being shunted to the side by his father as well as the rest of the clan. He was ready to be given missions and not just be passed on like just another useless mouth to feed. The hate he sometimes felt from his father was enough to make even the witch cringe if she were to ever find out about his family and how he had been treated his entire life.

Not even his own mother had given him some proper respect. She had stood by his father's side with any major decision that may have involved him. Although he had to admit that she had stood up to him whenever he had been in a truly foul mood and called him a disgrace to the clan.

Thinking about all of this made him miss his mother terribly and he wanted to be hugged by her so badly, but in the same breath he knew that it was a very important part of his mission to not get in touch with any of the clan unless it was absolutely imperative. He craved his father's approval, not just to get a little bit more respect from him, but it was an integral part of him taking over the clan one day.

If his father declared that he was to be the leader after his death then the others would not be able to stand up and say that he was not fit to do so. His biggest dream, besides his father's approval, was to be the leader of the clan one day and to hold his families name high. Destiny declared that he would be the next successor, but if his father named someone else as his successor then there would be nothing that he could do about it.

It would be a disaster as they would change everything that their clan had stood for in the last thousand years or so. They might just have said that half-bloods would be allowed to join them, as if they had been pure blood for the last millennia. It had been a hard battle to get it the way that it was at that time, but it had been worth it. He would put his life on the line just to keep the clan in the family and he knew that if they were to take over the forest it would be the first step in many.

The most important and biggest step was to keep Alexandria distracted for as long as possible, as well as to keep her from getting suspicious about why he was trying to stall her. If everything went according to his father's plan, then she would be dead soon enough, the forest would be theirs and the magical Creatures that resided in it could be banished.

The war would be started as soon as his father felt confident enough that their army was strong enough. While he was on his mission his father was busy recruiting more Centaurs as well as some of their other old allies. They all knew that without Alexandria the magical Creatures would give up without a fight and they would just stand there while they made this world theirs.

But he knew that before the killing blow to her head, his father would whisper to her what had really happened to her parents all those years ago and who was really responsible for their deaths. The old saying of power lying in numbers was true. The thought of his father congratulating him at the end of the mission would be the best day of his life and he was looking forward to it...

***

Alexandria was lost in her thoughts and was not really paying much attention to Justin, who just a few feet behind her. She was walking along the path but her concentration was not truly on where her feet were taking her. It was more an instinctive action. She knew that she was on the right path.

The forest was her home after all and she had wandered around so much that she just knew where to go. Thanks to her powers she would know almost immediately if there was any danger up ahead or even behind. With Shadick also lurking around, she knew that she did not have to worry about anything.

Her mind was on her parents, real and adopted, as well as her powers that seemed to grow daily. Smiling she thought of all the fairies and the other magical Creatures that had watched out for her when she had been younger. If it had not been for them, she was not sure if she would have been able to survive.

When the news of her parents' death had reached them, she had not known much about her powers nor had she really mastered any of her powers that her parents had taught her about. She had learned a few things from the fairies that she may not have known about if it had just been her parents.

Valencia had been a big part of her studies. She had been insistent on Alexandria learning how to use her powers the correct way, to not be tempted by the dark side of her powers.

She knew that if her parents had been alive and they had been able to teach her everything they knew, and not just about her powers but theirs too, that she would be stronger than she was now.

She did not blame anyone besides those monsters who had murdered them. She was grateful to the fairies, as it would have been a disaster without them. If it hadn't been for them, she would not know how to control her powers and she may have destroyed not just herself but the entire village.

Or even worse than that was if she had turned to the darkness that lived within her powers and she had become evil. She remembered how long it had taken her to learn how to transform and the mishaps that had happened while she had learned. Valencia had always tried to keep a straight face when she failed and it turned into something completely different than what she had been aiming for.

Valencia had always been strict during their studies, but the moment she was happy with what they had accomplished for the day she would laugh and treat any wounds she may have acquired that day. She and Amethyst had worked harder than her mother had expected just to impress her and to show that they really wanted to learn.

The day that she had started hearing voices she had believed that she had lost her mind. She would either believe that it was her own voices or she would answer the creature's thoughts. People gave her strange looks and muttered under their breaths about what a freak she was.

Having to concentrate on cutting the voices out and still listen when it was important to do so had been difficult. In the beginning, she had slipped up a few times. When she had been in the village when this happened, the villagers had stared at her as though she was some kind of monster. As she was an orphan, they could not really mention anything, as they did not want to come across as heartless beings.

So they smiled and pretended that she was nothing out of the ordinary while quickly backing away from her and acting as though cared. As soon as she started talking about her parents just to hear from them what their thoughts had been, they would quickly change the subject or make an excuse to get away.

It had been up to the Fairies to make sure that she knew as much about them as they could supply her with. It helped that they had been friends since before her birth and could tell her a lot. Yet she longed for them on a daily basis and some nights she cried herself to sleep.

With all the time that she spent with the Fairies, she had acquired some unexpected powers. Although they were shocked that she had these powers, she was happy that she had been able gain all of it. She liked the thought of knowing more than just one kind of magic as she believed in her heart that this would make up for not having her parents as teachers.

She loved knowing that she would always be able to help people even if they did not know that it had been her that had helped them. It was also one of the reasons why she was so happy to have gone on this *mission* to hopefully find out who was responsible for the attacks as well as to stop it from happening again.

***

While he was following Alexandria and Justin, Shadick had a lot of time to reflect on what had made him the man that he was right now. He was also contemplating what he knew about the occurrences during present events.

First and foremost was that he did not like or trust Justin at all and something was yelling at him that nothing good could come of this. A bad thought had been plaguing him ever since they had started this trip and how Justin had just *stumbled* upon the Fairies. It just did not sit right with him.

After overhearing the conversation from the previous evening, it had just cemented that feeling in his mind. He was determined to keep any trouble from happening. He had cursed silently when he had not been able to get closer and see who Justin had been talking to. He had known though that if he had made a move that the boy would have noticed him.

Alexandria was in enough danger as it was and it would not have been good if he was the cause of a sudden attack that could have been avoided. He did not want her in any trouble. He shook his head frowning, wondering where those feelings for Alexandria were coming from? Was he making more of the feelings than were strictly necessary? From what he knew this could not be normal at all. Then again, he did grow up in small villages.

There was no way he could feel this way for a witch... No, that was not right. He could not feel this way towards anyone, never mind just one specific person. Yet, the feelings made him think that perhaps it wouldn't be such a bad thing having feelings for someone. His parents would have been happy that someone made him smile.

"You do not fit in with Alexandria and the people or Creatures that she is with," Shadick muttered softly, shaking his head. "I am not mortal and it is always risky living with *normal* people when you aren't normal."

Being a Wolfane meant that he was not just different from mortals, but magical Creatures as well, as he was more wolf than human. Then again, he had never thought that he could love anyone besides his parents or that he could be loved by anyone besides them. To top all of that he was sure that he had seen something in Alexandria's eyes that had given her feelings for him away.

Perhaps he was just imagining that he could fit in with someone. It was not secret that he was no virgin and that he had bedded a lot of women over the years, but he did not have any feelings for those women. It had been more of a fleeting meeting than anything else. He would not allow his feelings for Alexandria to develop into anything more than friendship as things always seemed to happen to him that he could not explain. He did not want to screw up her life any more than was strictly necessary.

It was the strangest thing. When people and Creatures attacked him for absolutely no reason, he would be walking around minding his own business when an attack would happen. He tried his best to hide the fact that he was different, but it seemed that sometimes people would just look at him and automatically know that he was not one of them.

To them, different was bad and they just had to attack. Luckily some of the powers that came along with being a Wolfane was useful, such as being able run as fast as the wind. He used it often when trouble came running and he had to make a quick escape so that the villagers would not be able to gang up on him and stab him in the back.

He was also stronger than the average man, although he never had a chance to see exactly how strong he was. The important thing was that he could move anything or anyone out of his way. He tried not to use or show off this strength unless there was no other choice. He had decided to only go into villages when there was no other way that he could get what he wanted. He had learned that he could live in the forest for quite a period of time.

Another of his abilities, which had been very surprising to him and his parents, was that he could control the elements, wind, fire, earth and water. These powers of course came in very handy when he was in a fight and outnumbered; when he needed a little extra kick. He would just concentrate on whatever element he decided would help the most and then watched the attacker run as far away from his as their legs could carry them. He had to admit that he had killed a some of the more persistent men, but it was a choice of either him or them.

His father had told him to not be afraid to fight, but only if there was no other way around it; any fight that could be avoided should be. And when it was absolutely necessary and there was absolutely no other choice, he would use his powers to just try and scare them away. It did not always work.

Most of the time when they realised that he was not normal, they would plead for his mercy as though he was some kind of overlord. Something that had always struck him as funny was the fact that if he was in a bad mood a thunderstorm would suddenly hit the area and would not stop until his mood improved.

It left everyone wondering what had just happened. It had happened a few times where he lost control of his powers. It had ended up in disaster and he felt really terrible when it happened. It was not something that he could control.

His favourite *power* was the ability to see a person's heart through their eyes. He did not know where he had gotten this amazing power, as he had always known that his mother never possessed this ability. His father had been a mortal so there was no chance that he had gotten it from him. He did not complain though, because this had helped him out quite a bit in the past and he knew that it would come in handy again in the future.

Perhaps as soon as he was able to look that Justin in the eyes. He knew though that would not happen anytime soon as he did not want him to know that he was around until there was absolutely no other choice in the matter. It was also one of the main reasons he knew that he could trust Alexandria. She had a good heart.

He did not want to be deceived by anyone so he had to

make sure that she was a good person. He had learned the hard way that some people are really good at hiding their true motives. When things had gotten really bad at one point in his old village, they automatically turned to him and blamed him. No matter what he tried to say in his defense, they had no one else to blame.

They were insistent that it had been him, which is why he had left as soon as he had been able to, even though he had grown up there. It was one of the reasons why he tried not to go into any other village unless it was absolutely necessary.

***

"May I ask how far we are from the troll caves?" Justin asked

"We are not too far from there. Is there any specific reason you are asking?" Alexandria asked, irritated.

"It's been a long journey. I'm quite tired and hungry."

"It should be just beyond those trees up ahead."

"That is exactly what you said an hour ago!" Justin complained. "And to make things worse it looks as though you have barely been walking."

Alexandria rolled her eyes at his exaggeration and listened insistently through Justin's complaining, smiling when she heard exactly what she wanted to hear.

"If you stopped complaining for a few minutes and actually listened carefully, you will hear a stream that is just out of eyesight from here. If we walk a few more feet then we will be there."

"I hear the stream, but truth be told it only makes the thirst and hunger more prominent."

"Stop complaining and keep up. I am sure that the trolls will have food."

She glanced at Justin quickly before continuing the walk, trying to ignore the silent complaints from him. She knew that if they just pushed up a little further, they would be there within minutes.

She sighed when Shadick popped back into her mind at that moment. She decided that it was exhausting having to think about two guys at the same time, as she had to make sure that she didn't accidentally mention the other's name when she meant the one. Every time she thought that she successfully rid her mind of him, he would magically appear right back where he had been.

She had to admit it was rather relaxing knowing that he was close at hand in case something went wrong, like an attack or something similarly bad. Not that she thought that she would actually need his help, but it was good to know there was another hand to help. She found it kind of weird though, barely knowing him yet feeling as though she could trust him with her life. She had never felt like this with anyone besides with her parents and the Faeries.

When he had revealed himself to her the previous night, she had for a few minutes felt panicky that he was about to attack. Yet it had faded and she actually felt relaxed enough to listen to what he had to say and not just shrug it off. It was as though his aura or something had told her that she could relax and that he wouldn't hurt her.

However, she had still been wary of him until the vision had hit her so hard and she did not have a choice to let him in. When she had initially fallen to the ground he had seemed genuinely concerned. The shock of him picking her up was not even as big as she would have expected and his touch calmed her somehow.

"Earth to Alexandria! Are you in there?" Justin asked suddenly

"Oh,sorry. I was in thought and lost track of... never mind. Yes?"

"We have arrived at the caves and you nearly walked right past it."

She looked around shocked and saw that they were indeed at the caves.

"I really did not realise that we arrived," she said sheepishly. "Sorry about that."

"No worries. I was just wondering what was going on when you did not stop immediately, which is why I thought that I should probably make sure that you are okay. I am just happy that we can stop travelling now. It feels like I have been on my feet for years."

"We better locate the trolls so that we can find out where to set up camp and get to work immediately. There is no time to waste on this. The sooner we find out what we need to the better."

"I kind of expected the trolls to be lumbering around all over the place," he said, looking around. "It is their home after all."

"It never crossed your mind that they are perhaps inside the cave or perhaps in the forest gathering food or something?"

"They've been expecting us! We told them that it would take us about a day or two to get here, so I was expecting them to be waiting for us."

"I can't believe you expect some kind of welcoming party!" Alexandria exclaimed, more irritated at him than usual. "This is their home and they still have to live. They should not stop doing whatever they do just because we are here to help them. And not just them, but the entire world."

"So you are saying that they see us than nothing more as an inconvenience, even though we are here to help them?"

"They have not contacted any magical Creatures for years and it was a big deal for them to come and ask for help in the first place. For them asking for help is as though they are admitting they are not strong enough to handle this on their own."

"Welcome to our home, Alexandria," a voice said from behind them, interrupting her. "I hope that the trip did not take too long."

She turned towards the voice smiling…

Chapter 5

Dolomite Caves

"I welcome you to our caves, Alexandria and Justin," Grog said, walking closer to them. "And please, you are not an inconvenience at all. We know that you would be able to help us as well as the other Creatures that live in the forest."

"Thank you for the welcome Grog, it is an honour to be here," Alexandria replied, biting her lip. "Sorry if we are a little late. Someone decided that they could not walk for that long."

"Yes... thank you for the welcome," Justin said, staring at the caves and ignoring her comment.

"It is not much," Grog replied, "but it is what we call home and we love it as it is, perfectly hidden by this mountain range. So, if you did not know we lived here you would just overlook it."

"I think that it is a fantastic home," Alexandria complimented him while studying the cave. "For one, it is close to nature and you are able to have your entire family as well as friends near you at all times."

"That is in fact one of the other reasons why we chose this cave system," Grog informed her. He appeared to be impressed with her appraisal. "It has many different sections, meaning that each has their own privacy and do not have to worry about stepping on each other's toes the whole time.

"Then there are some bigger *rooms* that are being used by the bigger families of the pack. There is a section where we eat. The biggest one of them all is where we have the meetings, which I regret to say has been hit the hardest by these beasts running around. We are in the process of trying to pull it together again so that it can be used again."

"I am sorry about the damage that was caused," Alexandria said kindly. "If you require any help we will help as much as we possibly can."

"Thank you for the offer, but for now we have everything under control. Besides, your job is bigger than just that of cleaning. You guys need to see if you can figure out who is responsible for the attacks on the Creatures." Grog frowned and looked around. "Is there someone else joining you or are we expecting only the two of you?"

"There is no one else with us," Alexandria said, nervously glancing at Justin. "I'm not sure who you expected to join us?"

"It is just that I thought I heard someone else with you," Grog said, his eyes flickering knowingly at the trees beyond them. "I am wrong, I guess."

"Just us for now, unless Amethyst decides to join us at a later stage. Could you perhaps point us in a direction where we can set up our camp? Just so we can take a breather after our trip?

"Do not worry yourselves about setting up camp. I will have one of my men set it up. The important thing is you figuring out who has been attacking us."

"That is very nice of you to offer Grog," Justin said smugly. "I do not exactly feel up to setting up camp in any case."

"Thank you for offering Grog," Alexandria said glowering at Justin before smiling at the approaching troll. "It is not necessary, but I will not argue with our gracious hosts. All our things are in the bags and it is all ready to be set up."

"This is Gargantuan. He is the one that will be responsible for setting up your camp. You can also ask him if you require anything," Grog said shaking his head.

"It is very nice to meet you Gargantuan and thank you for helping us with setting up our camp."

"It is only a pleasure. We have heard so many good things about you, so if this is what I can do to help you then I am happy to do so. If it helps you catch the culprits quicker, then that is even better."

Gargantuan stalked off to an open area with their bags.

"If you could just please follow me into the caves," Grog said, leading the way, "then you can get started on your mission. Perhaps there is some clue that we missed in our investigations that you can pick up."

"I apologize in advance if this a too personal question, but what is wrong with Gargantuan?" Alexandria asked. "He seems to be angered about something. Is it our presence in your home?"

"The problem does not lie with your presence here; Alexandria, please rest assured."

"Is it something that we can help with?" Alexandria asked, not willing to let the matter die.

"If you are able to stop any further devastation to the forest, you will be helping," Grog informed her. "You see, the monsters that did this to the cave also took his wife and child hostage the night of the attack and he has not been able to find any trace of them."

"Oh no!" she exclaimed as she clasped her hand over her mouth. "That is terrible and I understand why he is upset. Any parent would be upset and mad if their wife and child got taken away and they were powerless to stop it from happening. I will work harder now than before; taking a child from its home is almost worse than murdering. It just proves that we are dealing with savages."

"When you see the state of the caves, the scratches and mess that was left, you will be asking the same question that we have been asking. If this is the state that they leave others' homes, how does their place look?"

A strange noise from behind her alerted her but she did not pay much attention to it until she heard the unmistakable wolf howl. She spun around just in time to see Shadick pouncing on Justin.

"Shadick!" Alexandria shouted in shock, dropping all pretense that she didn't know him. "What has gotten into you?!"

"Justin was about to attack you and if I had not jumped in, he would have had you on the ground faster than you could have responded," Shadick told her snarling at Justin

"Why would he attack me if I did not do anything wrong?"

"I have no idea who you are, but I assure you that you are making a really big mistake as I would never harm Alexandria!" Justin shouted, staring wide eyed at Shadick.

"Then answer me this; why were you ready to ambush her?! I saw you crouching, ready to attack at just the right moment."

"I don't know what you mean!"

"Can the both of you just stop and act like adults?!" Alexandria exclaimed at the top of her lungs, the sound reverberating through the caves. Both men looked up at her in shock. "You are both acting as though you are children who do not know how to talk things out like normal people. This is not the time or place to demand attention."

Shadick quickly stood up off Justin and walked towards Alexandria and looking her in the eyes.

"I apologize if that is what it looks like," Shadick said, sincerity shining in his eyes. "My concern only lies with you as he was making a strange noise, something I had not heard before."

"What strange noise did I make according to you?" Justin said angrily, quickly trying to regain his composure. "All I can do is sound like a human, that includes any and all noises that a human would make. But I cannot say the same about you. I am sure that I am not the only one that heard the howl that came from you."

Shadick bared his teeth at Justin, getting ready to jump at him again and this time willing to bite the other man. Alexandria's placed her hand on his arm, stopping him in his tracks as he straightened.

"Neither of you can judge the other as you do not know each other," Alexandria asked closing her eyes angrily. "We are here to help friends and figure out who has been attacking not just them but all of the Creatures. Fighting amongst ourselves will not achieve anything, so I ask the both of you. Could we please continue doing what we came here to do?"

"I have to agree with Alexandria," Grog grumbled, clearly irritated. "If you wish to fight each other, there will be a time and place for that. You are getting distracted from the real reason why you are here in the first place."

She quickly turned her back on the two men and walked on, hoping to distract everyone. She felt a hand land softly on her shoulder and she knew that it was Shadick. She shrugged it off. She was about to ask Grog how far they still had to go, but froze in place when she walked into the room and saw what devastation was within it.

When Grog had mentioned the unsightly look of the place, she did not expect it to be this bad. It looked as though a tornado had been through there. How was any creature able to cause so much destruction to another creature's home? This was not human behaviour at all. They killed any other living creature as though it was child's play and did not expect anything to happen to them. Grog did not have to tell her that those dark marks on the floor were blood, as she could see it clearly as though she had just decided to cut open her own arms.

"I apologize for the unsightliness of this place," Grog said breaking through her shock. "We have tried several times to clean, but we cannot seem to get rid of some of the marks."

"You forgot to tell me that they killed some of the trolls!" Alexandria said, swallowing past the lump in her throat

"Yes, I regret to say they did kill some of our best men when they refused to lay down like useless dogs."

Alexandria felt hands settling on her hips and relaxed a bit, although she knew that it was not wise to feel too much for Shadick. It would only cause trouble for the both of them. It would mean that she had to put her heart on the line and she was not ready for that. She was scared that she would get hurt if she allowed herself to get involved with him.

She knew that, at the end of the journey, they would go their own way. They both had lives to live and families to look after. Taking a deep breath, she stepped away from his touch, feigning preferred interest in the hoof print that was in front of her.

"This is not a normal horse's hoof print," she said, frowning deeply. "It has a different kind of pattern than those of a regular horse. As though the weight is set out differently."

"I do not understand what you mean," Shadick said bending down next to her.

"If you look at that part of the hoof print, when you look closely you will notice the slight differences between that of a horse's hoof and whatever creature this belongs to. A horse's hooves are more oval in shape; these are rounder."

"I see what you mean. You really do have beautiful... I mean good eyes to notice such a slight difference. The differences are really not that prominent."

"I love horses and I think that is why I am able to discern the differences; I doubt that it is anything special."

"Everything about you is special Lexie; never forget that."

Alexandria blushed at his off-handed compliment and tried to concentrate on the hoof print once again.

"I think that this could possibly be a Centaur's hoof print, but Amethyst does not want to believe that the Centaurs are trying to take over the forest, unfortunately."

"But do you really think that it is a possibility though? That the Centaurs are trying to make some kind of play for the forest?"

"Yes, it could very well be. I have said so from the very beginning. I will not tell Amethyst this just yet; without proper proof she will not believe me. She can be very hard headed about some things."

"What is your opinion, Justin?"

"Hmm? Oh, sorry! I was not really concentrating on what you were saying. Could you please repeat the question?" Justin asked looking around at the all the blood.

"I was asking you what you think about these prints we

found," Alexandria repeated. "If I am not mistaken, you work with horses?"

"Yes, I do work with horses, you are right. What about the prints makes you think that it is anything but normal? I have seen plenty of hoof prints like these that do not necessarily fit with what people expect them to look like."

"I have been around horses for most of my life," Alexandria said. "I had my own horse that was very dear to me."

"Like I mentioned before, sometimes it happens that hooves are shaped a little differently."

"That is wrong and I am sure that you know that. The only reason that it would be different is when the owner marks the hooves," Alexandria said seriously, glancing at the marks on the walls. "And if I am not mistaken, they favoured swords for the attack."

"I just did not think that it would make much of a difference if there was a slight discrepancy."

"It does make a difference," she pointed out. "It could be the difference between pointing the fingers at the wrong people. I now have proof that it is not one of the villagers that did this and I am certain that it is indeed Centaurs."

"Have you completely lost your mind? You heard what Amethyst said before this trip started! They have been banished from the forest."

"They may want revenge for being banished," Alexandria said, suggesting a motive.

"Never underestimate your enemy, Justin," Shadick said glaring at Justin. "They can take any shape or form. It is why it is dangerous to believe just anyone. Your enemy could turn out to be your best friend."

"Is there anything you can tell us that could help us?" Alexandria asked. "Anything that stood out during the attack?"

"As I said, most of us were sleeping at the time and when we did wake up there was to a lot of screaming," Grog said, ashamed. "They knocked us out with our own weapons."

"Were you able to tell if the trolls shouted something specific?"

"It was such a chaotic night that we never actually found out what they were looking for. At first, we thought that they wanted the cave for themselves, but when we awoke, we were still in our home, albeit a messy one. All they took were some of the woman and most of the children; we believe that they are to be used as some kind of bargaining chip."

"I promise that if it is at all possible we will return them to you," she told Grog with sincerity ringing in her voice. "We will stop these Creatures that are committing these mindless acts. I see no sense in all this violence and death."

"I have been telling you the whole time that it is only

mortals that are attacking the Creatures. Not these Centaurs that you keep blaming," Justin said angrily.

"You have no idea what you are talking about Justin!" Shadick burst out. "All the signs are there pointing right at the Centaurs! What do you even know about Centaurs, besides what you have heard or been told?"

"I disagree with you wholeheartedly!" Justin responded in kind. "It is most likely some of the villagers that have been trying to take the forest back from the magical Creatures. Those prints mean nothing besides them being from completely normal horses."

"And I disagree with you and I am sure that Lexie would agree with me! Mortals have nothing to do with this at all!"

"Just because you want to be in her good books does not make the splatters on the wall anything but normal."

"Are you saying that only humans use swords?" Shadick retorted, stepping forward. "In the tales that you have heard of the Centaurs, do they not use swords? They either salvage the weapons from fights they won or they craft their own."

"From what I have heard they were banished from this forest years ago and have absolutely no reason to want to come back!"

"Can the two of you please quiet down!" Alexandria shouted, her power throbbing in her head, threatening to explode from all the tension. "Otherwise I will hit the both of you with one of these clubs lying around! We are supposed to be working together, not fighting amongst each other as though we are wild animals."

"I do not trust him, Lexie," Justin said angrily his hands shaking. "There is absolutely no reason for him to have just appeared and offer to help a fight that is not his. And please remember that he tackled me without warning, not the other way around!"

"Guess what," Shadick replied, his ire moments away from physically lashing out, "I do not trust you. How could you possibly know where the Faeries lived unless you purposefully followed Lexie? It is nearly impossible to find Antithia unless you know where it is or a magical creature takes you there. Which in my opinion is even less likely as they do not even know you."

"And what gives the two of you the impression that I trust either of you?" Alexandria stated "But guess what, at the moment there is not a lot of choice, but to trust each other or this mission may as well be a failure. We are not here to judge or shout at each other. But we are here to help *all* of the Creatures in the forest. And perhaps even the humans in the villages."

"I apologize if I came across disrespectful Lexie," Shadick

said, bowing his head "You are right, of course."

"Please just do not do it again. If at the end of all of this mess you still do not like each other, then I give you permission to beat each other to a pulp. But for now, *get along*."

"For the sake of everyone inside as well as outside, I will do my best," Shadick said, not spending a single moment to stare at Justin.

"Sorry about our little disagreement," Justin said, scornfully. "It is just that *wolf boy* here thinks that he is in charge or something."

"Justin, please just stop it!" Alex said despairingly. "Can you please just stop trying to get everyone around you mad? Actually, can the both of you just stop it?"

"I am sorry if I disrespected you with the *wolf boy* comment, Shadick," Justin said through gritted teeth.

"Do not let it happen again, because next time I might just attack you for real and not stop until there is nothing left," Shadick said disdainfully.

Alexandria just shook her head and turned her back on all of them, walking towards some of the broken chairs.

"They are being disrespectful to you by not trying to get along, so do not worry yourself over their little quarrel," Grog muttered to her.

"I know that, it is just that they just met and they are already fighting. It is getting tiring trying to stop them from ripping each other apart."

"The important question is which one of the two you trust the most? Justin or Shadick?"

"I have known Shadick for only about a day, but I trust him more than I do Justin. The first time he showed himself to me he could have easily attacked me, but he didn't. In my eyes, that means everything."

"And has Justin attacked you at some stage during the trip?"

"No, he hasn't attacked me. But I can't explain it, there is just something that I do not trust about him, since the first time he arrived at the waterfall the other day. I do not know what exactly it is about him, but something is warning me to be careful."

"Perhaps you should just trust your feelings, especially about Justin. What did Shadick want last night, if I may ask?"

"He gave me a warning about something and it rang true," she replied, looking closer at the walls. "The blood on here doesn't just belong to trolls. There is another creature's blood on here as well."

"How can you tell the difference? It looks the same to me."

"I am not saying that you have bad eyes or something, but if you look at it in a different light you will notice that some of the blood is slightly thicker than the rest. I am sure that you can confirm this, that a Troll's blood is thicker than a normal creature?"

"I can confirm that as well," Shadick said, suddenly appearing by her side. "If you look over here, the blood is less consistent than those next to it. I have no doubt in my mind that one of your Trolls were able to get in."

"Sure, but that still doesn't tell us *who* attacked the Trolls and their cave, now does it?" Justin asked angrily.

The three of them turned towards Justin and looked at him suspiciously.

"You know what, Justin?" Grog said seriously. "I think that Shadick might just be right about you, that you are in fact on the side of those responsible for the attacks."

"Of course, I am on your side! How could I be on the enemy's side if I do not even know who they are? How can you accuse me of being in on something with the enemy? How is that fair judgment at all?"

"Unless we can prove that he is in fact helping the enemy there is no reason for us to point fingers," Alexandria told them, walking to the opposite wall. "I think that we all need some fresh air to think about what we have found so far."

"We can also have dinner as some of the Trolls have been preparing a meal since we have been busy," Grog said nodding.

"That is highly appreciated, Grog."

"If you would please follow me outside, they have set up your camp, as well as prepared an area where you can just sit and relax," he said, walking out of the main cave with Alexandria, Shadick and Justin following him.

Shadick walked faster until he caught up with Alexandria.

"I apologize if my earlier behaviour was inappropriate in any way. But it really did look as though he was ready to attack and I could not allow that."

"I really do appreciate it Shadick, it is just that I am not used to anyone besides the Faeries caring about me."

"You have to admit that I am not just *another person*."

"Truthfully... in my eyes you are just as normal as I am, and any other person who just met you would say exactly the same thing."

"That means a lot coming from you, Lexie, and I appreciate your honesty. Although I have seen how people react when they see me, and I have witnessed some of them say exactly what they meant. Some have even acted on those feelings and things have gotten ugly just because they thought I was a danger to their families."

"You tell them the truth, though?"

"Some do not take well to strangers; they think what they think because of past experiences. I have tried once or twice to explain that I was not there to cause any trouble but they do not believe me."

"I am really sorry that you have had bad experiences and if it has happened in our village, I apologize if they treated you unfairly."

"I have not been in any village for quite some time now. I scavenge what I can in the forest and only venture to the villages if there is a real need."

"And do you like that kind of living?" Alexandria asked as they stepped out of the caves

"No, I do not, but it is one of the downfalls of being different. But I have kind of gotten used to it and just make it part of your life."

"Alexandria! Shadick! If you come over this way you will find your camp," Grog shouted at them

They walked into the clearing and sat down on the logs that had been placed around the fire. They thanked the trolls who handed them their food, and their mouths watered. They ate until they felt as though their stomachs were ready to burst.

"So what do you believe our next move should be? Perhaps we should investigate further into the caves?" Justin asked suddenly.

"I think that we can call Amethyst and tell her what we have been able to find out so far," Alexandria replied. "Or we can try and see if there is anything else that we can pick up."

"I doubt that there is anything else to be found in the caves," Shadick said taking a sip of his water. "Grog mentioned that they mostly attacked that meeting area."

"That is true as well; we made sure to check every part of the cave. Perhaps we should relax for a bit before I call Amethyst to tell her what we have discovered."

"Alexandria, the Faerie Queen gave us this object, but we are not sure what to do with it," Grog said, handing over the item. "She told us that we had to give it to you as soon as you arrived, but everything that happened made us forget. She also mentioned that you would be able to get more information from it if you were to figure out where she had gotten it from. I am not sure why she did not give it to you, but mentioned that old friends of hers gave it to her."

"It is stone of some kind, but I cannot be sure what it is exactly," Alexandria replied turning it around in her hands.

"May I have a look at it please?" Shadick asked.

"I don't see why you can't. Perhaps you can make out what kind of stone it is."

He looked at it carefully, turned it around then spoke with confidence.

"This is a water stone."

"And what exactly is a water stone?" she asked.

"If someone gave this to Amethyst it could hold a thousand meanings. It basically means a promise was made that cannot be broken."

"Do you mean like a favour or something similar?"

"Whoever was given this stone can ask for anything he or she wants. As long as it is obtainable."

"And how do we know where she got this stone exactly?"

"I do believe that our next destination is the Atlantican Ocean, Lexie," Shadick informed her. "This stone originates from Trilantica. It is only a couple of miles from here."

Alexandria stood up suddenly and looked at Shadick shocked.

"Then let's get going!"

"Just when I thought that we would be stopping for a while," Justin said despondently. "I am so tired of walking."

"What exactly do you mean by *us*? It will only be myself and Lexie that will be traveling to Atlantican Ocean," Shadick replied, his gaze daring Justin to defy him.

"You can't be serious?" Justin replied, ignoring the look. "Do you trust this stranger over me? I mean you barely know him!"

"And I barely know you... I have to agree with Shadick on this one," Alexandria stated. "You will stay here and see if you can find anything else. We should not be gone that long.

Shadick would not attack me; I trust him in that at least."

"Lexie is correct in that assumption. There is no reason for me to attack her as I am here to help her find the Creatures responsible for the attack," Shadick said standing up

"That remains to be seen," Justin muttered

"We will see you in the morning Justin. Look around if you want, but make sure to get a good night's rest!" Alexandria shouted as they disappeared in the forest...

Chapter 6
Mermalani Twins

It felt kind of otherworldly walking to Atlantican Ocean with Shadick. As though she was in some kind of dream. He walked so quietly, it was as though he was purposefully not stepping on any leaves or branches. She could not even hear his breathing. She kept glancing at him just to assure herself that he was still next to her and had not disappeared.

"You seem to be in deep thought?" he asked her unexpectedly.

"I am just running through everything that has happened so far," she replied

"I noticed that you keep glancing at me. As though you are scared of me for some reason. But as far as I can tell you were fine with me a few minutes ago, so I'm not sure what could have happened since then."

"I apologize! It was not my intention to stare and make you uncomfortable."

"You worry too much about hurt feelings, Lexie. You forget

that I am used to being stared at."

"I am not looking at you in contempt or anything. Neither am I scared of you for that matter. Truthfully I am just checking that you are actually still there."

"Is that why you look at me then quickly away? As though you have been caught with your hand in the forbidden cookie jar? So tell me, why do you keep checking on me?"

"You walk without making a noise. I can barely hear it. And I keep thinking that you disappeared... that I just imagined you from the start."

He did not reply to her statement, just kept walking and looking straight ahead of him. Keeping up with him was easier than she would have thought it would be. And she was walking along the path as though she had been traveling it for years. Shadick seemed to always be on the lookout for the both of them.

He was such a strange person and she was not sure what to make of him. It was not as though she considered him anything other than a human; to her he was just like her. She was a human, albeit with special abilities just like him. Sure, their powers were vastly different from each other, but it was what made them special. If someone were to ask her if he looked like anything but a human, she would have said no. It did not matter to her that he was a... Wolfane.

She wondered why he was not living in the village where he had grown up. Or in any of the villages that were scattered around the area. She suddenly stopped when the feeling of being alone overwhelmed her. She glanced around and did not see him anywhere.

"Shadick?!" Alexandria whispered urgently, but there was no reply. "Where could he have disappeared to; it was only a few minutes ago that he had spoken to me. Shadick!"

"I am still here, there is no need to worry," he said from behind her. She blushed as she realised she had spoken her thoughts out loud.

Slowly taking a deep breath she turned towards him.

"Where did you disappear to? I got concerned when you weren't there when I looked."

"There really is no reason to worry; I just needed to check on something."

"Amethyst calls me a worrywart as I tend to worry about my friends, especially if they just disappear. And the attacks lately have not helped that at all."

"I understand, so no need to apologize. But rest assured that I am capable of looking after myself."

"I never said that you aren't able... never mind."

"In case you were still wondering, we are nearly there. It's only a couple more minutes until we get there."

"As you know it has been a long day and I am feeling a little tired. But do not take that as a complaint or something."

"You can relax, Lexie. Traveling can take it out of you and I understand that completely."

She nodded and kept walking, biting her lip and twirling a strand of her hair thoughtfully. It was a minute or so before she realised that they had reached the shoreline and she took a deep breath of the fresh air. Shadick led her off the path a little, walking towards the rock pools.

She was not sure what to expect from the Mermalani twins. All she knew were their names, Roslata and Starlansha. When she had questioned about them, he had told her that they were half mermaid, half human. Just like he was half werewolf and half human. Their mermaid mother had been married to their human father.

They had met when they had just been children and had fallen in love immediately. She had watched him for month before approaching him, but of course not telling what she really was. After that they met up almost daily and things had gone from there.

When they were both 18, they made love for the first time. They did not think about the consequences that might happen, for their love was too real. After a year they found out that she was expecting. She knew that her parents would realise soon enough that something was different so she told them that the baby belonged to a human.

They were furious with her and disowned her without listening to anything else she had to say. She knew that he had to go to William, but she was not sure where he lived and had to stop the first people she ran across. They were helpful enough to point her in the right direction. He organized with the priest to marry them before too many questions could be asked and that is how they bought the house where the twins still lived in.

The twins were born in the house and for a couple of years all went well. Until Mylesha decided that her children had a right to know her parents. After a few weeks, she was able to convince him to let her go. What they had not known was that the sea witch had gathered an army and was constantly patrolling the area in the hopes of capturing one of the King's people.

She was killed. A few days later, the Queen and a personal guard came to inform them of what had happened. Their father was so distraught that he dived into the ocean and drowned not too far from where his wife had been killed. The twins had no one to turn to so they were forced to go live with grandparents they had never met before.

They lived with them for a few years before they had

decided that they needed to be back in the home where they had spent most of their lives. They felt the need to be closer to them and their grandparents did not argue.

"I was just wondering, have you spoken to them before?" Alexandria asked.

"A few times yes. I do not know them that well though. I learned their story from the few times we have spoken, although they have admitted that they aren't sure about some of the facts," Shadick said quickly.

"So they wouldn't be too surprised if we just showed up?"

"I have to warn you that they can a little infuriating at times when they do the twin thing or start muttering about other stuff."

Alexandria was about to ask what he meant, but spotted a small house ahead.

"Is that where we are heading?"

"Indeed it is. It doesn't look like much, but it is an awesome place."

"Shadick?! Is that really you?" a voice drifted towards them

"That is Roslata. She's had a crush on me for years," Shadick whispered urgently. "Yes, Rosy your eyes are not deceiving you; it is indeed me."

"We have not heard one little peep from you in years and then you show up on our doorstep as if you own the world,"

Roslata stated. "Is there a reason why you have been so scarce the last while?"

"Life has been keeping me kind of busy the last while and I have not gotten around too much of anything. But enough about that, I am here on important business. Roslata meet Alexandria, a friend of mine."

"It is an honour to meet you," Alexandria said smiling

Roslata looked her up and down not even pretending to hide her disdain. She turned towards Shadick and grinned.

"Sweetie, tell me that you will be here for a while and that this is not just a quick hi and bye."

"If I were to say that we are staying that would be a lie," Shadick said sighing "As I have mentioned before we are here on business. Is your sister around perhaps?"

"She is neither here, nor is she there."

"Sorry if this is mean or something... but what do you mean by that?" Alexandria asked frowning

"That is for me to know and perhaps for you to find out," she sneered

"Will you behave like the lady I know you are? And give me a straight answer, where is your sister?"

"Ignore my sister Shadick, she woke up on the wrong side of the bed this morning," a voice drifted from behind them. "How have you been the last while?"

"Things have been good thank you for asking. How about you?"

"No real complaints besides the normal things. Now... please introduce me to your lovely friend."

"Starlansha, please meet Alexandria. A new friend of mine that I have promised to help with a few things."

"It is a pleasure to meet you, Alex!" Starlansha said, unexpectedly hugging her.

"It is an honour to make your acquaintance, Starlansha. I love your name!" Alexandria said smiling

"My mother and father chose it and I thank them for it every day. Did I hear that you are here on business?"

"We are indeed. Although it is more the retrieval of a favour than serious business," Shadick stated.

"You should know by now that favours are earned and not just given, Shadick."

"I remember that very well. But if you see what we have you will realise that a favour is owed to us," he said taking the stone out of his pocket and holding it out.

Starlansha's eyes widened and she nodded.

"You are right of course; with this we have no choice but to help you. What is it that you want exactly?"

"That is something we are not completely sure about and we were kind of hoping that you would be able to help us. All

I do know is that we need to figure out who has been attacking the magical Creatures as soon as we can. They need to be stopped before it spills over into the non-magical community."

"We have heard about all of the attacks that have been happening. Some of the underwater Creatures have also been attacked and King Celeriac is furious that no one can give him concrete proof on who is really behind all of this."

"King Celeriac?" Alexandria asked confused

"It shows how much you really know," Roslata sneered. "He is our grandfather, the kind of Trilantica."

"Oh! Shadick mentioned the King and Queen on the way here."

"Stop pretending as though you know everything."

"They are guests of ours, it is only proper that you show respect, Rosy," Starlansha chided her sister.

"I am being nice... to Shadick. The girl has not shown me that I need to be nice to her."

"If you could keep your personal feelings out of this it would be appreciated," Shadick told her angrily. "You should be nice to people whether you know them or not."

"Don't worry about it Shadick, I am used to not being liked," Alexandria said smiling sadly.

"There is no reason for you to feel the way you do. The way Roslata's words are making you feel," Shadick told her touching her cheek.

"Than... thank you Shadick, that means a lot to me," Alexandria replied wide eyed.

"I have to apologize for the way my sister is acting towards you. She normally has a lot more manners," Starlansha apologized.

"Really, there is no need for you to apologize over anything. Everyone is entitled to their own opinions."

"Stop talking about me as though I'm not here!" Roslata shouted angrily.

"We were talking about our grandfather and the attacks. When the news first reached us, he thought that it was nothing. But when the first attacks on his people happened, he was furious that anyone would dare to try anything with him."

"I give you the promise that I have made the Centaurs. We will stop whoever is responsible for all of these attacks, they can't hide forever."

"You are right that they cannot hide forever. But there is absolutely no reason for you to put your own life on the line. Be very careful with whatever you do."

"I have given Lexie my word that I will help her with this fight. So, nothing will happen to her," Shadick told Starlansha.

"In case you have forgotten, I am not completely useless!" Alexandria told him heatedly

"There is no reason for us to fight amongst ourselves," Starlansha said quickly, then glared at her sister as she opened her mouth. "I am sorry to say that we do not know any more than you do at this point. But I do feel like I should warn you... the enemy is closer than you think."

"That is exactly what you told me the first night," Alexandria said turning to Shadick.

"It is not someone that you would expect it to be. Be careful of who you trust to be your friend."

Alexandria's eyes widened and her mind drifted to Justin. Was this the reason why she had felt so against him the whole time? That he was truly working for the enemy and only misleading her? She thought she heard voices, but it did not really get through to her.

"Lexie! Is everything okay?" Shadick asked, shaking her by the shoulder.

"Why are you asking me that? Of course, I am okay."

"You were not listening to the conversation. It was as though you had travelled to another planet or something."

"I was just running through what Starlansha had just said. But I apologize for my moment of distraction."

"Do not worry about it, it happens to the best of us. But as I was saying... I have a feeling that the ones responsible for the attacks will be discovered sooner than they would have liked,"

Starlansha said smiling. "As though something is forcing them to reveal themselves."

"Really?! Is that a good thing?"

"It could be. But you need to be careful that you do not underestimate them."

"Thank you so much for the help, it means a lot more than you think."

"As long as you know that no matter what happens, we will be here for you."

Roslata snorted before blowing Shadick a kiss, diving into the ocean without another word to any of them. Alexandria stared after her, wondering if she had insulted the girl in some way.

"She has been acting so strangely lately and I cannot explain it to you," Starlansha said shaking her head. "For now, it is time for me to say goodbye as I have some things to do. It was nice meeting you Alex."

"It was a pleasure meeting you."

"One more thing... Shadick would it be okay if I had a moment with you?"

"I will excuse myself and go take a long walk on the beach. It's been years," Alexandria said smiling.

She walked off feeling Shadick's eyes on her back. She took a deep breath.

"Is something wrong?" Shadick asked Starlansha.

"Not exactly wrong... but I did see that something will happen between the two of you. I was not sure if I should tell Alex this, but decided that you can make that decision."

"What did you see that made you question yourself?"

"This relationship of yours will develop into more than what it is."

"What relationship are you talking about? We are just friends... besides I do believe that she likes the mortal that she has been travelling with."

"Why do you think Roslata is acting the way that she is? She saw it as well and it irks her that your affections may be wandering away from her."

"So, she is acting that way because of jealousy?"

"It seems that you have forgotten what you have learned about us all those years ago... we are never wrong."

"I am not sure what to think about that. Not that I am complaining that something *maybe* happening between us. It is just that I have my own mission to get back to once I help her."

"You have known her longer than I have so I cannot tell you how she would react to this. But it is something I thought you really should know so that it does not come as too much of a surprise."

"She has been hurt before and I am not sure that she would

take too well to it. From what I have picked up, she only believes that ours is just a friendship. Although she hides her feelings so well that I am not even sure."

"Most women are like a closed book, Shadick. Besides my sister of course, she will let you know exactly what she is thinking."

"Do I need to go for another walk or is it safe for me to be here?" Alexandria asked smiling.

"I have told Shadick what he needs to know."

"This is such a gorgeous place that I would not complain about another walk. My experiences with the ocean and beach are limited."

"We are very happy here. And the view from our home is absolutely breath-taking!" Starlansha said smiling. "Would you like to stay for dinner? Or do you need to get back to your friend?"

"I think that it would be for the best if we got back as soon as possible. We can't be sure if we would be safe in the forest after dark," Shadick said frowning slightly.

"One never knows which Creatures lie in wait in the dark. It is for the best to be careful."

"It really was an honour to meet you Starlansha. Perhaps when things are less unsure, we could meet up again and get to know each other better," Alexandria said.

"I apologise if my sister was being rude, she woke up on the wrong side of the bed this morning," Starlansha said hugging her. "But I agree that we have to meet up again at some point."

"It was good seeing you again, Star. I will have to make a plan to come through and catch up properly," Shadick said.

"We understand that you have your own life and that it isn't always possible for you to come through. But do not become a stranger."

Alexandria waved at her smiling, then turned and walked back toward the forest her mind buzzing with what she had just learned. Why did it seem to get more difficult the longer she was on this journey?

She sighed softly and kept walking…

Chapter 7

Truth Revealed

If she were to sit down and think about everything that had happened before, she would probably have fallen over. It seemed to get more complicated with every step they took. Starlansha had not told her everything that Shadick had that first night and she was not sure how she was supposed to feel about that.

Were they being followed by the enemy the entire trip? She was sure that they would have noticed if something was amiss during the trip. Before the attacks started, she had sometimes wished that something more exciting would happen just to spice it up a little. She was having second thoughts about that now.

"Is there a specific reason why you are so quiet, Lexie? I thought that you would want to talk about what Starlansha and Roslata had told you?" Shadick asked.

"I am just trying to work through some of the things that I have learned so far. It feels like the threat is right there in front of me and I am just missing it," she replied, shaking her head.

"Perhaps if you talk to me about your thoughts, we can work through it and find what is missing?"

"I am not even sure about any of it. Starlansha said exactly what you told me. 'The enemy is closer than you think'? Does that mean that they have been following us the entire time without us noticing? Is it Justin that is a double agent or perhaps even you? Am I over thinking this?"

"Sometimes putting some thoughts aside helps more than constantly thinking about it. I have a feeling that you will figure out the meaning soon enough. I did not expect them to tell us what we already knew, though."

"You seem to have so much trust and confidence in me," she replied, stopping and turning towards him.

"I have seen and heard what you are capable of. And one of these days you will reach your true potential! I am confident in you because I can see the determination in your eyes."

"What makes you so sure that the enemy is closer than I think?"

"Because I looked into someone's eyes and saw that they were nothing but bad news to the magical Creatures," he replied "I have seen some of the destruction that these beasts created and it is worse than you think. They would not think twice about killing you. Your parents would not want you to join them so soon, they would want you to work as hard as possible at this. Besides that... I do not want to lose you either."

"Are you trying to tell me that you actually do know who is behind these attacks? Or that I shouldn't trust you because *you* are behind the attacks? I am not sure why you think you can talk in place of my parents, you never even met them. Neither have I met you before last night!"

"The magical Creatures have always been there for me when I grew up, so I would not hurt them at all. If I were to do that it would be going against what is in my heart, against how my parents raised me. If you think about it, I never said that I ever met your parents. Amethyst told them about me."

"Amethyst told you about my parents? Why would she do that? And when exactly did this happen?"

"She told me a few years ago that the day they found out they were expecting you was their happiest day. That they did everything for you as they wanted you to grow up happy."

"That still doesn't mea..." she started, but Shadick suddenly wrapped his arms around her waist and kissed her deeply.

She did not fight the kiss, even though she was shocked. It was an automatic reaction, but she started kissing him back. Before she could properly process it, he pulled away.

"...that you know my parents... Wow, that was... unexpectedly, unbelievable."

"I have been wanting to do that since I first revealed myself to you."

"Thank you... I think?"

"It is meant as a compliment. I would never insult you, Lexie."

"Then thank you... most guys would probably throw themselves off a cliff before giving women a compliment."

A sudden whoosh from behind them had them both ducking out of the way and rolling on the ground. Alexandria looked up to see an arrow shivering in the tree trunk where her head had just been.

"What the hell?" she asked, shocked. "That came out of nowhere!"

"I am not sure, but I am happy that it didn't hit you," he replied. "Are you okay?"

"Besides a few scratches, I am absolutely fine."

"As long as you are not too hurt. I would blame myself if you were to get hurt."

"It seems that you like saving me," she whispered.

"What do you mean?"

She looked down at where he was still protectively lying half on top of her and she blushed, closing her eyes.

"Oh, you mean with us being so close? I am not complaining about that at all; it is a position I would like to be in more with you," he growled softly, smiling.

"Would it be too forward for me to say that I kind of like it?"

"No, it is not too forward. It makes me happy thinking that you might consider more between us than just a friendship."

She blushed as she realised what he meant and squirmed slightly, pausing when she realised what she was doing. The slight friction seemed to affect them both and she was not sure how to feel about that.

Before she could ask him if he could move, a sound in the nearby bushes made her freeze. He quickly jumped up and stalked closer to the bushes while she stood up slowly frowning. She shivered when she realised that she had felt safe when he had had his arms around her.

"Please don't go too far Shadick; it could be dangerous," she whispered

"Centaur," he whispered urgently as he sniffed the air.

"Do you mean to say that there is a Centaur close by?! They have been banished from the forest years ago!"

"You have been saying that it's Centaurs responsible for the attacks from the very beginning. Why are you doubting it now?"

"Because I don't really want to believe it? I know that they would love to get back at the magical Creatures, but it kind of seems silly for me to have believed it."

"They are a hateful breed and would do anything to get back into the forest, especially if they believe that they had been wrongfully banished."

"There was only trouble in the forest when they were around. And having them back would be the worst. I would hate to see them back here causing trouble again. Although I am ready to fight them if it came down to that."

"I never doubted the fact that you would be ready to fight, Lexie. Or the fact that you have it in you to fight anything. You have a fighting spirit."

"A fighting spirit?"

"It just means that if it came down to it you would kill someone. You would not be happy about it, but if it was for the better you would do it without a second thought."

"Is there any rational person or creature who would kill for fun? But you are right of course, if it came down to it I would kill someone."

She screamed softly when something jumped out at her and pinned her to the ground. She thrashed out hoping that she would get it off of her but to no avail. Shadick was so shocked that he did not react immediately, but he quickly ran towards her and pulled the creature off of her. He threw behind him where it crashed into a large tree.

"Lexie, are you okay?!" he asked pulling her up.

"I am now yes, thank you," she replied breathing hard. "I was not expecting to be attacked."

"Neither did I and I apologize for my slow reaction."

"It did not hurt me; I think that it was more of a fright than anything else. Did you see who or what attacked me?"

"I was concentrating more on getting the thing off of you, but I threw it against that tree," he said pointing to the tree across from them. "I can still see it there, meaning I may have knocked it unconscious."

"Maybe we shouldn't get too close," she said as he walked towards the prone figure.

"What?! How is this possible?"

"What's wrong, Shadick? Is it someone you know?"

"It is someone that *we* know."

"I know who attacked me?"

"I do believe this is where the puzzle pieces start falling into place, I'm afraid. If you walk towards me you will see what both Starlansha and I meant with 'the enemy is closer than you think'. I did not trust him from the very start, but without any proof I could not just point fingers," Shadick said as she joined him.

Alexandria gasped when she saw the face of the person lying there.

"But... It's Justin! Why would he attack me if he is on our side?"

"Lexie, the proof that he is anything but good is right in front of you. How can you doubt what I have been saying?"

"Are you trying to tell me that Justin is the one responsible for the attacks?"

"I doubt that it is just him attacking the Creatures. He has a lot of help, I am sure of it. From the very first time I saw him I was suspicious of him, but you insisted on trusting him."

"We left him at the troll caves... perhaps there was another attack and he was trying to get help!"

"Why do you insist on making excuses for this human? He is not worth your trust. I have noticed him sneaking around the forest when you fell asleep. And I have heard him talking to a friend of his although I was not able to see who it was."

"Perhaps he mistook me for someone else? If it was really him responsible for the attacks, I am sure that he would have attacked me ages ago."

"He has been following us ever since we left the Troll caves! I did not realise it because I was concentrating on getting to our destination, but the proof is right in front of you."

Alexandria stared at him flabbergasted before glancing at Justin's prone form. She closed her eyes and took a deep breath. She trusted Shadick and, no matter how much she argued, the fact remained that Justin attacked her. She was confused as to why he did exactly. Also, as to why he had followed them.

"If you do not believe me, you can ask him yourself," Shadick said as Justin stirred.

"Sorry I did not realise that I was thinking out loud again," as she opened her eyes wider.

Justin sat up and looked around him confused.

"What happened to me? And why does it feel as though I was pounded on the head with a hammer?"

"That is something that I should be asking you, Justin. Why did you attack me without any provocation?" she asked frowning.

"What do you mean?! I did not attack you, there is no reason for me to attack you."

"Then please tell me why you left the caves when we told you to not to follow us? It is safe there and it is too dangerous in here alone."

"Did the Wolfane say something against me? He made you believe that I attacked you? I followed you for the simple reason that I do not trust your so-called *knight in shining armour*. I am not sure why you trust him."

"I am more trustworthy than your little finger. I would not harm her no matter what and she knows that. You on the other hand scream danger," Shadick growled.

"And how would I, a lowly mortal be able to hurt her? I see no reason to hurt her!"

"Lexie is getting in the way of your plan which is why you have been trying to side-track her the whole time."

"I think that you have been sucking your thumb for too long. That reasoning does not make any sense."

"I have in fact seen you sneaking off at night when you think no one is watching. Unfortunately, I was not able to figure out *whom* you have been meeting up with, but I have heard some of your plans."

"That is a very nice, almost believable speech, Shadick."

"When I first saw you, I thought that you were a good pretender. But I see now that it is more the tendency to lie that you are good at."

"What are the two of you talking about? You lost me completely on the part where Justin is trying to side-track me," Alexandria asked confused.

"No need to worry, I am just trying to make Justin admit to the truth."

"Where he gets these farfetched stories, only he would know." Justin said defensively. "If you look at the facts, you will notice that I am in fact correct. He is only half human... and he does not even trust anyone enough to live in a village."

"Why do you insist on not accepting that he is a normal

human just like you and me?" Alexandria asked "The fact that he is a little different should not matter to anyone."

"You can try and convince yourself that he is just a normal human, Alexandria. But he is half werewolf and that makes him dangerous."

"I have to admit that when I first heard about you sneaking off at night, I thought it was just gossip mumblings," Alexandria stated. "But the more I heard about it the more I started wondering why multiple villagers would lie about one specific thing. Some said that perhaps you had heard a noise and went to go look into it.

"But it seemed that you came back with a huge grin on your face every single night. That means that you had heard something good from whomever you had been talking to."

"You should know better than anyone that the villagers love starting rumours. And if there is nothing interesting, they will start the rumour mill with something odd."

"Not about something as serious as this."

"So, you are calling me a liar now as well?"

"That is exactly what she is saying Justin. So just admit that everything thing you say is a lie," Shadick stated aggressively.

"I think that you are planting these preposterous lies and theories into her head. Just so that she would believe you and no one else."

"Shadick has not been planting any theories into my head. You make me sound like a child who falls for every story she has been told. I have had a bad feeling about you ever since you showed up at the waterfall, but I was not quite able to pinpoint why. From the stories that you have been spinning you are anything but a normal human. Is this in fact a lie?" Alexandria asked crossing her arms.

"My father has been right from the get-go... you are too smart for your own good. Just a bothersome witch with the insane need to always help everyone."

"How do you know I am a witch?! I have been very careful during the entire journey to not use my powers," Alexandria asked, astonished.

"You being a witch is the main reason why you have to be killed. Our plan will not work with you alive."

"Have you and your father been planning my death?"

"If I were to take a guess, I would say that their plan was to kill as many of the magical Creatures as possible. When they are too scared to fight back, they will be kicked out of the forest to fend for themselves," Shadick said, stepping closer.

"What our plan is, is none of your business. You are nothing but another hurdle. One that can easily be gotten rid of."

"And are you planning on killing us by yourself? You have no idea what I am truly capable of," Alexandria said, concentrating on her powers.

"There is no way for him to take us both on, by himself. So, there is no need to gather your energy," Shadick said, shaking his head.

"I am never alone, Shadick. There is always someone watching and ready to help," he said confidently

"Have you completely lost your mind? I cannot see nor hear anyone else in the forest."

"Do you really think they would let you hear them if that is not their wish? They are in fact right at this moment ready to help me if the need arises. My father would not let anything happen to me; I am his only heir."

"From what I have been gathering the last while it seems that you are not the only heir. Your clan has come under threats more and more lately. And unless you successfully take out Alexandria your clan will be taken over by someone else."

"Our clan has been run by the same blood line for centuries! We refuse to just give it up as though it is some kind of toy. We will fight for what is ours."

"Sorry to interrupt, but what do the two of you mean by clan?" Alexandria asked.

"It is just another word for an extended family. They are willing to stand together and fight for what they want," Shadick told her seriously. "Just like the Faeries and all the other magical

Creatures."

Justin suddenly ran towards Alexandria, but Shadick jumped in front of him, kicking him to the floor.

"How dare you try and attack Lexie while I am here?! Are you so stupidly desperate for your father's approval that you would attempt a doomed attack?"

Shadick was kicked in the stomach with enough force to send him flying a few feet and he fell hard to the ground. Alexandria ran to him and bent next to him, touching his face concerned.

At that moment it felt as though an earthquake had just hit. The entire forest was shaking beneath her feet. They looked around the area trying to discern between trees and whatever was coming towards them. Shadick quickly jumped to his feet, pulling Alexandria close to him as the Centaurs finally emerged from the darkness...

Chapter 8

Centaurian Enemies

There seemed to be thousands of them emerging from all around them. They were all holding some kind of weapon, ready to attack if they deemed it necessary. Alexandria looked around, alarmed to see so many Centaurs together after so many years.

She automatically knew that Shadick was ready to attack any of the beasts if they made a move to hurt her. She wished that she could have told him to not worry and that everything would be okay. Yet, she knew that those would only be lies. Concentrating on her energy she called it to her once again, ready to help him as much as she could. Why had she insisted on not bringing any of their weapons into the forest?

"Well, well, well... I assume that this is the witch that you have been talking about, Justren?" the largest Centaur asked. "And I see that the Wolfane has also joined her journey. Although it is earlier than what we had planned, I have to congratulate you. You did a whole lot better than any had thought you would do."

The Centaurs did not notice the plants react to her call. They were too distracted by what they seemed to consider a victory. Shadick on the other hand squeezed her hand in warning, but did not say anything.

"Yes, this is indeed the little witch, father. But she is no friend of mine. Even though you had to reveal yourself I was able to get her away from the Trolls and other magical Creatures," Justin said, sneering at Alexandria. "The Wolfane is easily taken care of and is just trying to play hero."

"If only they would have realised how easily it is for us to get rid of so-called *heroes*."

"We are not as easily disposed of as you seem to think! We will not let you just do what you wish..." Alexandria suddenly shouted "And Shadick is a great guy!"

"How dare you address me, witch?! Show some respect and kneel in front of me."

"I refuse to bow to someone who laughs at killing innocent Creatures. And I will speak to whomever I wish. You are the ones lying not just to yourselves but to those that may look up to you."

"Be careful what you say Lexie; they are not known for being lenient," Shadick whispered in her ear.

"Do not worry about me; I know exactly what I am doing.

And there is no way that I would allow a Centaur or anyone else to speak to us as though we are nothing. I will stand up for what is right and what I believe in."

"Would the both of you just stop talking?!" the Centaur shouted angrily making some of the other shoot arrows towards them.

Alexandria lifted her hands making a barrier jump in between them and the arrows. She watched as they fell to the floor.

"If you kill her now all our planning would have been for nothing!"

"What exactly is your plan? To kidnap me in the hopes of me joining your side? Or perhaps torture me for information? I assure you that I do not break easily and you will die long before I tell you anything."

"Oh please! Your parents were not even able to escape our best traps. It was quite funny watching them try and fail over and over again. And we know more about your family than you do."

"Wait... you knew my parents?!"

"There is no reason for us to want you on our side, besides perhaps as a maid and a harlot. As I have already mentioned I know all your family secrets," the Centaur continued as though she had not spoken.

"I would love to know what you know about my parents."

"Does everything always have to be about what you want witch? How do you know that we aren't just planning on killing you when we get tired of entertaining you?" asked a female Centaur.

"Take a deep breath honey. You will have the honour of killing the witch when the time is right," the main Centaur said, putting his hand on her arm.

"This is my true family, Alexandria. Both my parents are alive and well, even though I had to pretend that I had no family," Justin sneered as he walked closer to the Centaurs.

"How can they be your family if you are just a human? You have nothing in common with them!"

"I have to admit that she is right, Justin. You probably had an accident when you were a child and lost your memory. There is no chance that this is your family," Shadick said frowning.

"If you could only see how wrong the both of you are," Justin said before letting out a scream of pure agony.

If they had not known better it would have looked as though he had been attacked by one of the Centaurs as he fell to the ground. After a few seconds he started changing. His neck elongated slightly and his face seemed to be forced back into his head. His clothing disappeared and his legs changed to the body of a horse. They watched as even his hair grew a couple of inches longer.

Alexandria stared at him in shock her mouth slightly open. If she had not witnessed it herself, she would have said that it was impossible. Yet he was the spitting image of the biggest Centaur.

"You realise now how truly wrong you have been? This is indeed my family... this is my father Balditha, the leader of our Clan. And that is my mother Diliante," Justin said pointing towards them.

"How is it possible for you to turn into a human when you are actually a Centaur? Or is it a case of being a human that has the ability to shape shift?" Alexandria asked turning towards Justin.

"My name is *not* Justin contrary to what I had been telling you. It is in fact Justren; named after my great grandfather Justren-Trai. He was one of the strongest leaders of our Clan and made it what it is today," he answered.

"You still have not answered her question, Justren. How is it that you are able to turn into a mortal?" Shadick demanded. "From the research I've done, there is no history of a Centaur being able to change their appearance."

"That is true, but you see I inherited a gene from one of my great, great grandmothers. Who of course was killed by her father when she had the nerve to mate and have a child from a human.

"I got this ability from her child, who was also murdered when she was of the appropriate age. We do not kill children you see. It is an unfortunate thing that we did not realise that she had passed on the gene. But it gave me the ability to change into a human at will. It is rather painful, but completely worth it."

"I do not agree with you at all, but I guess that it could be a handy little trick," Alexandria admitted, frowning.

"So, are you going to tell us your so called 'big plan'? If there really is a plan," Shadick asked looking at Balditha.

"And why do you think that we would tell you of our plan? You are our enemy and you have no business knowing anything about what we are planning. And as we are planning to kill you there is even less of a reason to tell you," Balditha said, sneeringly.

"You just admitted that you will be killing us, so you may as well tell us..."

"I guess that you have a point, Wolfane. But unfortunately, it is not yet time for your death. It would make all our plans fall apart. She is an integral part of the plan you see."

"If it is the last thing I do, I will make sure that you never get your hands on me or anyone else. I will personally kill you even if it took my very last breath," Alexandria said angrily.

"Such an empty promise, from a useless little witch."

"Your downfall will come when you realise that she is not useless," Shadick muttered in her defense.

"How is it that you defend someone you barely know? It is honourable for sure, but it is to no avail."

"If it is worth fighting for, it is not useless. I would fight until my last breath if it meant I got to save my friends."

"That anyone can have such a ridiculous belief is beyond me. There is no use for silly feelings," Justren said, shaking his head.

"I do not see what need a Centaur has for feelings in the first place. You take what you want and it doesn't matter who has to die," Alexandria said sarcastically.

"Such flattery from a lowly being. But do not think that you have us all figure out. We are not some kind of animal that you can tame and call a pet. We have kept to ourselves for years, getting ready to take what is rightfully ours," Balditha added.

"You have one thing right, though. We will kill anyone and everyone that dare stand in our way," Justren told them.

"You seem to be under the impression that we will just bow to your power. Or not fight for our lives? When in fact we will stop you one way or another," Alexandria stated.

"And you can rest assured that I will be there right next to her, along with all the other magical Creatures," Shadick added.

"The age of chivalry has come and gone, Shadick. You are living in the wrong time period for that," Justren said, laughing.

"I am curious though, when exactly did you figure out that you are able to transform into a human?"

"My very first transformation was at the age of two, but it took me four long years before I was truly able to control the change. As I am sure you saw, it is quite a painful experience."

"So, you are telling me that you have been a snot-nosed Centaurian transforming idiot since the tender age of six?! What an accomplishment for a pain in the butt," Shadick said grinning.

"I am not an idiot! How dare you?!" Justren roared angrily.

"If you ask me, you really are an idiot."

"Father! Tell them that I am not an idiot."

"You are now acting like a spoiled brat that didn't get the toy he wanted. A daddy's brat at that," Alexandria added.

"I do not run to my father because I am useless! It is simply not true. I can defend myself when I have to."

"You are wrong once again," Balditha said angrily. "He has not been given anything throughout his life. I have always seen him as a disappointment, until recently of course. So I can assure you that he is neither spoiled or a brat."

One of the Centaurs closest to them loosed an arrow, but

Shadick quickly caught it and broke it in half. Alexandria flinched when another Centaur spoke, his voice booming in the clearing.

"They are a bunch of arrogant children. Why do we not just get rid of them now and save ourselves the trouble for later?"

"I have told you over and over again that she has to be killed during a full moon, Mattson!" Balditha shouted at the Centaur.

"They insult your son and you are just standing there as though it is nothing. You would let them get away with it? How can you just stand by and let them insult your family?"

"For now... but the time will come when I will show absolutely *no* mercy."

"Very well then. The minute you give us the command we will kill them without a second thought."

"I am happy to see that you still know your place, Mattson."

"We should get out of here, before the rest of the army gets restless and starts causing trouble. It will take us a while still to get there," Diliante implored her husband.

"You are right of course."

"So we are just going to leave them unharmed?" Justren asked angrily.

"Yes we are. You promised me that you understood that when I first gave you this mission. Just let the anger build for her and you will be able to kill her easier."

"Can we not just beat them up a little, father? Not kill them, just hurt them enough to prove that we are not useless."

"We are not some kind of wild creature with the need to show off our prowess! We do not prance around hoping that someone finds us attractive."

"I am sorry father; I did not mean any disrespect."

"Then let us get back to camp! Before I lose my temper with you."

Justren turned angrily on them and ran past the army surrounding them. Alexandria could only guess that their camp was in that direction.

"We will meet again soon enough and it will be at that moment, I will have the honour of running my sword through you."

"You wish..." Alexandria whispered, watching them disappearing into the forest. It was only after the noise stopped that she let her guard down and sighed. How was she going to tell Amethyst about all of this?

***

"The arrogance!" Alexandria muttered pacing up and down.

Shadick did not move from his sitting position on one of the rocks. He knew that interrupting her would not be a good idea, so he just watched her as the wind picked up around them.

"How can they think they can just come into the forest and demand that we give it up? They were banished from the forest when my parents were still alive and now they just come prancing back expecting us to just accept it. And the way they spoke about the magical Creatures, as though they were nothing but fleas! You would think that they banished the Creatures and not the other way around."

"You do realise that they can't hear you, right sweetie?" Shadick asked his eyes bemused. "also... your temper is making the wind go all crazy."

Alexandria turned towards him blushing slightly.

"Sorry about my behaviour; I guess that I lost control of my temper."

"There is nothing wrong with losing your temper, Lexie. I have to admit that you are cute when you frown and pace."

She closed her eyes and tried to get her temper under control her, cheeks still bright red. She smacked herself against the head lightly and groaned.

"What is wrong, Lexie?"

"Amethyst is going to be so disappointed when she hears

about this. She trusted Justin... I mean Justren... I mean.. Oh, whatever his name is. She was going on as though she had known him her entire life."

"Ah yes, you will have to contact her when we get back to camp and break the bad news."

"I need to give her an update on what has been happening the last few days. Although I had to do that last night, but I didn't feel as though we had much to tell her."

"Then we should get back to the camp so that we can start working on a plan to get rid of the Centaurs. Perhaps we are lucky enough to stop them before a war breaks out."

"But you heard Balditha! They are determined to start a war no matter what kind of plan we come up with."

"True, but you also heard that they plan you as soon as the next full moon."

"This has nothing to do with me. I care more about the Creatures living in the forest than my own life."

"It that really the right attitude to take?"

Alexandria looked at him incredulously.

"I mean no disrespect," he continued. "It is just that it is a fantastic attitude to have in the long run. But the Creatures living in the forest have to be happy with that decision as well. As it may very well make or break the Centaurs next move."

"It would be impossible for me to do any of that alone...

there is no way I can defend the entire forest on my own."

"But who said that you would be alone? You have the Faeries as well as the Dwarves along with all the other magical Creatures that call the forest their home. And most importantly you have me."

"We have the Centaurs to concentrate on. It is no use dwelling on what might happen."

"Of course, you are right. But just so you know, I have mentioned this before. I have my own mission to get back to once we get rid of the Centaurs."

"You have mentioned it before. And it makes me wonder what your mission is?" Alexandria asked, sitting down across from him.

"If I were to tell you now it might endanger the entire mission. Once I have succeeded, I will tell you all about it. All I can tell you is that I will be even stronger than I am right now."

"Is it a dangerous mission?"

"It is in an area that has been known to kill some men."

She nodded and stood up glancing up at the stars barely visible through the treetops.

"What is fascinating you so much up there? Or is it just an excuse to not make eye contact?"

"I was just trying to figure out what time it is."

"Alexandria!!!" a voice drifted towards them.

"Is that not Grog's voice?" Shadick asked suddenly next to her.

"Yes I do believe that it is him. Grog?!" she shouted back.

"Where have you been?! It has been more than six hours since you departed for Atlantican and we were getting worried for your safety... also... I have some bad news for you."

"I apologize if we took longer than we said it would, it really felt as though it had been only an hour or two."

"What is the bad news you are talking about?" Shadick asked frowning.

"Justin disappeared not long after your departure. We have searched for him, but there is no trace of him anywhere. I can only hope that he did not run into the evil beings while out here on his own," Grog said looking down.

"If only it was as simple as the enemy taking him and killing him. But unfortunately, there is no chance of that happening anytime soon," she muttered.

"What is she talking about?" Grog asked turning to Shadick.

"Justin... or rather Justren is just fine. However that isn't good news for us," Shadick replied and Grog stared at him confused. "Justren is in fact a Centaur, one of the evil beings responsible for the attacks."

"But they were banished from the forest years ago!"

"They were banished, but they are back angrier than ever

before and determined to take over the forest."

"How could I have trusted him? There was a little part of me that hoped that he would truly help us," Alexandria burst out.

"Trusting him was a mistake. But now that you know the truth you can move on from that."

She glared at him before walking towards the caves, leaving Shadick and Grog staring after her.

"We better follow her back to camp; Lexie needs to contact Amethyst and tell her the latest news."

"Amethyst will be devastated by the news. From what I could tell she trusted him even more than Alexandria did."

"She did trust him, but it was just a manipulation trick on his part. A trick to get closer to, Lexie."

"Are you guys coming or not?!" she shouted from the forest.

"We are right behind you, Lexie. Do not worry about us," Shadick said then sighed and followed her voice to the caves…

Chapter 9

Bad News For The Faerie Queen

Alexandria was pacing up and down around the camp, trying to delay the inevitable. She had to tell Amethyst about what they had found out about Justin. Her friend had for some reason believed the man so much that she had sent him with her on this mission. Why had she not been able to figure out the visions earlier? It would have saved all of them the heartache.

Shadick was sitting on one of the logs around the fire and talking to one of the trolls they had learned was named Rudolf. She could not concentrate on exactly what they were saying, but it felt irrelevant in the current situation. He kept glancing at her while every time she froze in her pacing. Her mouth opened as though she was finally going to make the call, but she kept changing her mind.

Without warning Alexandria spotted red lights through the tree line and she backed up quickly. Shadick jumped up and grabbed her by the shoulders reassuringly.

"It is just friends of mine that I called so that they could help us. I wanted them to see if they could locate the Centaurian camp."

"Oh, alright then. More help is always appreciated," she replied in a weak voice.

The wolves stopped a few feet from them. Shadick walked towards them and bent next to the one. He tilted his head as though listening to what the wolf was saying; not that she could hear anything. He stood up after a few minutes and he turned back towards her.

"The Centaurs have returned to the Wastelands."

"But the Wastelands is a two-day trip from here! And that is with no rest. It has only been a couple of hours since they revealed themselves."

"Anything is possible with the Centaurs, Lexie. It seems that you are still underestimating them. I would not put it past them to be able to make that trip in such a short time."

"I do not see how that is possible, but very well."

"Alexandria... I do believe that you should make the call now. She will start panicking if she does not hear from you soon," Grog said from behind her.

She sat down on one of the logs and lightly removed a butterfly pendant from beneath her shirt. She held it in her hands as though it would bite her. Gently bringing it to her lips and kissing it lightly, she watched as the coloured wings fluttered. It shot into the air and floated in front of her. After a few seconds of bright light, a hologram of Amethyst appeared.

"Just when I was starting to worry about you! You were supposed to call me last night, but I just shrugged it off as you being you," Amethyst said.

"Am..." Alexandria smiled, "you are the Faerie Queen. You know about things; things that isn't necessarily possible."

"Oh... you are right of course. But if I was to be honest with you it still does not feel real. It is as though my mother would walk through the Waterfall and take over because I am a disappointment."

"That will only happen in your wildest dreams. But I have to admit that it would be nice to see her again."

"Yes, it would be fantastic to see her again. I still have those dreams you know."

"Lexie, it is time that you told her," Shadick said, sitting down next to her.

"Shadick?! Am I overtired or is that really you? I haven't seen you in years! How have you been doing?" Amethyst asked grinning.

"I am well as always; there is no need for complaints. But thank you for asking."

"Oh and hello Grog! How are you doing this... early morning?"

"Always well m'lady," Grog grumbled.

"Are the lot of you having a party without me? Everyone is there that I know, including Shadick. I did not even know that you knew him, Alex!"

"Am..." Alexandria said softly.

"Did my invitation get lost or something? It seems to be a very jovial affair," she said, ignoring Alexandria.

"Am, I have some news..."

"But where is Justin? I can't seem to see him in the crowd. Is he hiding like a little boy? Scared of the big bad trolls?"

"Amethyst!" Alexandria shouted at the hologram and everyone stared at her. "I have some bad news. And I can promise you that you will not be happy with what you hear."

"Did something happen to Justin? Did the evil beings capture him?!"

Alexandria stared at her friend's shocked and worried face and her courage seemed to slip to her feet. Shadick hugged her gently and squeezed lightly trying to lend her his strength.

"Am... Justren is one of the enemies that we have been looking for."

"Justren? Who is this person you speak of?"

"We found out that Justin's real name is actually Justren."

"Perhaps it would be best for you to start from the beginning. It doesn't help if we throw her the facts and she doesn't know the back-story," Shadick said.

She nodded and started telling Amethyst about what had happened on the trip ever since they had left. From how he had kept delaying her to how they had found out that Justin had been working with the Centaurs to gain her trust. How the Centaurs wanted to take over the forest once again as they felt robbed of their true home. And how they had found out who Justren really was only a few hours before.

She informed Amethyst that they were planning on killing someone during a full moon, but she did not mention that it was her destiny. Amethyst would be outraged and probably do something dangerous. As she was telling the tale she felt Shadick next to her, supporting her in silence. What she noticed most was her friend's face and how smile slowly disappeared only to be replaced by sadness. She was trying to hide the fact that she was upset, but Alexandria knew her better.

Amethyst suddenly disappeared from the hologram and Alexandria jumped up, holding onto Shadick's hand.

"Am?! What happened?"

"I am just very shocked about what I have just been told. I trusted him and sent him with you."

"I know that has come as a shock. We both trusted him and

he stabbed us in the back... figuratively of course."

"Please do not feel bad Alex, this is not your fault."

"But perhaps if I had paid my premonitions more heed, I could have prevented all of this."

"No, Alex. This is not your fault at all. There is no way that you could have stopped any of this from happening."

"Your mother always told me that I should spend more time on my premonitions if they happened. But I just thought that she was being silly."

"Lexie, sweetie... she is right. There was no way how you could have prevented any of this."

Amethyst covered a smile as she noticed the use of endearments and the way her friend was clutching Shadick's hand; something was brewing between the pair.

"From what you have told me so far it's easy to see that they have been planning this for years. And unless your premonitions happened to show you exactly what would happen there is nothing that we could have done to stop this. Unless your visions suddenly showed you the past and years into the future and you forgot to tell me about it."

"You would know if that suddenly happened, although I have to admit that it would be useful little trick. But..."

"There is no need for 'but', Alex. We need to make plans to ensure that nothing more happens with the magical Creatures.

It is time that we send out a call to arms to all of our allies. This does not just involve us, but them as well. I will send the messenger Faeries at once."

"Our caves are open to those willing to help with the war. There is also a little more space over here than at your Waterfalls, your majesty. If we get to work soon, we can organize proper camps for everyone," Grog said in a serious tone.

"That would be a lot of help Grog, it is greatly appreciated. As well as an excellent idea! But it is of utmost important that the camps are separated so as to keep the peace, as not everyone gets along. I know that they will not be happy about this, but it has to be done. It is time for differences to be put aside."

"I will give my men the proper instructions and we will make sure that there is no discord."

Alexandria watched astonished as Grog walked away and grumbled something to his men. They started working on the camp immediately without any complaint.

"As soon as I am done talking to you, I will send the Faeries to the leaders so that action can be taken."

"Am, you know very well that the Unicorns hate having to travel by magic. Why not get everyone moving at first light? I know that you will not be able to rest after this news, but that energy can be used to plan this properly," Alexandria suggested.

"Truthfully, I have not slept the last few days anyways. But you are right of course. The Unicorns are going to love this, as they have been trying to warn me of a coming war for months now. But I have been wondering, Shadick... when did you arrive? At last report you were still in Crenaphe?"

"I got to your Waterfall just as Lexie and Justin started their journey and I sensed unrest. I introduced myself to her that first night just so she knew that she had help."

"I know that you wouldn't just drop your mission without any real cause. What is it that you spoke about exactly?"

"I had been getting a bad feeling about something going to happen for a few days. But I did not just jump into action at nothing so I spoke to some of the villagers to see if they knew anything. They mentioned rumours that had been flying around about unexplained happenings in Aribatiath. So I thought that it would be best to come and investigate.

"I knew my best bet would be speaking with you when I noticed Lexie and Justren leaving. I quickly assessed the situation and figured that I would be of more help to her. From the first time I saw him I was uneasy and wanted to do something, but you know that I do not just act."

"And how is it that the two of you know each other? Was he another orphan that your mother decided to take in?"

Alexandria asked

"No, her mother did not take me in. My parents were around until a few years ago when they died due to natural causes," he replied sadly.

"Oh! Sorry for my thoughtlessness."

"We also met years ago at a party my mother threw for her friends," Amethyst said absently. "He stumbled upon the Waterfall again about a year ago and we caught up."

"Why was I not there?" Alexandria asked frowning.

"You, my dearest friend, were busy fighting off the thousands of proposals from the young men in the village. It was during that week where you were unable to visit because of the constant attention."

"I will never forget that week! They proposed to me about seven times a day. They luckily stopped bothering me of their own accord, just as I was going to put a spell on them."

"Yes, and now you are stuck with all the other women telling you how their wedding plans are going. And all the secret babies that will suddenly appear."

"Don't remind me! It is tiring hearing about all of their dresses and the plans for a big wedding."

"So, is there any immediate wedding plans in your immediate future?" Shadick asked curiously.

"No! It is rather difficult getting to know someone when

you have to fight evil guys the whole time. And most of the humans in the village would call a major witch hunt if they were to find out about me."

"Surely you know a spell that would stop them from telling anyone? Or just not use magic when they are around?"

"That would not be fair to either me or any guy that I might like. I want true love, nothing forced. Besides... magic has been part of my life for so long that I would not be able to live without it for long," Alexandria said sadly then frowned. "Am, is everything okay? You blanched just now when I mentioned the village."

"I am fine, really. There is just something that I need to do before we get moving," Amethyst replied biting her lip.

"Alright then..." she said just as she heard the horn go off at the Waterfall.

"I just informed Juasta to blow the horn for an emergency meeting. So I should get going so that I can inform the Faeries of the move. They need to get ready."

"It still amazes me that Juasta has the ability to appear when he is needed."

"It is an amazing ability of his and I will not complain about it at all. And he is the only one that can blow that darn horn."

"We will see you in the morrow then, Am."

"Yes, it will be good to see after so long," Shadick said

smiling, still trying to not stare at Alexandria.

Amethyst nodded then disappeared, a few seconds later the butterfly pendant lightly floated into her hands and became absolutely still.

"That is not something I want to do ever again. She may not be showing it, but she is heartbroken," Alexandria said sighing softly and glancing at the wolves.

"She is a strong person and she will get over this soon enough. You will see in the morning that she will be fine," Shadick told her.

"Why are you looking at me so intensely? Is there something wrong with me?"

"There is absolutely nothing wrong with you Lexie. I am just wondering what is going on in your head, as per usual."

"Too many things to worry about, truth be told."

"Do you wish to talk about some of your thoughts? Perhaps I can clear some of the confusion?"

"Thank you for the offer, but I first need to sort through it all. But I now know that I can turn to you," she said smiling.

Shadick stood up and walked towards the wolves; they barely looked at him from their relaxed positions. Alexandria not wanting bother shuffled to where the trolls were busy working on the camps, she was amazed at what they had already accomplished.

"Is everything okay with the Faerie Queen? It seemed as though she took the news worse than I thought," Grog asked her.

"She was surprised by the news yes, although I have to admit it was more than even I thought," she replied sighing.

"Why is it that she trusted Justren so much when she barely knew him?"

"I think that she still hopes that the humans and magical Creatures can be friends again. After so many years it is her biggest dream. But as you saw, he seemed to wrap everyone around his little fingers when he arrived at Antithia."

"It is not something I truly understand, but even we were a little entranced by him. He knew just what to say to set us all at ease."

"You were all fools for falling for that scoundrels lies," muttered one of the passing trolls "I just knew that he would bring us a lot of trouble. But as I do not trust the witch next to you or the Wolfane. I guess that does not really count for much."

"I have told you many times not to speak about things you know nothing of, Leastatam," Grog said. "You only saw Justren here in camp and that is not enough to judge. And surely you can see that Alexandria as well as Shadick are good people."

"But just look at that! He has brought wolves into our home

and we have not had any wolves here for years. And within two hours there is an entire pack here."

"Are the wolves a problem Leastata?" Alexandria asked him coldly.

"There is no problem at all, Alexandria. Leastata just needs to learn that in times of war all Creatures are even and should stand together," Grog assured her. "Now get back to work and keep your nose out of business that is of no concern of yours."

"I did not realise that Trolls and Wolves did not get along and I apologize for that. I am sure that they could go into the forest so as to not bother you."

"There was just a *slight* disagreement with a pack a few years ago, but it is no time to bring that up."

She nodded and turned away from the working Trolls and looked at Shadick who was still talking to the wolves. He had not noticed their discussion and she was kind of happy for that, as she was not in the mood for trouble.

"What do you feel for Shadick, if I may ask?" Grog asked, glancing at Shadick.

"He is a good person and from the little I have seen he is an excellent warrior..."

"I do not mean as a warrior, Alexandria. It seems that you are falling for him, because I have seen you get lost in thought just looking at him. And your eyes light up when he speaks."

"What?! No that isn't true at all. I barely know him, but he has shown true friendship the past day or so. I would have been in a lot more trouble if he had been on the side of the Centaurs."

"Then answer me this... why does it look as though you wish to be the wolf that he is petting so lovingly?"

"That is insane! There is no reason for me to wish that," she replied turning away from Shadick

"Perhaps it is time for you to step back and have a good look at your feelings. You might learn a thing or two," Grog said walking away.

She shook her head trying to ignore the effect Grog's words had on her. She walked away from the Trolls' who was still busy building and moved towards the fire that was still burning. She sat down and stared at the logs, her thoughts mile's away. At first, she did not notice the wolf approaching and started a little when it sniffed her hand before bumping it lightly.

Biting her lip, she cautiously lifted her hand and scratched its head trying to not move too quickly. It was with a relieved sigh when the wolf closed its eyes. Smiling she glanced up and found Shadick staring at her.

"Am I doing something wrong?" she asked quickly lifting her hand away from the wolf's head while the wolf whined softly.

"I am just surprised. Managwa is the leader of the pack and is normally very cautious of people. He does not allow anyone to pet him besides me," Shadick replied, staring at the wolf shocked as it rested its head on her leg

"Really?"

"You really do have a way with people as well as animals, Lexie. And it has nothing to do with you being a witch. You seem to attract people to you as though it is a natural thing."

"Thank you Shadick," she whispered, blushing.

The wolf licked her hand then trotted back to the rest of its pack and lied down. Her attention was pulled back to the fire and she lost herself in it once again. She felt Shadick sitting down next to her, but did not look at him.

"Are you sure that everything is okay? Your thoughts really are miles away from here."

"Nothing is wrong, I am just trying to figure out what our next move should be."

"Everything will work out for the best Lexie; you should not worry so much," he said, lightly touching her shoulder.

"No, there is absolutely no reason for worry... I should just allow the Centaurs to kill all of the magical Creatures and take over their home. It is not a big deal at all," she muttered standing up and walking away from him.

"Lexie! That is not what I meant at all!" he shouted after her and all the Trolls turned towards him curiously.

He shook his head and just stared at her disappearing back. It had not been his intention to upset her the way that he had. He just wanted to make her feel better so that she could get some proper rest.

Managwa walked over to him and looked him into his eyes. Shadick laughed softly when the wolf growled softly and bit his hand softly before staring in the direction she had disappeared to. The wolf was telling him to follow her.

He stood up and patted the wolf before walking to the forest. He had to find her and apologize for not being more supportive. It was not as though he did not know what a war did to people. Alexandria had a good heart and it was her family and friends that had been suffering the most. He wished that he could assure her that there would not be any lives lost but it would only be a lie. Without really thinking about it he followed her tail and ended up at the stream that was situated a few miles from the Caves.

She was sitting next to the stream, thoughtfully running her hand through the running water. He was glad that she was smiling at least as it meant that she wasn't too upset at him. But it made him curious as to what she was thinking about...

Chapter 10

An Unexpected Event

She felt completely drained after dealing with not just Justen's betrayal, but Amethyst's disappointment. It was as though she had just summoned some kind of Creature and it had drained all of her energy. Or as though she had not gotten any sleep for days on end.

Yet she knew it was because she knew exactly how Amethyst felt about the lies that had been told. No one had really lied to Amethyst as they had respected her too much. She had truly believed that he had just been a helpful human wanting to help. It was with relief that she did not have to be alone when she had told her the news. Shadick had been there, silently supporting her.

After she had stormed away from camp, she had automatically come to the stream situated not far from the caves. She needed to be alone for a bit and just play through all of the events of the day. Her thoughts were a mess and she wanted to get them sorted before having to deal with anything or anyone.

There had to be a way to make up for what had happened, perhaps a plan that would help them with all of this. She still felt responsible for not paying attention to her premonitions. It felt like she should have taken more than just a few minutes to think about what she had seen. Why had she not listened to the voice in the back of her head when it had screamed at her about danger? It had seemed too impossible as evil had not plagued the forest for so many years.

Her parents had been a big part of getting the forest to the way it had been. They had fought until their last breaths to keep the evil from returning. Of course, there were some evil Creatures living in the forest, but they were not stupid enough to try anything.

There was a standing agreement that as long as no one bothers the other they were willing to live in peace. As for the humans in the villages, a treaty had been drawn up between them and the Faeries. They stayed out of the forest unless there was an absolute necessity for them to be there. It had been a good thing that the forest was bordered by another they could use for hunting and foraging. There had been mutual agreement that each of them would take care of their own problems and not drag the others into it.

She turned and leaned against a tree, sighing softly as her

thoughts turned to her parents. Even though she had only been six years old when her parents had died, Valencia had always ensured that she did not feel like an orphan. She had been whisked away to the Waterfall to live with them and so that she did not end up in a human orphanage.

When she was old enough, she moved back to her parents' home. In the beginning the villagers had brought her bread, milk or a freshly baked pie. And when the flowers were in bloom, they gave her flowers hoping to cheer her up a little. She had not regretted moving back to village for a second as she loved the tranquility and she had made some friends.

Some of the villagers had been shocked that she was able to recall small details about her parents. She remembered every single detail of her parents faces. How her dad had been the handsomest man with raven black hair. He used to call her his little angel and had always been ready to fight if there was no other way out.

He had always been so serious when a meeting had been held and when he thought she was not close at hand. But when they were alone, he was in the happiest of moods and would ensure that she always laughed. And when she got the frown line on her forehead, he would make a joke and all would be well. He had truly been in love with her mother and they had been the world to him.

Her mother used to turn head at her beauty. She had striking grey eyes and had the loveliest smile. Alexandria remembered how her mother had smelled like fresh roses just after the summer rain. When she was around the house, she would be humming songs and smiling while working on the house. When she was sure that no one would pop in for tea she would teach her some spells.

She had learnt her first spell when she was only two years old, and her parents had laughed at how she had been able to learn so fast when she could barely talk. Her father had insisted that she know how to ride a horse properly and had taken her hunting several times. He had found it funny when she tried picking up his sword only to fall over, but he patiently taught her how to properly hold weapons.

The villagers had joked with her mother that she had been born a fighter and not the lady that she had hoped. Her mother would just smile and tell them that she would rather know that she would be able to look after herself than having to worry about how she looked. There were times though that she dressed her in fancy and frilly dresses and she would pull a face at how ridiculous she felt. She smiled and pretended that she loved it and would thank her mom for thinking about her, quickly coming up with excuses to not wear it for much longer.

She sometimes wished that she had been able to stop their

deaths, but knew that it would not have been possible. It had been years ago and what would she have been able to do that her parents had not been able to do? A young girl of six was not strong enough to protect her parents.

Sighing, she pulled her thoughts back to the present while lightly putting her feet in the stream. She had been watching the young men as they realised that there were things besides violence to be seen. Running after a girl they thought they might like, flirting shamelessly and throwing compliments around without care. Some of her friends had already been asked to get married and they had been so happy that they ran to her to show her the ring.

When they weren't looking, she would just roll her eyes at what she considered frivolity. When the first guy had asked her for her hand, she had been so shocked that she had slipped over her own words trying to say no.

Alexandria doubted that she would ever get married; what was the use when they would never accept her for who she really was? She was sure to not sow any interest in the guys and kept to herself as much as was possible. If she really thought about it, she did not feel any connection with the guys that lived in the village. The only guy that she may have considered turned out to be a Centaur.

Yet he had not given her the time of day and she had moved

on from it. A blush slowly formed on her cheeks as she thought about Shadick and how he made her feel. If she closed her eyes, she was still able to feel his arms around her and it felt like home. Tilting her head, she wondered how it would be if she were to give herself to him.

She quickly shook the images from her mind and took a deep breath. Why was it that she came to the stream to try and figure out some kind of plan and she ended up imagining a naked Shadick? It was of great importance that they stopped the Centaurs from taking over. She was not ready to see the major loss to life if they were to start the killing. They would not care about families and friends.

Groaning softly, her mind drifted to Shadick on the battlefield, sword at the ready with sweat dripping down his face.

"Is something the matter, Lexie? It seems as though you would feel more comfortable inside the water," Shadick asked, appearing behind her.

"Why is it that you always move so quietly? I would have thought that by now I would be able to tell when you are approaching," she answered shaking her head.

"I did not mean to give you a fright and I apologize."

"No worries, I am still breathing," she bit her lip then turned on him again. "How long have you been standing there exactly?"

"Not that long, only a minute or so. I would have said something, but your thoughts seemed to be somewhere else. May I ask what is making you look as though it is the end of the world?"

"I was just remembering my parents and everything they had taught me when they had still been around."

"I thought that they had died when you had just been a girl?"

"They did yes... I was only six years old when they died. But I seem to have almost perfect recall of them, which I'm happy about. Of course I wish that they were still around; they would have known exactly what to do next."

"And how can you be so certain that they would be able to fix everything so easily?"

"Because they would not have let this get as far as it has. They would have been able to tell that danger was approaching and would have stopped it."

"You are blaming yourself for wanting to trust Justren."

"Maybe a little... I keep thinking that perhaps if I had read his mind. Or just listened to the gut feeling. Or even sat down to interpret my visions that it would have gone differently."

"It is not your fault that he had manipulated you or that he turned out to be evil. You are a good person expecting the same from everyone else."

"But what if I had just used my powers to find out more about him?"

"Things happen for a reason Lexie and we do not have the control over any of it. As for not using your powers, you thought that it would only cause you more trouble than would have been necessary."

"And what am I supposed to do now? Just watch my friends and family get killed?" she asked standing up, wanting to get away from him again.

"Lexie, wait! My words seem to be getting me into more trouble than it's supposed to," he said, grabbing her arm. "I can see that it is not just the Centaurs causing havoc on your mind. Neither is it the war looming either. I can see the unhappiness in your eyes and I want to take it away, but I am not sure how."

She glanced down at his hand chewing her lip, feeling torn. She wanted Shadick to let go of her and to just let her walk away from him. Yet, she also wanted him to pull her into his embrace and to make her forget everything and everyone for a while.

How was it that she was feeling so confused about all of this? She barely knew the man but she was ready to just go for it and let him make her squirm. It was the first time that she really noticed things about a guy and wanted more than just the occasional hug. Why now all of a sudden did it seem like she would throw caution to the wind and to just go with it?

Looking into his eyes she saw his blazing blue eyes and how his hair just touched his shoulders. He seemed to get irritated with it at times and she wondered why he not have it cut if it bothered him so much?

It truly felt as though she had known him for her whole life and not just a few days. She felt comfortable with him around, although she sometimes wanted to hit him out of frustration. It was as though she would be able to just forget that she had been raised right. To fall into bed with him and pretend that nothing had happened the next day.

If she let her heart fall for him, it would only get broken as he would be leaving for his own mission as soon as he was able to. Would she be able to do that? Move on as though he had never existed and did not make her heart soar? Yes, she would be able to move on from him. The problem was that she would not be able to live with herself... he was already a major part of her life and it would be empty without him.

"Lexie are you even listening to me?" his voice broke through her reverie.

"Hmm? I'm sorry! I was lost in my thoughts there for a few minutes and did not hear anything," she said, blushing.

"I was just asking you if you wanted to get back to camp?"

"I'm ready to go back whenever you are."

He looked down at her frowning, opening his mouth as though he was about to say something, but changed his mind at the last minute. He turned his back on her and shook his head; she shrugged and stepped past him. Before she got too far he pulled her to him and kissed her deeply, making the world around her disappear.

Her arms seemed to have minds of their own as they wrapped around his neck and pulled him closer. She moaned softly as he lightly bit her lip, her eyes closed in the joy she was feeling. He ran a finger down her cheek and she shivered slightly opening her eyes. It was through misty eyes that she saw the desire in his eyes and knew that he wanted the same.

She scratched his neck and he growled in the back of his throat, while her hands drifted down his body, magically undoing his shirt. His heartbeat was erratic, but not in a bad way. In the back of her mind she felt his hands slipping underneath her shirt and cupping her breasts.

She started kissing him again and gave up the part of herself that wanted to stop this before it could go any further; it was without a thought that she let his shirt slip off his shoulders. It was as though she was unable to stop touching him; he felt so powerful and she could not get enough of it.

"We can still stop this before it goes any further. And I

would rather have you stop it now than you hating yourself later," he whispered through her kisses.

"It is already too late for me to put a stop to this... and I do want it. You have no idea how much I want this."

He growled a little louder before removing her shirt and throwing it to the floor; he swept her into his arms and carried her to the stream. She kept kissing him as he laid her down on a patch of grass a soft moan escaping from her lips as the passion took over.

***

At some point in the early morning she woke up and was confused why her body felt as though it had been drained of all of its blood. Looking up at the stars she tried to figure out what had happened the last few hours to make her feel this way. Her mind was fuzzy and she was unable to concentrate on anything besides the sleep pulling back into its arms. She frowned as she felt the weight on her stomach as well as across her leg.

She turned her head to the side and saw Shadick lying there, next to her his arm across her stomach and his one leg between hers. It was as though the lights in her head suddenly came back on and she blushed scarlet. She dared not move in the fear that he would wake up. She did not want that; she just wanted to relive the previous evening as though on some kind of loop.

She was more relaxed than she had been in quite a few years and it felt good. She wondered how he had known to be gentle with her... or perhaps that was just how he normally was? It had made her fly and she would want to experience it again.

After it had all been done, he had pulled her head onto his chest and held her tightly not saying a word. How she had fallen asleep right before she wanted to thank him. Her muscles tightened as the war came rushing back; why had she let herself get lost in all of this when there were more important things happening?

She took a deep breath and forced herself to not think about it, not to let the moment be spoiled by the worries of the morning. It was something that could wait until she felt more coherent and had help from her sister. What would Amethyst say if she was to find out what had happened? Shocked? Or completely unsurprised?

She had always been the good little girl, never stepping out of line, and here she was. In the arms of a guy she had only known a few days. Perhaps she would not tell her yet... not until it had really sunk into her own head that she was not the *pure* one anymore. The one everyone looked at thinking that she was weird because she had not done it. She grinned as she slipped back into sleep. She did not regret anything...

Chapter 11

Amethyst's Arrival

He woke up with a smile, knowing exactly why his body felt more relaxed than it had in years. It was no question who was lying next to him; he slowly turned his head to look at her. She was still fast asleep, but there was a smile curving across her lips and it suited her. The previous evening had been perfect, but in the new light of day it seemed that perhaps he had been foolish.

It had started off so well, although he thought that perhaps he should have just walked away before it had gone too far. He was a little upset by the fact that she had not told him that she had been a virgin; not that he would have rejected her, but it would have been nice if he had known.

Quietly slipping from her embrace he got up and started getting dressed. He gathered her clothes as well, putting it next to her still sleeping form. The smile was gone and her thoughts seemed to be bothering her. What had gotten into him?! Why had he let this happen as though they were just helpless teenagers that were head over heels in love with each other?

He distracted himself by catching a few fish and starting a fire to cook. How was he going to explain to Amethyst that he had taken advantage of her best friend... no, her sister? When he had gone to visit her all those months ago, she had told him about how she had lost her parents at a young age. Even if she would not admit it that she was still hurting.

She had told him what a free spirit she was and always saw the good in everything. How even when the times were tough, she was making jokes and making sure that the bad did not take over. In all the time that he had been with girls it had always been the same. Where he would get with them, only to make himself happy and disappear before they could want more. A trick he had learned from his best friend.

When he had come this way, he had not expected to meet her. It had been his intention to come and find out what was happening with these attacks after the rumours that had been flying around. It had never crossed his mind that he would walk away from talking to Amethyst about everything and to follow the vivacious girl she had told him about.

He had shrugged it off as just fate. He was there to help the Faerie Queen and that was it, and the best way to do that seemed to be to follow Alexandria. She seemed to be one of the main players and it would be the easiest way to find out as much as was possible.

He shook his and thought about why he not just stuck to his original plan. It would have been easy enough to pass along the message via Amethyst and asked her to tell Alexandria, but he had been intrigued. It was as though his body had a mind of its own and he was unable to make his mind convince him of anything else.

When he thought about it now, it had been as though he had been attracted to her from the get-go and he just had to see what happened to her next. Yet, why had he not just given her the message and moved on? It should have been an easy decision. He did have his own mission after all and he was distracting himself by following them.

It had been his second plan, but the minute he had seen Justren acting so scaly he had he had thrown everything into the wind and kept following them. He turned towards Alexandria's still sleeping form and wondered what he had gotten himself into...

***

She was watching him through half closed eyes; he did not realise that she was awake. The moment he had moved to get dressed she had woken up. She was not sure what would happen when he realised that she was awake. He seemed to be distant and distracted and it was with a heavy feeling in her heart that she thought that it was her fault. Perhaps she should not have gone into his arms so willingly. If he was regretting it so much though perhaps, he should have stopped it and not waited for her to pull away.

For her it had been the best feeling being in his arms, only hidden by the darkness. Yet, the sun was out now and it seemed that it changed everything. Maybe he was beating himself up for ever meeting her in the first place. It was not as though she had actively been looking for him, he had come after her.

She quickly closed her eyes and pretended to be asleep as he turned towards her. When she was sure that he was not paying her any attention, she slipped into the stream and disappeared into the slightly deeper water. If she washed hard enough would it make everything disappear?

She swam up and took a deep breath, staring at rocks fighting against the tide. She had thought that the previous evening had been a good thing. Something to be appreciated and not looked on as a bad thing.

"Lexie?! Where are you?" his voice broke through her reverie and she heard him mutter. "I could have sworn that she had been right there a minute ago."

She sank lightly to the bottom of the stream for a few

seconds wondering if it would hurt if she were to drown herself right here. She shook her head and swam back to the edge of the stream and slowly got out.

"Lexie?!" he shouted again panicked.

"I'm over here Shadick; there is no need to panic," she said taking a deep breath.

"You almost gave me a heart attack! You just disappea..." he started then froze as he realised she was standing there naked. "I apologise; it did not cross my mind that you were bathing."

"Could you please pass my clothes?" she asked trying not to blush.

"Yes of course... right away," he said handing her, her clothing.

"It is not as though it is the first time you've seen me naked..."

"I did not mean to stare."

"I was not thinking about last night in that comment," she said then as he looked confused. "The very first night we met... I was also getting out of the stream and you were right there watching me. It seems that awkward moments are something we excel in."

"I really am sorry about staring Lexie..." he started, but saw the smile on her face. "I am not sure why, but yes we do keep ending up in these kinds of situations."

"Perhaps the Fates are having a good old giggle at our expense," she whispered as she got dressed.

"Well, whether it is them just having a good giggle or not, one thing remains true. You have a gorgeous body."

"Why thank you... I have to say that you don't look bad either," she said, grinning cheekily.

"You must be starving! If I am not mistaken, we have not eaten for an entire day," he said pulling her towards the fire.

"I am absolutely famished! But with everything that has been happening the last day or so it is not a surprise that food was the last thing on my mind. First the Troll caves and everything we found out there to having to travel to Atlantican and meeting the Mermalani twins. Finding out about Justren's and his family. Then the fact that I had to be the bearer of bad news to Amethyst. And then..." she sat down cutting her own sentence short.

"About what happened last night..."

"It was a mistake I know and I should have known better... I just got lost in the feelings and trying to forget."

"Is that what you think I meant?! No, that is not it at all. I don't regret last night at all and I would do it again in a heartbeat."

"It was fantastic yes, but you do not have to pretend that

you would do it again. I saw how you were beating yourself up earlier and I understand it completely. But it is what it is and I promise that I will not fall in love with you and get all needy." He opened his mouth in shock but she spoke over him. "I do believe I smell food; is it ready yet?"

"It has been for a while now, but I thought that you were still asleep."

"Positive thoughts for this day... that is all that I need, until Amethyst arrives."

"Here you go; breakfast!" he announced handing her food.

"Oh wow, well done. It smells absolutely scrumptious!"

"It is only my pleasure and I do hope that you enjoy it. It is an old family recipe."

She took a tentative bite of the fish and closed her eyes dreamily. When she opened her eyes once again, she saw that Shadick was staring at her quizzically.

"This is the best fish that I have had in years!"

"I was not sure what was going on. Whether it was completely disgusting or what."

"There is absolutely nothing wrong with it. It is mouth-watering."

He took his own fish, sat down and watched her as he ate. Handing her water that he had scooped up earlier. After a few minutes she squirmed under his scrutiny, looking everywhere but at him.

"I guess that we should probably get back to the Troll caves... Amethyst should be arriving soon. And the Trolls are probably worried about where we had gotten off to. I am actually surprised that they have not come looking for us yet."

Shadick quickly grabbed everything that they had brought with them and started walking back to the caves, he hesitated for a second then grabbed her hand and held it tightly in his own.

"Alexandria! Shadick! We have been worried about where you had disappeared to last night," Grog said as he spotted the two of them walking towards the Caves. "Some of the other Trolls mentioned that they saw you disappearing into the forest, but there was no sign of the two of you returning. Whenever we tried sending out some of the men to go searching for you the wolves would get in the way and would get rather angry."

"There is no need to worry about us, although it is gallant of you," Shadick answered.

"And how were we supposed to have known that?"

"Well if the wolves had gotten irritated and had disappeared into the forest it would have been a good way for you to know. They always know whether I am safe or not. Which is most likely why they were stopping you from entering the forest."

"Very well then... Alexandria there's a Faerie here looking for you. We believe that she has a message for you, but we cannot understand her."

"Where is she?" she asked walking forward just as the Faerie flew right at her making her gasp and stumble a few steps back. "Shana?! What's wrong? Is Amethyst okay?"

The Faerie slowed down and settled on her shoulder whispering in her ear while the Trolls and Shadick watched worriedly. After a few minutes, just as he was about to ask what was going on the Faerie flew up and sat down on Alexandria's head.

"So, what did she tell you? Is there something wrong with Amethyst or the other Faeries?" he asked looking at the Faerie on her head

"That we have to prepare for the arrival of the first group of Creatures. In about five minutes time. And that apparently that was already a few minutes ago and we only have a minute left to prepare," she said shaking her head.

"And how exactly are they going to move such a big group of Creatures? If I am not mistaken, they are traveling on land, aren't they?"

"Something like that yes," she replied just as the Faerie's light brightened. "Oh dear, Amethyst will be arriving first."

Shadick was about to ask how exactly she had this information and how they were planning on getting there when one of the trees on his left radiated energy. It was in shock that he watched the image of a woman appearing and slowly solidifying and becoming clearer. What was first a bark covered skin slowly changed to that of a person. A second later Amethyst stepped forward, looking as though she had not just randomly appeared through a tree.

"You will never get tired of that little trick, will you Am?" Alexandria asked stepping closer to the Faerie and hugging her.

"No I will not... ooh! I have to show you this new trick I recently discovered," Amethyst said excitedly and they watched in amazement as her wings disappeared. If they had not known that she was a Faerie, she could have passed as a human.

"When exactly did you learn that little trick?"

"I have been playing around with it for a few weeks now. It is just that I thought it might be safer to not have them out on display, especially if there is going to be fighting. And we wouldn't want to give them anymore power over us, now do we?"

"You have changed so much Am... the last time I saw you, you were still getting used to being Queen," Shadick commented as he stepped forward.

"Speak for yourself, Shadick! You have gotten so much stronger since we last spoke," Amethyst replied hugging him.

"You have gotten stronger as well, the power is radiating off of you! I am happily impressed."

"Why thank you, young man. It is true what they say after all. With knowledge comes power and all that."

"Am, when is the other Creatures getting here?" Alexandria asked.

She lightly smacked her forehead and stepped back to the tree, lightly drawing a strange design on the bark. It slowly turned to a deep red before changing to what seemed like a swirling mess before it calmed down and some of the Creatures stepped through the newly created portal.

The Faeries flew over to Alexandria and she almost disappeared within their light. Shadick watched in shock as her dirty clothes changed into clean black leggings and a dark blue shirt. It complimented her complexion and as he watched they pulled her hair into a ponytail and secured it there with the same blue hair tie.

"You seem surprised for some reason." she said smiling.

"I never really thought that Faeries were able to change someone's clothing, but it seems that I have been wrong."

"They love changing my clothes, for some reason. If you

want, I am sure they would give you some clothes as well."

"I am happy with the clothes on my back, thank you," Shadick bent down and whispered in her ear. "You look great, although I have to admit the outfit from last night is much better."

"I see that they couldn't wait to change your outfit again," Amethyst said just as Alexandria blushed scarlet. "Is everything okay with the two of you?"

"Why would you think something is wrong?" Alexandria asked.

"The two of you are standing almost a foot apart from each other! And a minute ago you looked rather happy so close to each other."

"I just thought that I should move a little so that there was more space for the Creatures still coming through," she lied quickly.

"I thought that I heard one of the wolves calling me," Shadick said at the same time.

"There is something fishy going on here and I will find out what it is," Amethyst said frowning.

"Malady, should we be expecting any more Creatures?" Grog asked, standing closer.

Amethyst looked around at the group closely then touched the tree.

"That would be it for now. I organised that the rest come later in the day. That way there won't be complete chaos."

***

It was a few hours later and Alexandria was standing with some of the Unicorns listening to them talk about what has happened since they last spoke. Amethyst was walking through the Creatures and checking that everyone was doing okay or if they needed anything.

Shadick seemed to be dosing off next to the fire, the wolves next to him. They had not spoken to each other ever since Amethyst and the Creatures had arrived and the atmosphere felt rather heavy and cloying. She knew that there was no way that Amethyst wouldn't eventually find out about what had happened, but it was not the time to tell her just yet.

"...the village was almost completely destroyed!" she heard Oliver saying.

"What village are you talking about?" she asked, turning back to the Unicorns.

"I was just talking about the village situated west from the Waterfall. Unfortunately, the name has escaped me."

"Do you mean McLeod's?!"

"Yes, that sounds right; do you know about it?" Ashley

asked.

Alexandria stumbled back a few feet, Managwa appearing behind her just as she was about to fall over. She was pale and felt as though she was about to faint, but took a deep breath.

"Yes, I do know it, very well in fact. It is where I have been living for years! That is where my parents' home is."

"From what I saw of it yesterday when I flew over, I doubt that it would still be standing. All I saw was smoke and destruction," Markus added snidely.

"Do you know perhaps who did it? Although with what has been happening lately, I am sure that I can guess."

"It was indeed the Centaurian army. I heard that no mercy was shown to anyone," Oliver said, lowering his head.

"Alex! Is everything okay? You look as though you are about to faint!" Amethyst shouted, running towards them stepping on Shadick's hand.

"She overheard our conversation about McLeod's, your majesty," he replied as Shadick walked toward them rubbing his hand.

"I was going to tell you as soon as I found the right time to do so."

"What about the villagers?" Alexandria asked, shaking.

"Most of them were able to escape into Pecan forest and as far as I know they are planning on moving to one of the other villages."

"*Most* of them?" Shadick asked.

"Some of them were captured and if they put up too much of a fight they were killed off," Markus said with a wicked smile.

"Markus this is not something to be joking about!" Amethyst said shocked.

"I truly am sorry, your majesty," he said unconvincingly.

Alexandria turned her back on the Unicorns, walked to the fire and sat down. How could they have done that? Just destroy a village as though it was nothing. Kill people just because they stood up to them? Just to show that they had the power to do it?

"Lexie, everything will be fine. There is no need to worry. We will make sure that the Centaurs get what is coming to them," Shadick said, wrapping his arms around her.

"And on the bright side, the villagers will probably come and offer to fight alongside us! If of course they don't decide to move to another village," Amethyst said hopefully.

Her words were barely out of her mouth when a wolf close to the edge of the camp howled. Shadick jumped up and ran closer just as a group of humans appeared, scared and unsure of what to do or say next.

"We are looking for the Faerie named Amethyst! We were

told that we would be able to find the Faerie Queen here at these caves," a man said, someone that Alexandria didn't recognise.

"I am Amethyst, the Faerie Queen," Amethyst said stepping forward.

"We are here as representatives from the three outlying villages, Dargona to North-West, Crenaphe to the South and of course from McLeod just West of these caves."

"Very well, how can I be of assistance? In case you did not hear, but Humans have not stepped into Aribatiath for years and even longer since they travelled here to the caves."

"It is as they say it is... desperate times call for desperate measures. When we originally heard about the attacks in the forest, we thought nothing of it and just shrugged it off. But when McLeod's was attacked and destroyed, we came to the unfortunate conclusion that it is probably the same monsters that had been attacking your forest.

"It was also then that we realised that we will need help fighting this. We then decided that perhaps it was time to talk to the Magical Creatures so that we can all fight these beasts."

"And what are your names?" Alexandria asked stepping closer.

"My name is Philiap; I am the general from Dargona Village. Over there is Christopher, general from Crenaphe. And from McLeod's..."

"Alex!" said a voice from behind Philiap running closer.

"Michael?!" she asked walking to the man and hugging him. "Is it really you or have I lost my mind? Where is general McShawb?"

"Luanda was going out of her mind of worry when we did not see you with the rest of the villagers that got away. I tried telling her that you would be fine, but you know her."

Shadick growled softly and she stepped out of Michael's embrace.

"Of course, I am fine; I was not in the village when it was attacked. I was busy with some other stuff."

"As for your question about general McShawb he was killed in the attack on McLeod's," Philiap said to her unanswered question.

"May I offer our caves if you wish to hold a meeting?" Grog said walking towards them.

"That is a good idea Grog, thank you for offering. It would be best if we were to decide what our next move should be. Would it possible to set up more tents for the new arrivals?" Amethyst asked nodding and watching Alexandria walking towards Shadick seeing his frown. "If you could lead us all to the general area, that would be appreciated Grog."

She watched everyone walking into the caves and glanced

again at Alexandria and Shadick who seemed to be in the middle of an argument. Promising herself that she would deal with it later, she walked into the caves hoping that they could figure something out.

"I will request that some refreshments be brought to you, your majesty."

"Thank you for that Grog, I would also like if you joined us for this meeting. These caves belong to you and it would only be right that you are there, representing the Trolls."

He nodded and they disappeared into the caves just as Alexandria stormed into the woods angrily, Shadick frowning after her...

Chapter 12

Separate Quests

"Lexie! Would you please stop walking away from me?" Shadick shouted after her.

She ignored him and kept walking. Without warning she walked into something and fell over. She looked up angrily and saw that Shadick was right above her. Glaringly she started getting up from the floor, but before she could properly get up his arms were pulling her up.

"Could you please just listen to what I have to say?"

"And why should I do that?"

"Because I am trying to have a conversation with you, which is being made difficult by your storming off."

"Why should I listen to your lies, yet again?" she asked shrugging away from him.

"Please tell me when it was I exactly lied to you? And if you could tell me what I have done to upset you this much it would greatly appreciated."

"Michael is one of my best friends from the village and that is how I greet someone when I was afraid for his life. And you acted as though I was a misbehaving child."

"Is that what all this is about? Just because I may be a little jealous if someone gets close to you?"

"There is no need to get jealous after last night! And it was a harmless hug, nothing to make a big deal of."

"I am still a person, and jealousy is part of the package. If that is such a big problem..."

"I never said that you aren't a person, if in fact if you think about it, I was the one trying to convince everyone that you are as human as I am. And the last time we checked, we weren't together."

"That is not what I meant either. Look I did not mean to come across as an unfeeling brute..." he started then stopped when a buzzing interrupted them.

He sighed when he realised that it was a group of Faeries flying towards Alexandria and knew the conversation would have to wait. The four rainbow Faeries flew around her head and he got dizzy watching the movement. Just as he was about to complain they flew a short distance away from them and transformed.

"Alexandria, the Queen request your presence in the cave, along with Shadick's," the blue Faerie said.

"If you asked me it sounded very important," said the green Faerie as she sat down on a rock, resting her chin in her hands.

"We *are* on the brink of war in case you forgot, so of course it is important! They are busy discussing strategies," the violet Faerie replied.

"You should cheer up a little, V! In case you have forgotten, it is important to laugh when things get a little too serious. Because without laughter, life would be very monotonous," the yellow Faerie said from her spot in the tree branch.

"Well who asked for your opinion?" the green one replied angrily.

"Will the four of you stop it?!" Alexandria interceded just then. "You are the rainbow sisters and one would expect that you would get along and whatnot."

They looked shocked at Alexandria then at each other and burst into laughter. The yellow Faerie nearly fell out of the tree while her green sister rolled around on the ground. Shadick looked at them curiously then glanced at Alexandria who just shrugged.

"Why do you insist on taking us so seriously, Al? I thought that you would have gotten used to us bantering with each other like this by now," the violet Faerie said, clutching her stomach from laughter.

The Blue Faerie stopped laughing and wiped her eyes.

"We were serious about Amethyst looking for you though. And she sounded like it was quite urgent."

"Shadick, please meet the Rainbow sisters. Brittany, Georgia, Viora and Yolanda... Thank you for coming to get us. If you would tell Amethyst that we will be shortly it would be appreciated," Alexandria said and they nodded before transforming back into their miniature forms and flying away.

Before he could reply in anyway, they had disappeared and he was left with Alexandria. The tension was still thick in the air and he was not sure what to say to make it better. Why was she acting like this? Perhaps she was lying about Michael just being a friend. She was very defensive when he mentioned him.

Then again, why would she have allowed the previous evening to happen if she was seeing him? In the same breath it could be argued that he could have put a stop to it as well. It was not as she had seduced him... much. Why was it that her energy seemed to call to him and made him fall for her ever since their first meeting?

"We should probably get back to camp. If Amethyst sent the rainbow sisters after us it is quite important," Alexandria eventually commented, not looking at him.

"That might indeed be so, but we need to continue our conversation," Shadick stated.

"And what conversation would that be? The one where you

talk and I just have to listen? Thank you but no thank you... I have a lot more important things to worry about than what problems we may have in our *non-existing relationship*! We slept together last night and it was fantastic, but we do not have the time to have a polite conversation about it."

"I think that we need to sort this out and that would include *both* of us talking... not just me."

"Right now, the looming war seems more important than a one silly conversation," she replied before storming off.

Shadick ran after her knowing that they will have to sort everything out before they got to Amethyst as the tension was just too much for anyone to handle. And she would then find out about everything that had happened the previous evening and he was not ready to face the consequences in that. He grabbed her arm and forced her to face him; he refused to move his arm even though she was throwing death glares at him.

"I think that it would be best if you let go of me, Shadick."

"No, I was serious when I said that we need to discuss this. In case you did not notice, the tension between us is so palpable that it might just come to life and bite anyone that might be around us. Do you have any idea how uncomfortable it would be if they found out about what happened between us?"

"Very well then! We will just pretend that last night never happened, that way there is no need to worry about them

finding out. Not that I was planning on telling anyone about it.
but alright then, if you want to talk, then talk.

"I have told you already that I do not regret last night at all,
in fact I was a lot more relaxed than I had been in months. I kind
of find it funny that you barely know me yet you judge me by
my friends, even though you haven't met them. But just to give
you some *food for thought*... I was the one that got Michael and
Luanda together in the first place.

"In case you forgot the conversation that you overheard
between myself and Amethyst, I am not planning on getting
involved with anyone in the village, nor any other place for that
matter. It would only mean trouble for myself as well as the
magical Creatures that I call my friends and family.

"And yes, before you say it... I know things are changing
and that soon it would probably not be such a *big deal* for them
to know that I am a witch. But I want to tell them on my own
conditions and hope that they won't hate me for it. So I think
that it would be best if I were to just stay single and not have to
deal with any of it."

He stared at her shocked and she slipped her arm out of his
grasp before he could gather his wits. She stormed away and
emerged from the forest and he knew that even if he would be
able to catch up with her, he did not want to make a big mess
for her.

He took a deep breath and followed her more slowly, trying to ignore the anger he felt still reverberating throughout the forest...

***

"Alex! There you are, we were waiting for you. Where is Shadick? The Rainbow Faeries said that they found you in the forest together," Amethyst said as soon as she walked into the caves.

"Oh... uhm... we were.. He.. Uh.." Alexandria stammered.

"I am right here. Sorry for my delay, I just had to speak with the wolves in the forest quick so I sent Alexandria ahead of me," Shadick said appearing behind them.

"Very well then, now that we are all here... you met the generals from the villages earlier and they kind of met you. Or rather, Alex knows Michael," Amethyst said frowning.

"I believe that you mentioned him briefly before but I think that proper introductions are in order," Christopher said suspiciously.

"Shadick is a personal friend of mine and he has offered his help in this war and as you have mentioned before we will need all of the help that we can get. So please do not sound as though you do not trust him. But I will tell you this, Shadick is a

Wolfane. Meaning that wherever he is the wolves will be, if that means anything to you," Amethyst said glaring at Christopher.

"And what exactly, in the high heavens, is a Wolfane?" Michael asked confused, sitting up straighter.

"The easy explanation would be that I was born from a werewolf mother but a human father," Shadick said shortly.

"But werewolves are uncontrollable beasts! They are vicious and attack anyone and anything that come into their way during the full moon!" Philiaps shouted.

"Just shows how much you know! As for him being an uncontrollable beast, you have no right to judge what you don't truly know. Perhaps the werewolves you ran across was murderous monsters, but please know that there is always a break in the rule. And honestly... if it was about who I trust more... it would be him and not you," Alexandria said, surprising everyone.

Three of the four representatives frowned at her as she finished her speech then quickly stepped back again, slightly behind Amethyst. Shadick grinned, but no one noticed. He wanted to run to her and hug her fiercely, but kept control of himself.

"And why are we supposed to trust you? You are nothing but a mortal, just like we are. And it has been decided that women will not be part of this war, it is too dangerous,"

Philiaps said, banging on the table.

"Do not dare talk to Alex like that! Her father made sure that she knows everything about swordsmanship and I would take a guess that she may just know more than you do about any of it. I have seen her handling a sword and it is impressive," Michael said calmly.

"And for your information... she is not just another *mortal*. Yes, she is an excellent swordsman, but more importantly she has magic behind her. Which makes her stronger than almost anyone in this room," Amethyst added, shocking them all into silence, while Alexandria blanched.

"Magic? What is this rubbish you are talking about? Is she a Faerie or something?" Philiaps asked frowning.

"History made everyone forget about them, but there are still witches out there in the world," Alexandria said. "Just because people outlaw something does not mean that they just stop existing. We all just find a way to blend in and not be caught, so as not to be hung for being evil. Which is why, no one but the magical Creatures know about me. I hid it just because I knew that people would freak out."

Shadick grabbed her arm to stop her from saying what may harm the tentative peace that had been accomplished so far. She shrugged off his hand and crossed her arms, looking at Amethyst.

"Let me put this out on the table before this conversation goes any further... You have come into the *magical* forest to ask for our help in the battle. And that means that you will fight alongside various of magical Creatures. You need to accept that and not judge them just because of what your history books have taught you," Amethyst said seriously.

"We understand that and we accept it. This coming war won't just be us having to fight them but it will be *all* of us fighting against the same enemy," Michael said glancing at Alexandria who sighed softly.

"Was there something specific you wanted us to be here for? Or just to discuss strategies?" Alexandria asked Amethyst.

"Oh right! It was something more specific than just discussing strategies. While the discussions have been going on, I remembered something that may just help us during this war," Amethyst said putting her hand against her forehead.

"And what would that be?" Shadick asked leaning against the cave wall.

"They are three stones... apart they may seem completely useless and powerless but if combined they can be very powerful."

"And you wish to send someone to retrieve these stones?

"Yes, I do, but it has to be done as fast as possible. You see if the stones were to fall into the wrong hands it may just cause more trouble for us as it could destroy everyone."

"And who did you have in mind, Am? And where exactly are these stones being kept?" Alexandria asked frowning.

"Well... the Trilate amethyst can be found in the far reaches of Trilantica, also known as Sorceral Deep. The Septer Quartz can be found deep within the Sangalon Mountains and the third stone is called Aquadious. If you do not know what you are looking for it could easily be passed over. It is normally handed down the family line by King Celeriac, who is also of Trilantica."

"Well there is no way that we can send mortals to any of those places," Philiaps commented. "It is not as though any of us can breathe underwater and who knows what dangers lay waiting in the oceans depths! As for Sangalon Mountains, it is known to be life threatening to anyone who got close."

"I had no intention of sending a mortal to retrieve these stones."

"So who exactly did you have in mind?" Shadick asked.

"I was thinking that I would send the two of you... I know that you would be able to retrieve the stones as soon as possible and that you would capable of dealing with any danger that may be thrown at you."

"That is very true. We are not scared to fight if it came down to it and together, we would make an excellent team."

"I have no doubt in my mind that you would make a great team... but you will have to test that theory out some other time. I need Alex to travel to Sorceral Deep for the Trilate amethyst and the Aquadious. While you, Shadick need to travel to Sangalon Mountains to retrieve the Septer Quartz."

"What?!" Alexandria asked, standing up straight.

"We need to retrieve the stones as soon as possible and if you were to go together it would take twice as long. And it will just be waste of time, time which I am sure you realise we do not have."

"And you trust the two of them enough to go on these missions? A witch and a wolf... whatever it was you called him?" Christopher asked.

"I would trust the both of them with my life and I know what they are capable of. And I know that they will do whatever is necessary to accomplish this. Unlike mortals who believe just because something goes wrong that it went wrong because of superstition."

"When... when did you want us to leave, Am?" Alexandria asked glancing at Shadick.

"As soon as the two of you are ready. The Centaurs know about these stones and I am sure that they are planning to retrieve the stones as well, so as to use it for themselves."

"We have all the necessary supplies that may be needed...

or at least we have the supplies that Shadick will need. Alex will be going into the ocean and unfortunately we do not own anything will allow her to breathe underwater," Grog answered.

"Do not worry about that; I have already sent words to the Mermalani twins and asked for their help. And they have assured me that they will be able to help."

"What exactly is a Mermalani?" Michael asked, although he looked like nothing would surprise him.

"A Mermalani is someone who has been born from a human father and a Mermaid."

"Alright then, it kind of makes sense I guess."

"I am not sure that they would help me..." Alexandria said sighing.

"As I have already told you, Alex. They have already agreed to it. Or rather, Starlansha did. Roslata on the other hand is more difficult to convince, but her sister will be able to do just that. She is a funny one," Amethyst replied. "If she decides that she does not like someone she will not be the most pleasant person."

"She definitely does not like me then."

"Very well then, Shadick do you need any weapons or supplies?" Grog asked.

"I have my sword and that should suffice. If you were able

to just give me some supplies and perhaps a horse to ride upon I would be grateful. It would be very difficult to carry supplies while in wolf form," Shadick replied.

"Would you be able to organise everything that he needs, Grog?" Amethyst asked.

"Yes, it will be organised within the hour. There is a horse that he can use and the provisions just need to be put in a satchel," Grog said nodding and disappeared outside.

"Thank you, Grog it is appreciated."

Alexandria frowned slightly as she watched Grog leaving. Why did she have to go alone on this quest when, if she thought about it, it would go quicker if they were together. And how was she supposed to retrieve a stone that was miles below the ocean?

"Is there anything that you think you may need, Alex?"

"How about the ability to breathe..." she started, but got distracted by the yellow Faerie that had just arrived.

She flew closer to Shadick and transformed into her human form and smiled suggestively at him. He did not move, but stared at the barely clad Faerie in surprise.

"Ariana.... How many times have I asked you to not dress so inadequately? That a Faerie should be respected not just by who they are but by their entire look?" Amethyst asked frowning at the Faerie.

"And I have told you that not all Faeries wish to look like nuns. If you ask me it should be more a case of *if you have it, flaunt it*," Ariana answered still smiling.

"Do you have any other news from the Mermalani?"

"I do yes... Starlansha said that it would be the biggest of pleasures to help Alexandria. Roslata on the other hand said that it would only be a pleasure to let her drown or have the sharks eat her or perhaps let the Sirens get a hold of her to kill or change into one of them. But she would be happy to oblige with whichever option you choose."

"I have not seen her so sour in years... she needs to get her priorities sorted."

"She seemed pretty happy to me when she gave me the message. It was all laughs."

"Oh, I'm sure that she was. Alex, are you ready to travel and retrieve the stones?"

"Of course, I am, it is not as though I need that much to go underwater," she replied walking out of the cave, arms folded.

"What has gotten into her? When I arrived, she seemed to be so happy," Amethyst wondered out loud watching her friend.

"It is probably nothing... surprised that you are sending her on a mission. I think that she thought that she would be helping you here, organizing the troops and whatnot," Shadick fibbed.

"It is not as though I have much of a choice! We need to get those stones as soon as possible."

"And we both understand that, Amethyst. And we are both willing to do what is necessary."

"I know that, Shadick... but she just seemed really upset."

"I will go talk to her for you."

"Thank you, Shadick. I appreciate all the help that you are offering."

"It is no problem at all," he said and straightened up before walking out of the cave and looking around.

She was standing next to a newly constructed fountain that Amethyst had requested. Fresh water was being pumped from the stream so that they were able to refresh whenever they needed to. She seemed lost in thought as she ran her hand through the water.

"Amethyst is really upset that you just walked out of the cave like that. She is really worried about you now."

"I have my reasons for why I walked out of the cave and I am sure that she will understand why, soon enough," she whispered trying to wipe her eyes before he noticed.

"Of all the things you are really good at, hiding your feelings isn't one of them. I know that you were crying just now, I'm just not sure why you were."

"I had just washed my face and the water dripping down

my face must have looked like tears."

"Why were you crying, Lexie? And do not tell me that you were just washing your face because your eyes are red."

"I was just surprised that she wants us to go find the stones. And yes, I understand that they have to be retrieved as soon as possible, but I just would have thought that it would have been easier if we were to go together."

"You know that it would take twice as long to retrieve the stones if we were to go together. And I have a really bad feeling that the Centaurs are already trying to retrieve the stones for themselves."

"I am sorry if I am interrupting something, but I was just wondering if everything was okay? The two of you seemed happy enough last night and this morning," Grog asked walking towards them.

"Nothing to worry about, everything is absolutely fine," Alexandria replied smiling.

"There is a feeling of heaviness whenever the two of you are around each other."

"I assure you that everything is fine, but your concern is appreciated Grog. We were just talking about the stones," Shadick told him.

"Very well then... and just so that you know. The horse has been saddled and the provisions have been loaded. It is now just up to you when you wish to leave."

"The quicker I get on the way, the quicker I will be able to retrieve the stone. It would be better for everyone involved."

"I tend to agree with you there, Shadick. I do not wish to rush you or anything but we may not have the luxury of just sitting around," Amethyst said walking out of the cave.

"Then I shall get going."

"And what about you, Al..." she said turning towards where Alexandria was, but she was nowhere to be seen "Where did she disappear to?

"I believe that she has already started her journey to Atlantican Ocean as she had just disappeared through those trees," Grog said pointing.

"It is not like her to leave without even saying goodbye... but I guess she has her reasoning."

"I better get on the road as well... time isn't on our side after all," Shadick added walking to the horse and mounting the horse and kicking it into movement. The wolves automatically followed him and Amethyst wondered if she had done the right thing...

Chapter 13

Sangalon Mountains

As he rode further away from the caves he frowned. Amethyst did have a point; it was not like Alexandria to not say goodbye. She had just walked away from them without a word. Yes, she was mad at him, but surely not mad enough that she would just completely ignore him. Amethyst had seemed really sad about that fact that she had not gotten a greeting and he wished that he could make her feel better.

The horse broke through the forest and started galloping freely. He glanced up at the sun and noticed that it was noon. It was so difficult to tell the time when you were within the forest that he had been feeling a little disconnected from the rest of the world. He was about to urge the horse to go even faster when his stomach reminded him that he had not eaten since earlier in the day.

He slowed the horse and decided that a break may not be a bad idea before he got to Sangalon Mountains. He looked into the bags and pulled out some of the food that they had given him. He was just relaxing when he heard scuffling from coming from the forest and he immediately jumped up and unsheathed his sword.

As he was taking a step towards the noise the wolf pack strolled towards him and sat down. Managwa looked at his sword then at him and gave a soft growl. Shadick smiled at the wolf and laid the sword next to him as he sat back down. He watched as they lazed around just waiting for him and wished that he could have been one of them. As always Managwa did not completely relax and kept wandering around the area as though looking for something.

He took a bite from the bread and glanced towards where he could barely see Sangalon Mountains, he knew that if he really pushed himself it would take about two days. Yet he was determined to get the trip over and done with as soon as possible so that he could sort out the trouble with Alexandria. It was strange how she was able to pretend that it did not matter when he could tell that it had. When she hugged Michael so excitedly, he had gotten a little pang of jealousy and he had not even been sure why.

Shaking his head, he jumped up and grabbed his sword, putting it back in its sheath. Jumping back on the horse and calling to the wolves so that they did not get left behind. They quickly overtook him and he urged the horse into a faster gallop.

When he realised that night had fallen, it was with happy surprise that he saw that he was already halfway to his destination. If he really wanted to, he could have pushed through, but he was not sure what was waiting for him and he had to get his rest. He quickly started a fire and cooked some food so his stomach would stop complaining and he could get to sleep.

The wolves had gone hunting in the nearby forest and were now sleeping around the fire. It crossed his mind that he may have to keep watch, but then saw that Managwa was watching the area carefully and knew that he was in safe paws. If there was some kind of trouble, they would either inform him of it or take care of the problem themselves.

He lay down and looked up at the sky; there was not a cloud in sight and it felt as though if he just stretched far enough that he would be able to touch the stars. He groaned slightly as he tried getting more comfortable and with a pang realised that he missed Alexandria next to him. How was it that she had gotten so under his skin so quickly? It was as though she had put a spell on him, but he knew that it was not the case at all.

He had made himself a promise not too long ago, that until

he finished his mission he would not fall for anyone or be convinced that there were better things to do. Perhaps once he had finished his own mission he would return and try and settle down. Hopefully it would with Alexandria, but he would not hold it against her if she moved on before he was ready. His journey at the moment though was almost as important and he knew that it would help Amethyst and everybody else.

It had been in some of his father's journals that he had found out about the Glacier Sword as well as the Breastplate Solaar and had wondered ever since why his father had given up on finding them. According to the books the sword had the ability to send chills up a person's spine as it paralysed them or killed them if it was placed just right. As for the Breastplate Solaar it could blind the enemy by the reflecting light, whether it be the sun or moon. Had his father still been alive he would have made sure that they found the weapons together so that he could realise his dream. Unfortunately, his parents were killed before this plan could ever be spoken about and it was now his dream to find them in his honour.

It was when he was about halfway to the Ice Caves when the rumours had reached him that Aribatiath had been under attack. And he had known immediately that he would keep the promise he had given her months ago that if there were any trouble that he would be there to help. He had not even been sure that it wasn't just stories that were being spread by bored old ladies or if it was in fact actually real but he always kept his promises. So, he had changed his course and had ended up where he was right now. After a few minutes of complete silence, he passed out with a soft sigh.

The next morning, he woke up early and made the decision to eat when he arrived at Sangalon Mountains. It was with that resolve that he saddled the horses and got back on the road. He had awoken ridiculously early and had not been able to fall asleep again so had decided to get on with the journey. It might help with the oppressive heat and he wished that it would rain for a bit, but knew that it would not. He kicked the horse's flanks and urged it to move faster. The sounds of the wolves' paws became almost like a relaxing song and he was able to relax a little, although not enough to slow down.

As the sun rose higher into the sky, the Mountains got closer and the earth was getting warmer again. He did not want the horse or the wolves to get thirsty, so he knew that they had to stop at least once more. Yet he wondered if he could push them a little harder than he normally would; he glanced down and saw that they did not show any fatigue yet and knew they felt the importance of this mission.

It was with a happy heart that he finally reached the bottom of the mountain three and a half hours later. He made sure to stop at the stream not far from the entrance of a cave, ready for the journey ahead but knowing that they all needed some rest and to drink some water before continuing. The horse seemed to know just where to go and ambled to the closest grass patch and stream. He quickly climbed off the horse and let it graze in peace. Sitting down beneath a large tree and glancing at where he knew the entrance was situated. It would be about another three hours or so before he would be able to arrive there and find the stone.

Lazily watching the horse and the wolves he felt as though he was going to pass out and shook himself before standing up and stretching. He tied the horse to one of the trees so that it would still be able to get to the stream and got back on the path. If it had been possible for him to have taken the horse, he would have, but it was going to get rough and he did not want the horse to get injured.

He finally reached the cave entrance about two hours later and he felt like he had walked for days. As far he could tell there was no immediate danger, but the wolves seemed restless and were growling at the entrance as though sensing something that he could not. He had found it strange that there had not been one fight as he had climbed, although he did notice some old bones lying around perhaps in warning.

Looking down at the wolves he wondered whether they would follow him in, but shrugged knowing that he would not be able to change that. So, he stepped into the cave and was immediately overwhelmed by the darkness. Hearing a slight slip of rocks, he realised that the wolves were not going to abandon him after all and he felt a little better.

Managwa ran next to him and sometimes urged him to go farther and if he had not known the wolf, he would have felt insulted. He picked up speed making sure that he was still able to hear what was necessary so that he could react if necessary. It was not long after that, that he froze in his tracks as he was thrown a loophole.

Ahead of him were two paths, both leading to what seemed the middle of a huge cavern. The wolves slunk forward slowly and growled softly; he noticed light bouncing off of their eyes and knew that he was at the right place.

As he was about to give a whistle to the wolves to get back to him, he heard the unmistakable sound of some kind of rustling coming from ahead of him and knew that it meant nothing good. He flinched at the ring of the sword as it resounded off of the walls and hoped that whatever was ahead of him were too busy to notice other things.

He groaned when he realised that the sound of wings was getting louder and he knew that it had not gone unnoticed. The wolves growled and their hackles raised in attack. A Pegasus flew past them and he watched in shock as it flew around the top before charging straight at them.

"There is no need for attack! We are not here to harm you!" Shadick shouted hopefully.

The Pegasus did not even seem to hear him and kept charging straight at him. He rolled out of the way and ran down the one path absently noticing the wolves taking the other path to get down. He knew as he watched the creature circling that it was considering who would be the easier target and knew the second it decided that it was him.

He dived out of the way as it flew at him barely able to get away in time. The wolves' strategy seemed to be to confuse the Pegasus as they barked up at it, running around. It landed in a gush of wind stomping the floor and snorting as it got ready for its next attack. Shadick quickly glanced around the Cave and saw a raised platform, on which he was able to see a bright stone that he assumed to be the Septer Quartz. Nodding thoughtfully, he quickly broke into a run, heading straight for the platform. If he was lucky, he could get out before anyone got hurt. He fell flat on his ass as the Pegasus appeared in front of him and he sighed.

"I will not allow you to touch the stone!" the Pegasus shouted.

"I was sent here by the Faerie Queen! She said that this stone would help in the coming war. It might even be the one thing that assures us victory or the loss of a thousand lives. The Centaurs only plan to use it to take over the world and I don't think that you would like that very much.

"My name is Shadick and I give you my word that I am not here to harm you or any other creature. I just want to stop the Centaurs before their plan goes too far." Shadick said, wide-eyed.

"And why is it that you think I should care what happens to this world? If there is a need for it, I will just return to my own. I was assigned here by the leaders of my world. But seeing that you told me your name, I shall tell you mine... they call me Miliantes."

"Sorry if this sounds... simpleminded. But is this not your world as well?"

"Eons ago perhaps yes, but we moved when the corruption got too much. But we received a message from the King of the Oceans that he required one of us to protect something valuable and that he considered precious. When we got here and found out that it was nothing but a stone, a lot of my kind went back knowing that they faced being turned away by our own King. In the end it was only I, who remained here."

"Would you not rather be able to go back to your own

world? To be able to see your friends and family again?"

"Do you not understand?! If I fail in this mission my family and friends will be killed, or even worse... rejected by all the other Pegasi."

"Then should it not be an obvious solution then? If you are so concerned about your family... do not let the Centaurs take over this world. They will be coming for this stone and they will not be leaving without it. It also means that I will lose those I love."

"Why should I care about those you love?!" it shouted its eyes reddening.

Shadick quickly parried a blow from the Pegasus's hooves as it attacked him; the wolves responded immediately. They ran up to him growling and biting at its legs. It was to no avail as the Pegasus was too fast and he dodged each attack. Managwa lunged for Miliantes throat and he took that as the wolf trying to distract him long enough so that he could get the stone.

Racing up the flight of steps and towards the platform and was just able to grab the stone when it realised what he was doing. He turned with it in his hands just as Miliantes reached him, his hooves smacking him right in the chest and causing him to land on the floor hard.

Just as he was trying to figure out how to get away there

was a sudden blinding light and he watched in shock as the Pegasus rose into the air. The wolves growled uncertainly as the light got blinding and in a flash it was over and Miliantes was drifting back to the floor cave.

"What in the world is going on here?" Shadick whispered confused.

"You were able to break my curse!" Miliantes shouted happily.

"There was a curse? And what did this curse do exactly?"

"I have been under an evil curse for the past five years; I had not been able to escape it."

"And who had put you under this curse?"

"Those blasted Centaurs! I am not sure how they had been able to convince a witch to do it, but she did. They said that they needed as much help as possible, even if it meant that they had to force their hands. I was then instructed to not allow anyone, but themselves come in here and take the stone. If I am not mistaken, they planned to move it somewhere more secure, but I have not seen them since the damned curse was placed on me."

"And how was it possible for them to put a Pegasus under a curse? Do you not have some sort of *immunity* to things like that?"

"Usually we are immune to most magic that is out there in

the world, but this witch was somehow able to make it stick and I lost control over everything."

"I assume that me picking up the stone was able to break this curse?" Shadick asked sheathing his sword.

"I will answer all your questions. But first I request that we get out of this darn cave as I have not had any fresh air in years."

Shadick sighed and looked towards the entrance of the cave and wondered how he would be able to get back out when he felt as though he had not rested in years. As he looked back at Miliantes he realised that they had moved and was outside.

"Wait.. What just happened?"

"I transported us outside as I gathered that none of us were in the mood to walk outside. It would just take too much time and it just seemed easier to do it quickly."

"Very well then; I just did not expect that to happen."

"It is not something that we use often as the effect is felt differently by everyone. For example, the wolves and the horse might start panicking and cause trouble. But you barely feel it and would not mind."

"That makes sense; animals are attuned to their surroundings more."

"Have you been traveling for long?" Miliantes asked him as he mounted his horse.

"It has been quite a while yes, although I have been helping friends the last few days," Shadick replied glancing at the sky and noticing that it was early evening. "When the attacks on the Creatures became clear I knew that I had to help in some way. We then found out that it was the Centaurs that had been creating all the trouble, wanting revenge or something similar for being banished from the forest."

"And how will this stone help you with the war?"

"I am not sure myself; I was just told that if you combine it with two other stones that it will become a powerful stone. As I mentioned before, Amethyst sent me here to retrieve it as she believes that it will be the key."

"If the Faerie Queen is so confident that it will help then perhaps, we should not question her. You mentioned two other stones, is that where you are going next or was someone else sent to retrieve those?"

"No there is no need for me to retrieve those stones; the Queen sent her best friend to go and get those. I am just hoping that she did not run in too much trouble."

"You seem to care for her. The moment you mentioned her, the world seemed to become much brighter in not just your eyes. But your entire being."

"I do care about her yes, even though we only met a few days ago. She seems to pull me towards her without trying very hard," Shadick said before his mind turned to something else.

"So, you said that you would tell me how I broke the curse?"

"When the curse was placed on me all those years ago, the witch was very powerful. And she was able to force it on me, but she knew that the Centaurs may turn on her so she cast it in such a way that if it was picked up by anyone besides a Centaur that the curse would break. I doubt that they knew about this or did not care. Or perhaps it was the fact that they never thought anyone would ever travel that far for just one stone."

"They seem to underestimate the magical Creatures quite a bit and that will hopefully help with their downfall."

"I am sure that it will!"

"I know that I need to get back to the Dolomite Caves as soon as possible, but another day of traveling seems to be impossible right now. I also know that they will start worrying if I take too long."

"Perhaps it would be best for us to rest for the evening? Just so that you can regain your energy before the trip?"

"It is very tempting and I know that I should probably listen to you, but I really do need to get back. I have food in my satchel that I can eat as I travel. And sleep can happen when I get there."

"And you of course want to make sure that your friend is still unharmed and back to the safety of the caves."

"That too."

"I shall walk with you for a bit... tell me more about her."

"Her name is Alexandria; her brown hair just reaches her shoulders and she has the most outstanding grey eyes. It is strange; she grew up without her parents, but it has not lessened the flame that burns in her soul. And she cares so much about the magical Creatures and would do just about anything for them.

"She really does sound like a wonderful person and I am sure that no harm has come to her. I am just wondering... why not send one of the wolves to check up on her?"

"There is that option, but it would be a lot more comforting if I was able to see for myself that she was still okay."

"Very well then, I will leave you for now so that you can properly start your journey back. I promise you that I will help you in this war as I owe you for my freedom."

"Your allegiance is greatly appreciated and I will make sure that the Faerie Queen knows about it as well."

"The fact that you helped me means enough already, but I will accept."

"If I had just killed you or just taken the stone without a second thought it would have gone against everything that I was raised to believe. And I know that if my parents were to find out about me just abandoning other Creatures they would try and smack me."

"Your parents sound like wonderful people, who knows what is right and what isn't."

"They were wonderful yes. I lost them a few years ago."

"I apologise if my words were insensitive; I did not realise that they had died."

"No worries... I miss them and wish that they were still around, but I know that it was probably their time to go. But with that I will have to say goodbye so that I can get back to the Caves."

"Of course, time is short. But rest assured that when the fighting starts, I will be right next to you!"

"Thank you once again for that Miliantes. I will then see you on the battlefield," Shadick said urging the horse to run faster. He glanced back just as Miliantes took to the skies and disappeared from sight.

"Farewell Miliantes and I know that you will be a great asset for this coming battle. I will see you again soon."

And it was with a slightly easier heart that he set his sights on the forest. He could barely see from where he was at that moment, but knew that once he got there, he would be able to relax...

Chapter 14

Sorceral Deep

Alexandria disappeared through the trees determined to get away from the camp as well as Shadick and the trouble he seemed to have brought into her life. It was rather funny how much chaos he had caused since he had shown up. She sighed as she figured how mad Amethyst would that she had not greeted her, but it had been difficult enough to not break down and knew that if she had stayed for a hug that she would have broken down.

If she had allowed that, she would be forced to tell Amethyst about everything that had happened between them and she was not ready for that. With a war looming she should be thinking about what the best way would be to prevent as little life lost as possible, but instead she was concentrating on the little things. The things that she could do nothing about.

She froze in her steps as she realised that she had taken a wrong turn somewhere. Why was it that the last time she had gone to the Ocean she had not paid attention at all? Oh, right... Shadick had been right there, silently guiding her in the right direction. She had not questioned him about why he was taking one road and not another; it had just been accepted.

"Why does it seem that my thoughts get me into more trouble than needed? I should have paid more attention the last time and not be thinking about some guy," she muttered to herself as she approached one of the trees and placed her hand on it.

A smile popped onto her face as she realised that she was indeed on the correct path and was not lost. It was only a matter of not falling flat on her bum with the roots seeming to want to cause her some serious damage. She could not remember that it had been this difficult the last time; perhaps Shadick had just guided her through a less treacherous pathway. Or she was concentrating on him so much that she had just not noticed how carefully she had to walk.

She ducked underneath some low hanging branches before stopping again and taking a deep breath. There it was, the smell of the ocean. It seemed to call to her and her heart lightened a little. In shock she realised that it was already early evening when she heard the sounds of the night time Creatures.

It felt as though the trip was taking forever and it made her worry that she was wasting too much time on silly thoughts.

Just as she wanted to force herself to speed up she felt as though evil was surrounding her and wanted to kill her. She froze again and looked around trying to see if there was someone there. The Centaurs presence was apparent and she realised that they had been there not too long ago. Breaking into a sprint she ran for the edge of the forest knowing that time was not on her side. As she broke through the tree line, she blinked in the sudden brightness of the beach area.

"Alexandria! We were just starting to get worried about you," Starlansha said, putting her hand on Alexandria's arm. "Amethyst had sent the Faerie and I thought that you would be here before sundown. But when you didn't show up, I was wondering what the delay was and was just about to send one of the water Faeries to go out and look for you."

"There is no time to waste! We need to go get the stones, right now!" she replied gasping.

"But we can't go right now; we would not be able to see anything going on around us."

"I felt the presence of the Centaurs in the forest! There was definite evil in the air and I can tell that it may not turn out for the best."

"There has been no one near the Ocean since Shadick and yourself left yesterday. I just had a feeling that we needed to keep an eye out for any trouble since then and I can assure you that there has been no one."

"Oh... but I'm sure that they have been here."

"I can assure you that this stretch of beach have not had any visitors. Perhaps lower down, but I cannot assure you of that. I think that we should get you some food at the cottage so that you can get your breath back. You can get some rest and then at first light we can go into the Ocean to get the stone."

Alexandria sighed and nodded knowing that Starlansha was right, but it did not feel right. But she nonetheless followed the Mermalani to their home hoping that they would still be in time.

It was a couple of hours later and she had forced herself to relax while Starlansha made dinner. She was listening to the singing from the birds that were outside and she smiled slightly. Roslata had not shown her any courtesy when she had walked into the house, but had turned her back on her before she could utter a word.

"I know that you have tasted Shadick's *world famous* fish, but I can assure you that my octopus rings are even better. It is normally an instant hit!" Starlansha said, breaking the silence.

"I am sure that it would be absolutely delicious. And yes, Shadick's so called *secret* recipe is scrumptious. You know I have been trying to get that recipe out of him, but he refuses to hand it over... something about how it will go to the grave with him."

"I know what you mean! I have tried to get it from him as well but he just shrugs it off.

"How long have you known him?"

"Hmm... if I am not mistaken it has been just over five years now."

"And where did you meet?"

"We met him for the first time when his parents sent him and his best friend here for some *thinking time*. They had been getting into some trouble and they had figured that it would be best if they had some time to themselves to think about what they had done. You see our parents had been friends with his for years and they vacationed here whenever they could.

"They stayed here for a month if I'm not mistaken and after they had returned home we would travel there just to stay friends. He was also one of the first people besides the Ocean community that I told when my parents died," she whispered and Alexandria kept quiet. "My sister was always the one flirting with Shadick and Chadromida hoping to get his attention. She was not the only one though as there were always other girls vying for his attention. But truthfully he was always too busy with studies and getting better with weapons to really care about girls."

"It would seem that he had a very *care-free* lifestyle when he was younger. But it sounds like he was very close with his family."

"Oh, they were! And they would not want a nothing to corrupt his mind into something that might just get him into trouble," Roslata said walking back into the room.

"Rosy! Take that back! Alexandria is not just a worthless person; she is a powerful witch," Starlansha said shocked

"And why should I take it back? If you remember correctly, his parents liked me and they had told me that they wanted us to get married."

"That is all lies! They liked you of course, but they never said anything about you marrying each other."

"You just don't believe me because you weren't there when they mentioned it."

"Rosy, why are you being so weird? There was not one time that you were alone with them. You seem to forget that we used to be half attached at the hip and did not go anywhere alone."

"Well whether you believe me or not, it is what they wanted. And Alexandria is a nothing. And they would be ashamed that their son was even talking to her never mind whatever else she has made him do."

"I have no idea why you are being so disrespectful to her! But you better take it all back."

"Just leave it, Star..." Alexandria said and started shaking.

"You are a friend of ours and she has absolutely no right to speak to you like that."

"I can do whatever I please... I have been an adult for long enough to be able to make my own decisions and to know what is wrong and right."

"And how does that give you the right to be mean to anyone, especially a friend?"

"Since when has she been a friend of mine? From the very first time she set foot here she has been a thorn in my side."

Alexandria quickly got up and walked to the bathroom to give the two of them some alone time. She splashed water on her face and leaned against the door, wondering how a friendly conversation had turned so deep and troubling. It had not been as though she had asked them the world; she had asked to know a little bit more about Shadick. And how they had met when Roslata had just stormed in and ripped everything out of order.

There was suddenly a soft knock from the other side of the door causing her to gasp in shock. She quickly straightened up and unlocked the door, a smile firmly in place.

"You have no need to pretend as though that didn't just get to you. I would actually understand if you decided to leave right now," Starlansha said sighing.

"Leave without getting the stones? For some reason I think that your sister would only find some kind of sick humour in me doing that. Besides... without your help I would drown as I have no way to breathe underwater," she replied smiling sadly.

"That reminds me! I was supposed to give you something from my grandfather. He sent a messenger here earlier today and told us that we were to give you this necklace."

"Not that I am not grateful or whatever... but why exactly would he send *me* a necklace?"

"My grandfather can be a very strange person and he has his own ideas about things. But this is a useful little stone that will allow you to breathe underwater. Truth be told he has never given anyone one of these as he believes that they would just cause trouble."

"And he decided to give one to me? Why would he do that? I'm sure that he just sees me as a mortal that would want to cause trouble."

"Oh no! He would not have sent this to you if he thought that."

"I am not insulted or anything so you can relax... you forget that I have been pretending to be a mortal for most of my life and it kind of feels natural by now."

"Very well then... the food is ready by the way."

"It smells absolutely heavenly, Star. Thank you."

They had just sat down to eat when Roslata appeared from outside and joined them, she did not say anything to either of them. Starlansha seemed to struggle with her sister not speaking with her, but she did not want to cause more trouble between them so she just kept quiet. When she had finished her meal, she stood up and walked into her room not saying a word to either her sister or Alexandria.

It was early morning and she was staring outside as the sun slowly made its appearance. She had not slept very well the previous evening, but she would not complain. She was unsure whether the twins were awake yet or if they were still asleep and did not want to bother. It was as the last of the stars disappeared that she thought about why Roslata would be acting the way that she was. Was it really just because she was getting close to Shadick and she was sensing it?

As far as she knew they weren't in a relationship so it was not as though she was interfering in a relationship they may have had. And was it true that his parents had told her that they should get married? It seemed rather ridiculous, but one could never really tell what went on in other people's heads.

The sooner she was able to retrieve the stones and get away from the negativity the better it would be for her own wellbeing. Yet she could not just leave without at least

Starlansha with her as she would not know where to go.

"Good morning, Alexandria! I am so happy you are already awake as I think that we should get moving as soon as possible," Starlansha said suddenly appearing in the room.

"Morning Starlansha; truth be told I have been up for hours now. I was trying not to bother you."

"I should have offered you my bed as I know that the couch is not very comfortable. We still need to sort out the extra room after my parents' death."

"It had nothing to do with the couch; I just had a lot on my mind with the upcoming war. Also wondering what the Centaurs are up to... although Amethyst thinks that they will be trying to retrieve the stones as well."

"I know that it is not my business... and I am probably overstepping some kind of line by saying this. But you were thinking about Shadick as well, weren't you?"

"Yes, I was, but it nothing important at all," she said standing up and folding the blanket.

"Very well. When I got to bed last night, I realised that your clothes aren't exactly fit for going for a swim."

"I should be fine... they are comfortable enough."

"As much as you think that... they aren't waterproof and would only weigh you down."

"I was so shocked that Amethyst had sent me here

otherwise I would have asked the Faeries for another outfit."

"There is no need for you to worry about it. I found something that you can wear and that should be very comfortable... if you want to that is."

"That would be very nice of you, thank you."

She watched Starlansha disappear into the next room, appearing a few minutes later with a box in her arms.

"Perhaps once the war is over you can come visit and not have to worry about clothes. It is a combination of a mortal swimsuit and that of the armour that the Mermaids wear. The King's wife... or rather Grandmamma Cece invented theses especially for us when we moved in with them. She also invented something similar for the other Mermaids if there was a need to fight."

"Oh wow! I really appreciate it. If you will excuse me for a minute, I will go put it on quickly."

"I am not sure whether it will fit right, but I am hoping that it would. And Grandmamma said that it should fit you just fine. And we have learned the hard way to not argue with her about things... truthfully I think that she might have some seer in her."

"I think that you should rethink that..." Alexandria said, walking out of the bathroom.

"But it fits you absolutely perfectly! And I can understand why Grandmamma designed it for you.

"I still feel as though I am wearing nothing though."

"Alex, honey... no one, not mermaid or human would be able to swim while they are covered by clothes. This has been designed specifically not to get in the way of the wearer. And the colour of the swimsuit brings out the colour in your eyes perfectly."

Their bedroom door burst open and Roslata walked out, looking Alexandria up and down. She looked as though she was looking for something to insult her on, but found nothing so she kept walking.

"That just confirms it! Even Rosy likes it."

"And you call that *like*?"

"If you knew her like I do, you would know that she would tell you straight. If she stays silent it means that she finds nothing wrong and would rather keep quiet than drag her name through the mud. Now let us get on the road... Grandfather wishes to meet you and it is best to listen to him unless you want trouble of course."

"Absolutely no pressure then..."

"You are not the only one that is nervous... we have not always gotten along with him. And if it had not been on my Grandmother's insistence, he would never have reached out to us when my parents died," she said, holding the door open and then walked to the cliff situated only a few meters from their front door.

"Wait... aren't we going to go to the beach and go in from there?" Alexandria asked as they reached the edge and she looked down at the water.

"I can assure you that it is quite safe from here. There are no rocks below us that could hurt us... if you want, I will go in first so that you can see."

"Uhm... okay sure, you do that."

Starlansha paced back a few steps and then took a running start towards the edge of the cliff, it was as though Alexandria was watching in slow motion as she jumped into the air and towards the water. Her legs and feet transforming into that of a Mermaids tail. She hit the water gently and came up a minute later and beckoned for her to join her. She took a deep breath and copied what Starlansha had done. It felt as though she was a clumsy child the way she spluttered as the water hit her.

That went better than I expected... I was expecting some screaming or struggling the first time your gills formed, Starlansha spoke in her mind.

I figured that it would be for the best to not scream and cause an unnecessary fuss Alexandria replied smiling slightly trying to hide her shock. *Besides, I think that I was expecting something worse. But truthfully it is so peaceful down here,*

This area has always been peaceful. Once we get to the Mer-

Kingdom, you'll see that it is bustling with activity. They are always out and about, either shopping or taking their little ones to school. But if I timed it right, we should not run into a lot of people as most would still be sleeping.

If only times were less unsure then I would have loved to take some time to explore the Ocean.

Perhaps one day I will be able to give you the grand tour. But for now, we need to get to my Grandfather's Palace.

Alexandria nodded and followed Starlansha to what seemed like a wall of really tall seaweed, but it was when they got closer that she noticed it had been planted in such a way to look impenetrable. Starlansha disappeared through the seaweed and without hesitation she followed. She got to the other side and groaned silently; she had expected it to be just there, but there was nothing to see.

I am just wondering... how far exactly do we need to travel until we reach the Palace? she asked Starlansha.

It is about an hour's travel north from our place, Starlansha replied.

She suddenly wished that she had a mer-tail as well; it would have made the journey so much easier. Her legs were already feeling tired from the swim. It had been quite a few years since she had a chance to go swimming and she felt very out of practice.

Taking a deep breath, she forced herself to concentrate on what was around her. It was no use complaining about something that could not be changed. Besides that was the only way to reach the Mer-Kingdom, so she may as well enjoy it while it lasted.

It was with that thought that she realised that this would have been an awesome trip to have taken with Shadick. It would have been one of those things that one just had to share with someone else.

Is everything okay, Alex? Starlansha asked of her suddenly.

Yes, everything is fine, why do you ask? she asked, confused.

You stopped swimming...

Oh! I'm sorry I did not realise that I had stopped.

Very well then... just so you know that we are almost there.

She would have asked why she said that when they had barely begun their journey, when she realised that an hour had passed in the blink of an eye and she was already able to see the walls of the Palace. They were pearly white and seemed to double in size as they got closer and closer.

For some reason she had expected it to be more colourful, but she realised that the houses perfectly blended in with some of the surrounding walls and it was rather pleasing on the eyes. It was so strange seeing the different houses that were there and it was with shock that she realised that each house was covered in stones. Instead of detracting from the surrounding it made them all the more special and perfect.

Oh my! The houses look absolutely brilliant, she said looking around.

Yes they do, and you will not notice it from this distance, but the walls of the Palace is actually a blue-green. It always feels as though it belongs in some kind of dream and I just love looking at it. Although that won't be happening today.

They swam closer and Alexandria noticed what Starlansha meant; it was a completely different look from close up than it was from a distance. She landed next to Starlansha on what she assumed was the balcony and waited.

His majesty has requested that he is not bothered today, a guard told them seriously.

Well I am his granddaughter and he is expecting the both of us. He has given me explicit orders to bring Alexandria here to meet him. So unless you want to argue over the situation and get into trouble... Starlansha replied.

But she is not even a Mermaid! Why would he wish to see a useless mortal? the other guard asked astounded.

Because I am more than just a mortal. I am a witch and I have been sent here by the Faerie Queen to retrieve something for her. Alexandria said frowning.

And you think that you would be able to defeat the Centaurs?

Our King had not even been able to do that, now you wish to do it yourself?

And what makes you think that I will be fighting on my own? All of the magical Creatures are getting ready for the fight, as well as the humans from the villages. Our army grows stronger each day. And truth be told I am sure that King Celeriac will join us.

"Joshua! Eric!" they heard someone shout from inside of the Palace.

Yes, your majesty? Joshua asked.

"How many times have I told you to allow my Granddaughters free passage to and from the Palace?" the Queen asked then waved them away.

Grandmamma! Starlansha shouted and swam through the barrier and straight into the Queen's arms.

"Hello, there's my Star! How are you doing on this wonderful morning? And where has that sister of yours gotten to?"

"You know how my sister can be Grandmamma. Here one second and gone the next."

"So very true! I do sometimes wish that she would be more like you and not as carefree. And who is this charming young lady?"

"Grandmamma, please meet Alexandria. She is the witch that we have told you about. Alex, this is my grandmother

Arabella."

"Hello there dear, it is good to finally meet you!" the Queen said giving her a quick hug. "And you really do look fantastic in the armour Star gave you. I have to admit that you have a great figure, not too thin nor overweight."

"It is truly an honour to meet you. And thank you for the compliment although I have to admit it is not what I am used to," Alexandria said blushing slightly.

"Well you have nothing to worry about as it fits you perfectly! Now shall we go find you grandfather? He has been rather antsy this morning while waiting for you to arrive."

"The sooner Grandfather talks to Alex, the sooner we can go to Sorceral deep to retrieve the stone," Starlansha said as they walked away from the entrance.

They walked along passages that felt as though they carried on for days and even though she was burning inside to ask questions she kept quiet. As she looked at the walls and glanced into some of the rooms, she was reminded of how her father had told her about Palaces. To her it had seemed as though he was just telling her stories and had never believed him. She now wished that he could have been there to see it with her.

She noticed that no one stopped them again but they did stare at her as she passed and she wondered if it was because of the armour she was wearing or the fact that she was not a

Mermaid. They finally paused in front of a door and two guard opened it for them and they all walked in towards what she assumed was the throne room.

"This is quite a magnificent Palace," Alexandria finally said.

"I am very happy that you are enjoying it... not a lot of people get the chance," Starlansha told her.

"Secrecy is an important part of our lives, unfortunately. Which is why so very few people ever get the chance to see it," Queen Arabella said softly.

"Perhaps once we get rid of the Centaurs we can come to an agreement. Something that will be good for both those from the water as well as the land. Although... I have to admit that I am sensing some evil." Alexandria said biting her lip.

"That would be true unfortunately. They seem to have recruited the Sea witch and her minions to their army and it has been chaos ever since. The only bad thing is that even though we can change our tails into legs we have no true control over it and if one drop of water touches us, we transform back into Mermaids. Which is why it is such a nice thing, that the twins do not have to worry about that."

"I understand that very well and we would not want that to happen. It would just be nice to know that we could depend on all the sea Creatures."

"That would be up to my husband so I can't promise you

anything."

"Grandmother..." Roslata said appearing at the top of a set of stairs and walked towards them.

"Rosy, I was just wondering where you had gotten to!"

"I travelled here ahead of, Star. And Grandfather is wondering where you are so he asked me to come and find you."

"As you see we just got here, Rosy. And we are right outside of the throne room so at least you did not have to walk that far," Starlansha said shaking her head and walking up the stairs. "So, I do hope that you will not go on as though you had to walk miles to find us."

"Whatever you say, dearest sister."

"Those two have such a love hate relationship," Queen Arabella said shaking her head as she walked into the throne room.

"I assume that you are Alexandria?" King Celeriac asked as they walked into the throne room. "It is very good to finally meet you."

"It is an honour to meet you, your majesty. I have heard quite a bit about you," Alexandria said bowing uncertainly.

"From what I heard you are basically a Princess, so there is no need for bowing. I am sorry to say though that I do not have a lot of time so I will be sure to get to the point. The Centaurs have not just started taking over the lands but the Ocean as well. They have somehow convinced the Sea witch to join their forces and with her comes the Sirens as well as all her other little minions... the witch was also able to change one of my guards into some kind of shark monster a couple of years ago.

"He now goes by the name 'shark-boy'. He can be quite a lethal fighter and it is never a good thing to meet him when alone. There is a fear that she will turn some of the other guards into such monsters as well, but we have not noticed any signs of it as of yet. I can't promise you a whole army as land is not our strong suit, but we can do to help as much as we can. We can discuss what you would expect from us and come up with a plan. The Faerie Queen has always been on good terms with us and we will not go against that."

"Of course, and please know that I will help you as much as possible as well. United we are stronger than if we were to take them on our own. I am unsure how much you have heard the last while, but the humans have joined the magical Creatures and they are planning on fighting together. There is already a small army gathered at the Troll Caves."

"Thank you for offering to help us, but it is not needed. We have a constant guard set up that is in charge of finding any of the Sirens or any other evil Creatures and ridding them of this world. Although I am glad to hear that the humans have overcome their irrational fear of anything to do with magic."

"I doubt that they have really overcome anything... it is more a case of they know that they stand no chance on their own and it was the most logical move for them to come together with the Creatures in the forest."

"Grandfather, do you know anything of Sorceral Deep?" Starlansha asked suddenly.

"Why of course I do, Starlansha. It is in the far reaches of the ocean as well as the most dangerous part as well. It is out of bounds to all of my people, especially my granddaughters. Perhaps you only want to go there to get yourselves into trouble!"

"There is no choice but to go there, Grandfather, and you more than anyone else know this. I'm sure that you would be just too happy if we were killed. It is not as though you care all that much."

"I took you in when your parents were killed; your grandmother basically forced me to accept it."

"Celeriac! You know for a fact that you would not have allowed anything to happen to them either. I just made the decision a little easier for you," Queen Arabella said heatedly.

"There is no need to worry Grandmamma, you should know that we are used to him being so cold to us," Starlansha said then rushed out of the throne room. "if it would make him happier, I won't be returning here."

"It seems that something I said brought up bad memories and I apologise for that," Alexandria said turning and following Starlansha.

"Shall we go to Sorceral Deep now?" Starlansha asked just outside the door. "And I am sorry if I kind of snapped back there."

"I think that it would be for the best to get going as soon as possible. It feels as though they are getting closer by the second and we should get moving as soon as possible."

Together they ran back through the long corridors towards the main entrance where the guards were watching for danger, without a word they dived into the water. Alexandria was sure that she had heard a shocked shout from one of the guards but they ignored it.

You know... I really thought that my Grandfather had changed his attitude towards us, but I guess that I was wrong. He accepted us into his home after my parents death but it seems that it is only because my Grandmother had been forcing him to show us any kindness, Starlansha said sighing softly

I know that my opinion doesn't count all that much, but I think that he does care about you. It is not as though he forbade you from contacting them. And when you asked about Sorceral Deep he really did seem concerned, Alexandria replied thoughtfully.

Starlansha shrugged and concentrated on where they were swimming. She wished that she could say something to make it all better, but she was not sure what would make her feel better. It was difficult to talk about something when you had never met your own grandparents. Without warning something swam past them and they both froze and looked around.

What was that? She asked.

In all honesty I can't answer that question... but I do not think that it is a friend of ours, Starlansha replied frowning.

She was just considering telling Starlansha that perhaps it had been nothing when she noticed Mermaids swimming right at them and she relaxed a little. This was just more proof that her grandfather actually did care more than he let on.

Oh no! Starlansha said.

What is wrong, Star? They were probably just sent by your grandfather as back up.

Those are not normal Mermaids, Alex! Those would be the Sirens that my Grandfather had mentioned.

That isn't good at all... she started but was suddenly being smacked in the face by a tail causing her to spin on the spot. She tried to kick back at the Siren, but she could not move fast enough.

Alex! she heard a shout.

I don't have much time for distractions right now, Star! she replied, trying to block another attack

Catch! she heard next and turned just in time to see two daggers being thrown at her.

She caught them and struck at the closest Siren, catching her just as she was trying to get out of the way. She straightened her shoulders and started slashing at the remaining Sirens that was around her. It seemed that even though she was not able to touch them without weapons; there was something that made it easier by the daggers.

It was automatic movements that guided her as she thrust the one dagger into a Siren's stomach that was behind her and was able to cut another's throat just as she wanted to bite her. Dodging lower, she just missed another smack to the face and breathed a sigh of relief when the remaining Sirens scattered. As she was smiling and looking around her, she noticed that Starlansha was still busy fighting and that she was not faring very well.

Sighing softly, she aimed and threw one of her daggers directly into the one Sirens back, a scream barely being heard before she was forever silenced. The remaining two Sirens turned towards her and she smiled at them in challenge. The one threw a spear in her direction and which she dodged with a graceful back flip; the other had no weapon but swam straight at her.

Her arms were outstretched and it was easy to guess that she wanted to strangle Alexandria, but she quickly grabbed her one arm and bent it behind her back. While gently pushing her other dagger into her back.

She heard multiple shouts from around them, but could not place where the rest had disappeared to. It was then that she looked around and saw that they were surrounded by murdered Sirens and she had killed them all... drifting to the ocean bottom and hiding her face in her hands she tried breathing around the lump that was stuck in her throat.

Alex! Is everything okay? I'm not seeing any marks on you but you are very pale.

I have never in my life killed anyone... and just look around us.

It was not as though you had much of a choice! If you had not stepped up and fought against them, we would be the ones dead right now. And have you not realised before now that there will be Creatures dying all around? Starlansha asked her seriously, handing her the daggers again.

I guess I had hoped that it would not truly come to that, but I have been mistaken, haven't I? Perhaps it would be best to just continue on to Sorceral Deep before they bring back reinforcements?

It would be better for us to get going yes, as they most likely went to go get the Sea witch or Shark-boy.

Do you know how far we are from there maybe?

I am not a hundred percent sure, and I have a feeling that there will be more fighting ahead of us... will you be able to continue?

Of course I will be; my father taught me how to fight for a reason.

You may keep the daggers... I never seemed to really master them, whether that is because I prefer the sword or because I don't know much about fighting, I don't know.

Thank you, Star. I really do appreciate it.

It was just as they were approaching a dark structure that she wanted to ask Starlansha if they were close to where they needed to be or if they would be able to take a break. It did not take her a long time to realise that this had to be the sought after Sorceral Deep.

They had been lucky enough to not be attacked again after the initial attack. Starlansha had admitted that her mother had always been very against 'girls learning to fight' which was why she hated having to use weapons. Her father had sometimes taught them a few things but it had never felt right, so she had always avoided it as much as possible.

They had swum a short distance, Alexandria still holding the daggers when Starlansha had smacked herself on the forehead before giving her holsters that matched the daggers. She quickly put the holsters around her legs. One on each of her legs, and it felt as though it was a part of her body. Starlansha also showed her that she had a sword behind her back, smiling.

When I heard Sorceral Deep I expected something completely different than this, Starlansha commented

You mean this charming place? It looks so happy what with all the stalagmites and stalactites all over the entrance as though its smiling at us, she replied sarcastically.

I am sorry to say that this is indeed Sorceral Deep, with all the gloom and doom added free of charge! Starlansha said giggling.

So very morbid...

Shall we proceed before any more bad guys show up?

Alexandria nodded before swimming closer to the entrance apprehensively. She peered inside and checking that there was no one waiting for them inside. One never knew how badly someone wanted to attack until it was too late.

I don't think there is any immediate danger, she told Starlansha. *Neither do I sense any evil presence in the cave, so I think that it should be relatively safe for us to proceed.*

It is not as though we have much of a choice...

Well we do... but it isn't a choice that we really want to make.

Oh yes. Get the stone and kick ass or let the Centaurs get the stone and have our asses kicked.

It is all about how you look at it really.

Hmm... I would rather have to fight the Centaurs than have them take over and destroy everyone and everything.

She was about to reply, but was interrupted by the fact that they were suddenly falling a few meters through an invisible barrier. She flinched as she stood up.

"Ouch! I think that I hurt my foot when I fell."

"If things can better now instead of worse it would be a whole lot better. I would try and help, but I can't even see my own hand in front of my face."

"I can help with the light situation..." Alexandria replied before concentrating on her hands a flame appearing in her hands, lightening the cave.

"Oh wow, that's much better! Would it be too much to ask for you to make it slightly bigger?"

"I can definitely do that," she stated, moving her hands a little and revealing the entire cave that they were in.

"Do you think that we reached the centre of the cave?"

"Why are you asking?"

"Because if I am not mistaken then that is the Trilate Amethyst over there," she said pointing ahead of her.

"I do believe that you may be right," she said testing her foot as she stood up.

"You think that it is some kind of decoy or something?"

"I can honestly not tell you, but I am sensing an evil aura approaching."

"Any idea how long until they get here?"

"About an hour, more if they take a few wrong turns along the way."

"Then it would be for the best if we were to hurry and get the stone so that we can get out of here. Do you have any idea how dangerous it can be to fight in here? It might just cause a cave in."

"Oh, I know that all too well and we do not need any more trouble in our lives right now."

Alexandria limped towards the slightly raised platform frowning. She knew that she had to be careful just in case the place had been booby trapped. The platform that the stone was situated on was something that people spoke about in fairytales.

Completely covered in coloured stones, shining in the light that she still held in her hands. She moved the light so that it was balanced on only one of her hands and reached towards the stone. As she wrapped her hand around it the entire cave shuddered and she squealed in surprise.

"If I am not mistaken, they just started blasting their way in here! So, we better get going," Starlansha sighed as she looked back towards the entrance. "I guess that we will have to fight again and I was so hoping that it would not come to that."

"Well, well, well... if it isn't young little Starlashoua and the witch we were told about," sneered the shark-boy as he walked into the cave with the Sea witch right behind him.

"Indeed it is her, Tobias. Although there is nothing to worry about, I cannot even feel her power. So, she should not give you any trouble at all," said the Sea witch shaking her head.

"Tobias? Oh yes, now I remember! You used to be the head guard up at the Palace who always chased after Rosy and flirted with her non-stop," Starlansha said back up towards Alexandria.

"It is good to see you again Starlashoua," Tobias said grinning evilly.

"It is Starlansha... not..."

"Star, as much as I know that you want to correct him this isn't the right time for that," Alexandria said putting the stone in a side pocket.

"No, the time for introductions is not now," Tobias said as he drew his sword.

She and Starlansha removed their own weapons at the same time barely glancing at each other. She twirled the daggers and waited for them to make the first move. They had to end this quick as this was not the place for a big fight.

"Do you really think that you would be able to beat us?" the Sea witch asked sneeringly.

"The two of you? Well of course we will be able to," Alexandria said.

"Oh, but we are not alone..."

It seemed as though the passageway behind them was suddenly filled with little lights seemingly getting closer and brighter. She was about to comment on it when she realised that the lights were actually eyes of Sirens and that there was about a dozen of them.

"Oh... I do not think we will be able to fight all of them at once," Starlansha said lowering her sword.

"I would not be so sure about that Star. I am sensing some of the Palace guards outside. If we can move them all outside somehow it would be very easy to take care of them," Alexandria noted softly.

"You wish to be outside? Very well that can be arranged quite easily," the witch said.

She started muttering under her breath and Alexandria realised that she had begun casting a spell. And before she could warn Starlansha they had been transported outside of the cave system. Starlansha glanced behind them and saw that it was not just the guards waiting for them, but King Celeriac as well.

Alexandria suddenly gasped and coughed as the gills formed once again and without warning. From where they were right then she could see that most of the Sirens had been left outside, probably in wait. They were still outnumbered, but she really hoped that the guards would make that not matter.

Morganasha, when will you learn to just give up? King Celeriac demanded of the witch.

And why would I need to learn that when my army outweighs yours a hundred to one? she replied

Because I knew that this battle would not require my entire army and selected only the best to join me.

Before long you will realise what a mistake that had been. Although I have to admit not even your entire army would be able to stand up against my fighters.

I see that you still underestimate not just me, but my army, the King said.

You are mistaken once again; I do not underestimate you. Instead I guessed that you are so pitiable that you would rather depart from this life before you allowed your family's nobility to get ruined.

I am of course talking about how you denied the existence of your own daughter when you were told that she was expecting a human's child, the witch continued. *How when she came to ask for help you threw her out of the Palace like some useless pup. And how when you heard that I had her in my clutches, you did nothing. I was not a complete heartless witch in case you were wondering. When she tried to escape for a third time was when I gave the order to have her killed. And I am sure that you would have just stood there and watched it happening just because you did not want to admit the existence of 'Mermalani's'.*

Starlansha gasped and put her hands in front of her mouth, shocked. Roslata on the other hand did now show much emotion besides swimming to her sister and completely ignoring their grandfather.

How dare you lie about something so serious?! It just shows how evil you are, King Celeriac said angrily

And why would I lie about that? Just ask Tobias if you want someone to back up my words. How he tried swimming after her, but lost her momentarily when she entered my grotto. He watched as I slit her pretty little throat and then I transformed him into the thing he is today! Morganasha stated.

I will not allow you to keep lying about my daughter! ATTACK!! he commanded and chaos ensued.

The Sirens rushed at the guards and the fighting started. If one had not looked properly, it would not have been obvious who was Mermaid and who was Siren. There was just the sound of weapons being drawn and it rang through the entire ocean.

King Celeriac was not just standing there; he swam towards Morganasha and hit her in the stomach with his trident, but dodging his next blow. She shot a spell at him, but he was able to move out of the way just in time.

Alexandria watched the fighting happening not sure if she was supposed to help or just watch. Roslata made the decision for her when she swam at two of the closest Sirens, swinging her sword at their tails. She was able to behead the one and use the movement to propel herself towards another who she was able to cut almost cleanly in half.

Starlansha swam to her sister, but was almost immediately surrounded by three Sirens. It was then that she realised, Starlansha had never drawn her sword and sent a spell at the Sirens, causing them to tumble away from her. She took the moment of aloneness to withdraw her sword and attacked the nearest Siren, letting the sword sink through its heart.

She pulled it out and span to another and thrusting it into its stomach. The third swam up to her and smacked her in the face with her tale making Starlansha gasp in pain. Roslata attacked the Siren from behind and thrust her own sword across its abdomen.

Alexandria watched Tobias swimming towards her and was just getting ready to attack him when he sent five sharks towards her. She panicked slightly not wanting to harm Creatures of any kind. She was able to turn in a full circle to avoid the attacking sharks and she sighed in relief but it was short lived as another swam towards her and she was forced to attack it with both her daggers.

Leaning back and letting it swim over her, she let her blades run across its belly and it started bleeding profusely. The blood seemed to confuse the other sharks as they started fighting each other for the kill. She was able to sink just outside of the spreading blood and saw that Tobias was staring at the sharks angrily. He got distracted by a guard reaching him and the two started fighting.

Roslata and Starlansha swam up to her and they watched that the chaos was still in full blast, although it looked as though King Celeriac had been right. His army was taking care of the Sirens as though they were just practice dummies.

Get out of here now! We can handle the Sirens as well as the Sea witch, the King shouted.

But we want to help! Starlansha replied desperately.

I am staying here until all of the Sirens have been killed as I wish to take care of the Sea witch myself. She is the one responsible for the deaths of my parents and she needs to pay, Roslata added.

I told you to get out of here! Everything will be fine here so just get going, he shouted at them again.

You heard your grandfather, you two. I know that you want to stay and help the army fight. But they are more than capable of handling the Sirens. And I promise that we will come back here and help him fight the war when it starts, but for right now we need to get going, Alexandria said desperately.

They both nodded begrudgingly before swimming away from the fight, Alexandria barely able to keep up with them. It went against everything in her to just leave the Mermaids to fight on their own but she knew that they would be okay and that Amethyst would want the stones. The twins slowed down and she knew that they were having second thoughts. So, she said a quick spell and they landed in the twin's cottage.

"We have to go back and help Grandfather! They are still in danger and we just left," Roslata said angrily once she realised where they were.

"As much as it hurts me to say Rosy... they will be fine. You saw that they were handling it all fine," Starlansha said, falling onto the couch crying.

Alexandria sat down next to her and hugged her.

"You are right, everything will be okay. When I glanced back I saw a whole lot more guards than Sirens."

"Why do you think that makes it any better?! The fight can turn at any moment and the Sirens will be able to kill my Grandfather."

"I understand that, but I really doubt that would happen. And you heard your grandfather, he told us to go. Now we can get the stones to Amethyst so that she can combine..." she started but Roslata suddenly slapped her through the face.

"Our family is in danger and all you can think about is yourself and how this might affect you. You should perhaps have another hard look at what is happening in the world right now and see that it is not just all about little old you! I am going back to bed before I jump back into the ocean to go help," she shouted and disappeared.

"I am sorry about all of this, Star. It was not my intention to cause you or your sister any heartache."

"Do not blame yourself, Alex. We knew from the very beginning what this mission would involve. We also knew that we may not be able to help my Grandparents once the fighting started."

"I just wish that I was able to help more."

"I have no strength left to make food and just need my bed," Starlansha said before disappearing to their room as well.

Alexandria sighed softly, feeling completely helpless... there would have been no way for them to have helped the guards fight the battle as they were already beating them back. They might just have gotten in the way and caused more damage than anything else. She lay down on the couch and tried to relax, but jumped up a few minutes later when the bedroom burst open.

"You know that we cannot go back right now, Rosy!" Starlansha shouted.

"I do not care what you think! I do not care if it is too dangerous! I am going whether you want me to or not." Roslata shouted back.

"Your sister is right, Roslata. I know that you do not like me and probably won't care what I say but it is too dangerous to go back," Alexandria said standing up.

"This is really none of your business Alexandria, so why do you not just keep your nose out of my... our business?!"

"She is just trying to make you see some sense, Rosy. You know that both Grandmamma and Grandfather would rather have us here safe than there in the hands of danger," Starlansha said shakily.

"And in case you forgot... your grandfather told us to get away from there. Did you really want to go against what he said?" she asked carefully.

"OUT! Get out of our house! Just get out of our house!" Roslata shouted suddenly. "Your invitation into this house has officially expired. And you are not welcome here anymore!"

"Alex, you will always be welcome here. But perhaps it is time to just go for now. We will help you in the war when it starts but for right now, we need to be alone," Starlansha said at a shocked Alexandria.

"Very well then... if you require any help just send a message and we will be here as soon as possible," Alexandria said automatically walking towards the door, pausing before walking out.

She took the Aquadious stone off from around her neck and

the Trilate Amethyst out of the pocket that had held it. Why was it that the stones seemed to create more chaos than what it was supposed to? How was she supposed to accept that these little stones would be able to help in this war when they were only creating trouble at the moment?

If only the Centaurs had not gotten it into their heads to come for revenge things may have been so much easier. She would not have to worry about so many Creatures getting hurt or killed. She could have lived in peace in McLeod's and just not have a care in the world. She sighed and walked towards the forest clutching the stones tightly and wishing that she could turn back time and just stop all of this from happening. Unfortunately, it was not in her power to do that...

Chapter 15

Reunion of Lovers

From previous experience, she would have thought that it was nearly impossible to just stand by as her friends and family fought. Yet it had been for the best that they had left King Celeriac and his guards to take care of the fighting. It would be of no good if they were to get hurt right now when there was a bigger battle not too far into the future. She knew that no matter how difficult it was to watch, that friends and family would want to help.

She glanced back at the cottage as she reached the edge of the forest and sighed. It was not as though she expected them not to worry about them, but for now there was nothing to do about it. The twins did realise it, but their Grandfather did care about them which is why he had shown up at Sorceral Deep. Yet how was one supposed to tell someone that when all they noticed were the bad things?

"Soon you will be able to make them happy, but for now there is nothing to it," she whispered to herself.

Taking a deep breath, she turned and walked into the forest, knowing that the more time she wasted the more time the Centaurs had at causing more havoc. She was going to give Amethyst the stones and she would combine it and... and... what could stones do? Make a pretty necklace for someone and they would just throw their hands in the air in surrender? Hardly... but perhaps she knew something about the stones that she had not told them. Alexandria sure hoped so.

When she had asked Starlansha if she knew anything about the stones, she had just received silence. Whether that was because she did not know anything about the stones or because she was not supposed to tell her, she was not sure. She had not even been able to sense any powers coming from the stones which made it even more difficult to believe that they could help any in the coming war.

She really hoped that Shadick had successfully been able to retrieve the stone and had not run into too much trouble. Taking the Trilate Amethyst out of the pocket she looked at it carefully, turning it over and over hoping for some kind of clue. She sighed and dropped it back into the little pocket; there was no way that these little stones could do what Amethyst was hoping from them.

It was during times like these that she really wished that her parents were still alive so that they could give her guidance as what to do next. Even better would be if they were to help her get rid of the Centaurs for good, if that was even possible. It seemed just like a waste of time to banish them as they would only gather support again and try it all over again.

She would not want to kill them as they were still Creatures that she had to look after, but if she really thought about it, it would be for the better. Yet she knew that would never happen. Perhaps they would get scared and run off to some far place and never bother them again. If only it could have been that easy.

She glanced around and noticed that the forest seemed to have opened up somehow and she was not sure how to explain it. And there seemed to be a permanent sense of evil hanging in the air, making sure that no one can truly relax. She knew that she wasn't that far from the Caves anymore and perhaps then she could get some proper sleep and not have to worry about anything or anyone.

"Alex!" a voice shouted from the pathway ahead. "Oh how wonderful! You're back! Amethyst was really getting worried when she thought that you were taking too long to get back here. I do believe that she has created a little road the way she has been pacing around."

"Ashley? Is everything okay back there? Has something happened to Shadick? Or any of the others for that matter?" she asked panicked.

"There is no need for worry! But you know Amethyst... she was having a panic attack the moment you disappeared into the forest."

"And have you heard anything of Shadick?"

"There has not been any news of him yet," she said then quickly added, "But it is a long journey and it is only natural that he would take a little longer with his journey."

"Absolutely... nothing at all to worry about."

"Come on, come on! Amethyst will want to see with her own eyes that you are back safe and sound! And to of course hear whether you succeeded."

Ashley disappeared through the trees and she sped up to try and keep up with her, clutching a stitch in her side and flinching at the pain in her foot. After this she needed a year's holiday where she could just lay back and not worry about anything.

"Amethyst! Your majesty! You will never believe what... or rather whom I found!"

"What is it this time, Ashley? Did you see trouble coming?" Amethyst asked from her seated position.

"No... of course I didn't see any trouble. If that was the case why would I be smiling?"

"You are right of course, Ash. I am just a little distracted as you should know."

"I have told you before, Am... that if you don't get proper rest you will look like a hag by the time you are thirty." Alexandria said stepping into the light

"Alex!" she shouted and ran into her arms

"Am, you're choking me."

"You have no idea how worried I've been! I am so happy that you are back, safe and sound."

"Really, Am. There is nothing to worry about."

"Why did you take so long? I had really thought that you would have been back earlier today."

"Starlansha insisted that we get a good night's rest before going to Sorceral Deep. We then had to first go the Palace and meet with her Grandfather, then we went to go find the stone. And we ran into a bit of trouble there when the Sea witch and Tobias showed up. But luckily King Celeriac expected foul play and they were waiting to help us fight. Although he ordered us away before we could really help much."

"You were attacked by Morganasha and Tobias?! I knew that it may be a little dangerous, but I did not think that the Centaurs power stretched that far already!"

"It was more of an ambush than an actual attack..."

"Ambush?! Why didn't I follow my first instinct and not allow you to go alone?"

"Amethyst, as you can see, I am absolutely fine. Although you are really starting to choke me and I'm afraid that will do more damage." She said just as her ankle gave way

"Oh my! Are you okay? And I put your life in danger by sending you there alone!"

"And all I have to show for it is a slightly twisted ankle, so can you please relax?"

"She is right, Amethyst. You need to calm down," Oliver said from behind her.

"Alexandria! I am so happy that you're back at last. We were all really worried about you," Michael told her as he walked out from the Caves.

Amethyst took a step back before sitting down heavily on a log, crying softly into her hands. Shana and Ashely rushed to her and tried calming her.

"I am absolutely fine. Although I only got back a few minutes ago," Alexandria told him giving him a quick hug as he helped her up

"If you were attacked by a Sea witch then what kind of danger did Shadick run into? It is a lot more dangerous in the Sangalon Mountains than at Sorceral Deep!" Amethyst sobbed.

"Am, Shadick is a *lot* stronger than I am. And please

remember that he had his weapons with him the whole time... as well as the wolves! And I am sure that he will be back here faster than you think."

"Alex, you do know that Amethyst have not slept at all in four days?" Ashley asked standing up. "She will not be able to be of any use if she does not get some serious rest."

"Please go have a nap, Am. I promise that I will handle everything around here for a while. And if it is a real emergency, or if Shadick shows up I will call you."

"Oh, very well then! I will go and have a nap," Amethyst said frowning.

"Sorry if you will find this inappropriate... but what are you wearing?" Shana asked still sitting on the log.

"This is the outfit that the twins gave me for the journey into the Ocean and I completely forgot to put my own clothes back on when we got there," she replied with a slight blush

"Oh, right then... I will go into the forest and keep an eye out for Shadick."

"Thank you, Shana!"

***

All of the traveling was getting to him and he was not sure how much more of it he would be able to handle. If someone were to ask him how long he had been on the road he may just have said weeks instead of days. Why had they never figured out easier ways of travel?

He knew that there was still a lot of traveling to do before he could finally declare that he had had enough. Once the war was over, he had to get back to his own mission and that would require yet more travel. He sighed as he realised that he had almost arrived at the Dolomite Caves and would be allowed to rest for a while. It was a good feeling knowing that he had succeeded in retrieving the stone. And to make it even better, the Pegasus Miliantes, would be joining them and he was sure that Amethyst had not expected that.

As for his feelings for Alexandria, he was sure that he had them under control. Or he hoped so. He shook his head and realised that he had strong feelings for her although he was not ready for just everyone to know that. Perhaps they could work on a relationship even with the looming war. They were both adults and they both understood the dangers involved.

He was suddenly overtaken by a yawn and he put a hand in front of his mouth. If he did not get to the Caves within the next hour, he would not be able to stay awake and would most likely pass out on the horse. Both he and the horse got a fright when a blue light shot straight at them. He only realised a few seconds later that it was a Faerie who quickly landed ahead of them transforming into her human form.

"Shadick, you are back!" she said grinning.

"It was Shana, right?" he asked sleepily.

"That is correct, I am surprised that you remember me. We were just wondering where you've been as it has been feeling like *days* since you left. Although I tried to remind them that it wasn't just a quick trip."

"Did something go wrong with Lexie's mission?!"

"I assure you that everyone is doing perfectly fine. Even though Amethyst has been worried and haven't slept and Alexandria did hurt her foot a little. But the minute Alexandria got back to the Caves she demanded that Amethyst go get some rest. Which was when I told them that I was going to come into the forest and keep an eye out for you."

"That is a strike of luck then..." he said shaking his head.

"Is everything okay with you?"

"I will be... I just need to get back to the caves so that I can sleep for a week."

"Very well then, shall we get back so that all of you can get some proper rest?"

"That sounds like the best plan yet," he said watching her turning back into her miniature form and flying off without him.

He urged the horse into a gallop and stopped on the edge

of the tree line just as she flew right at Alexandria.

"Shana! You are making me dizzier than wine on an empty stomach!" Alexandria sighed and Shana transformed once again

"I have some really good news!"

"And what would that be, Shana?"

"The news of my return, which I hear has been highly anticipated," Shadick said jumping off the horse and leading it forward.

"I am so glad that you are back!" Alexandria said jumping up and running straight into his arms, kissing every inch of his face. "I was really missing you the last few hours... or was it days... oh whichever."

"You see! I told you that I had good news," Shana said grinning.

"Well if this is the way that I am greeted after a long trip then perhaps I should go away more often," he said laughing.

"I'm sorry! I am just so happy that you are back here safe and that no harm has come of you," Alexandria apologised blushing.

"And I am happy that you are safe as well. Although you do have me curious over this outfit that you are wearing. Don't get me wrong... it is absolutely breath-taking, but isn't it a bit too more than what you normally wear?"

"Oh, this little thing...? It's been laying around in my closet just waiting for the right time to be worn," she joked.

"I never thought that you would be into wearing something like that."

"Starlansha gave it to me... so that I would not be slowed down by normal clothes once we got the swimming part of the mission. And I didn't want to go there naked so I didn't have much of another choice," she stammered.

"Take a deep breath, sweetie. I was just pulling your leg."

"Oh... right... I knew that!"

"Have I told you that you are cute when you blush?"

"Were you able to retrieve the Septer Quartz?" Michael asked suddenly.

"I was able to find it yes."

"That is truly good news! Now Amethyst will be able to combine the stones and we will make short work of the Centaurs."

"Shadick! I am so happy that you are back. I was really worried when you had not returned by earlier today," Amethyst said appearing all of a sudden.

"As I am sure you know, it is a long trip to Sangalon Mountains. And truthfully I did not think about sending one of the wolves as I just wanted to get back here," he replied still holding Alexandria.

"Well as long as you are back here, safely then I am happy. Especially when Alex told me that they had been ambushed at Sorceral Deep. I could only imagine what kind of trouble you may have run into."

"You were ambushed?!" he asked angrily.

"Well... kind of," she started.

"And what does 'kind of' mean, exactly?"

"Fine! Yes, we were ambushed while at Sorceral Deep, but we were lucky enough to have King Celeriac and his guards there and they helped us. And it was only a small battle between us and the Sea witch, Tobias and some Sirens... and we didn't get hurt... much."

"And I was wondering what Shana had meant by you had hurt your foot! It could have been so much worse! I should not have let you go; it should have been up to me to go to both Sangalon Mountains and Sorceral Deep."

"I promise you that no serious harm has come to me. And you know that I would not have approved of you going to Sangalon Mountains *as well as* Sorceral Deep."

"Besides, from what I am seeing of you now, you can barely stand on your own two feet from exhaustion," Amethyst said stepping in.

"Speaking of which... a little Faerie told me that you have not had any rest for the last four days!"

"There is no need to worry about me. I will go have a long nap as soon as I'm assured that the two of you have been fed and taken care of. Otherwise I will not be moved."

"Their food is right over here, Amethyst. So, you can go and have your rest. I will stand over them until they finish eating if it's completely necessary." Ashley joked.

"Please tell me that it isn't fish," Alexandria said desperately.

"And here I thought you loved fish?" Shadick asked surprised.

"I never said that I don't... but I have had enough fish to last me a lifetime!"

"It is not fish, promise," Ashley said giggling.

"Then food it is!" she said and walked to the table and sat down while Shadick just shook his head.

"They really do seem happy together."

"As long as it stays that way and they don't start fighting again," Amethyst replied.

"You really think that they would fight again? They were separated for a while."

"You make it sound as though they had been separated for months instead of days."

"From what I can see, to them it was an eternity. Just look at them, your majesty. They are smiling and laughing, something that I do not remember before they left."

"You do have a point. Truth be told, Ashley... I doubt that Alex has truly been happy since she had been a young girl. She has been good about hiding her true feelings but I have always known."

They both looked at Alexandria and Shadick sitting around the table, joking around. They were laughing at Alexandria who were pulling faces as Shadick picked up a fish and put it close to her. She glared at him until he put it down and started tickling her.

"But she truly does seem happy," Ashely said smiling.

"Stop! Stop it, Shadick!" they heard Alexandria's giggles.

"And I am glad that she is happy, even if it is just temporary," Amethyst agreed.

"Why would you say that it is only temporary?"

"We have a war being held over our heads and from what I have seen the Centaurs will go through with it unless something really big gets in their way."

"You're right... but perhaps we will get lucky?"

"We can always hope and believe me that is what I am doing. Unfortunately, we have no real control over that."

"Could you imagine the things we could do if that was the case? The control and power that would come with powers like that."

"You forget that we are Creatures with pure hearts. And it would go against everything we stand for if we were to abuse power like that."

"I know... was just saying."

"Relax! I was trying to make a joke," Amethyst said then added to Alexandria and Shadick "You *eat* food, not play with it!"

"Who in the world is playing with their food?" Alexandria asked innocently.

"That is a very good question that I would love to have answered as well," Shadick added nodding.

"The two of you aren't as funny as you believe! Such immaturity from adults," Amethyst said jokingly.

"Truth be told... I am stuffed," Alexandria groaned softly.

"Are you sure? There is still a lot left."

"I am as sure as I can be."

"All I need right now is to find a comfortable spot and to pass out," Shadick added, standing up.

"That sounds like a good plan. It feels as though I have not slept in da... oh, wait. I haven't slept in days."

"Then I do think that it is time for us to get some sleep."

"There has been a spot set up for the two of you in the Caves, so you can just go there and get some rest," Amethyst stated.

"No... the Cave is way too busy and full of life. We will not be able to get any rest if we stay here. I do believe that we will go sleep next to this spot next to the stream. It is peaceful and it is where we had been the night before you arrived."

"I understand that, but is it safe enough to do that?"

"Yes, it is... and if it makes you feel better, the wolves are already throughout the forest and will send a warning if trouble were to appear. Although I doubt that would happen."

"Very well then. Go and get some rest and I will see you in the morning."

"Night, Am. Please make sure that you go sleep as well," Alexandria said hugging her friend.

"I assure you that I will go rest."

Shadick grabbed her hand and pulled her away, she waved at everyone sleepily. She barely noticed where they were going. She heard whispers, but decided that they could get over it and that she really didn't care all that much anymore.

"I can barely keep my eyes open, that is how tired I am."

"Don't worry, I am with you on that one. But I knew that I would be able to sleep as soon as I had you in my arms," Shadick agreed.

"You are talking about *only* cuddling, right? I do not have strength for anything else right now."

"I promise you that is the only thing on my mind right

now."

As soon as they got to the spot, she felt the worry and stress of the day melt off her shoulder. She sank onto the floor gratefully and watched as Shadick drank some water before joining her, immediately pulling her into his arms and closing his eyes.

"Goodnight, Shadick," she said, kissing his arm.

"Night, Lexie. Sleep we..." he started, but passed out.

Alexandria giggled...

Chapter 16

Fraternal Revelation

"It seems that Shadick has a good effect on you as you have been absolutely glowing," Amethyst commented the next morning. "Where did he disappear to anyway? You showed up, but I do not remember seeing him at all."

"When I woke up, he was still fast asleep and I did not have the heart to wake up him. He has really been exhausted with everything going on," she replied

"Now that you mention it, I did notice the exhaustion. If he hadn't been distracting you, I am sure that he would have fallen asleep right at the table."

"You know that he would rather pretend as though nothing is wrong instead of just saying that he needs a break. How did you sleep by the way? You were barely standing when we left last night."

"I did yes. It has been the best rest I have had in a while. But I think that the Faeries may have slipped something into my evening tea."

She giggled at Amethyst's surprised face and glanced absently into the forest and sighed. Absently scratching the table her cup was resting on. A frown formed on her head as her thoughts turned to McLeod's and what was probably nothingness by now.

"There is something serious on your mind all of a sudden."

"I really want to go to McLeod's; I need to see what is going on there."

"You heard what Oliver said... there is nothing left. Besides, it is too dangerous to go there, especially alone."

"But it is something that I have to do, Am. And I don't want to put anyone's life in unnecessary danger.

"Then take Shadick with you. But I will not allow you to go by yourself!"

"You have no reason to worry, Amethyst. I will go with her," Michael said from behind them.

"But I have already said that I do not want to take anyone with me! And you should know by now that I won't go out just looking for trouble."

"The fact remains... it is too dangerous for anyone to go," Amethyst said seriously.

"I need to see what they did to my parents' home. That is the only memory I have of them and I would hate to lose it."

"The important memories is still in your head."

"I need to see it for myself..."

"Ask, Shad..."

"I am not going to ask him neither am I taking anyone with me."

"I have also been wanting to see what destruction they have caused. And whether you accept that I am going with you or not; just know that I will follow you," Michael said seriously.

"Fine then! I would rather have you coming with me than going on your own and you getting hurt."

"So, when are you planning on leaving? As soon as Shadick has woken up?" Amethyst asked nodding.

"No, I want to leave within the next few minutes. Perhaps you can go ask Grog if we could borrow two horses so long, Michael."

Michael nodded and walked off to find the Troll; Amethysts smile had faded. Alexandria really hoped that she would not continue arguing about the fact that they were going without Shadick.

"I promise you that we will be fine. Besides... you should be happy that I said yes to Michael joining me when I could have easily just transformed into an eagle and flew off. But I didn't..." she glanced at the forest as a growling emerged from behind her and she bent down next to Managwa. "Of course you are welcome to come with us! At least this way I can say that you were with me the whole time."

"Well at least the wolf would be able to come for help if something goes wrong."

"I do not just want to use Shadick like that, as though he is some kind of faithful dog. He is a person who needs rest."

"And you know that if you were to ask him that he would go with you in a heartbeat! He knows how much McLeod's meant to you."

"The village has been given a new name..." Markus sneered as he walked towards them

"You have got to be kidding me!" Alexandria said shocked.

"I am deadly serious."

"And what is this new name?"

"Justren Village," was his reply before walking away laughing.

"The nerve of them!"

"It is a terrible thing and I'm sorry."

"This just gives me more reason to make sure that they pay for what they have done!"

"Will you be taking any weapons?"

"Yes, the twin daggers that Starlansha gave me will work well. Although I will try my best not to use them."

"I was able to find these two horses; I hope that they will suffice?"

"They will do just fine, thank you."

"Please be careful the both of you! I do not wish to explain to Shadick or anyone for that matter that I just allowed you to go to this village and then got killed," Amethyst said as they climbed onto the horses' backs.

"You should know by now that I am always vigilant," Alexandria replied smiling as she urged the horse forward.

"You better be careful!"

It was about two hours later when they cautiously approached the edge of the forest. They could have taken a shorter and quicker route, but she did not want to risk running into of the Centaurs or any of their guards. If it hadn't been for Michael, she would have just flown there but that wasn't possible right then. She had to admit that it was kind of nice to travel with him right there. It was different than it was with Shadick, but this was just a friend of hers. Sighing she let the horse pick its way through the underbrush.

"Is everything okay, Alex? You seem to be troubled for some reason," he asked her.

"Everything is fine, there is no need to worry about me."

"Would you like to talk about it?"

"It is nothing that has not been discussed before, about how we are heading for a war and nothing can be done about it. I just wish that we could stop the Centaurs somehow, but know deep down that wouldn't be possible."

"And have you raised these thoughts with that guy you have been running around with?"

"He has a name you know..."

"I know that, but for the life of me it has escaped me."

"His name is Shadick and he is a fantastic guy! He would do anything in his power to help us, even though he could have turned his back on everything."

"Relax, Alex! There is no need for you to get onto your high horse. I was only asking whether you have spoken to him about these things that are on your mind."

"Oh... I apologise, Michael. I have been on edge the last while. But to answer your question, yes I have talked to him about all of it and we know that no matter what we do there is no way to stop what has been started."

"Do you really think that the village is as bad as what Marcus said?"

"Do you want the truth or have me tell you a sugar-coated version?"

"I would expect nothing, but the truth from you as you are an honest person."

"From what I have seen of not just Justren but of the Centaurs... yes, the village is as bad as he says it is, if not worse.

And whether or not we like it, we will have to face what happened at some point and I would rather want it to be now than later."

"I was afraid that you would say that," he said sighing. "May I ask you another question?"

"You should know by now that you can ask me anything, Michael."

"Why are we being followed by a wolf?"

"He is a close friend of Shadick's who seems to have taken a liking to me. All he is doing is making sure that no harm comes to us and will even fight if necessary... he will even run back to get help if he had to."

"I can see the use of having a wolf as a pet."

Alexandria slowed the horse down and took a deep breath before forcing herself to move forward. She had wanted this and it would only be stupid to turn back now. A soft gasp escaping her lips as she looked at the destroyed village. Smoke was lazily drifting from some of the houses while some had been destroyed so badly that they were not able to distinguish between one and another.

There were red splatters on some of the walls, which she quickly realised was blood. She jumped down from the horses back and tied its reigns to a tree before inching closer to the destroyed buildings. Managwa looked at her then at Michael before crawling forward carefully

"What is our plan exactly?" Michael asked.

"I don't exactly have a plan... but I do want to try and go in as deep as possible. Perhaps see if we can find out anything more."

"I will not allow you to put us in danger!"

"Will you relax please? I won't be putting myself in danger... I will be hiding behind buildings... or rather walls. It is not as though I would just mindlessly walk up to one of them and start demanding that they answer questions."

"Neither Luanda or Shadick would be very happy with me if I just allowed you to do this! They would tell me that I was dim witted or something."

"And this... is why I wanted come alone," Alexandria muttered under her breath before running into the village.

***

"Am!" Shadick shouted as he dodged Trolls and Dwarves.

"Why good morning, Shadick. I do hope that you had a good night's rest?"

"I did yes, thank you. Do you perchance know where Lexie is? I have looked all over and I can't seem to find her."

"Oh..."

"Please tell me where she has gotten herself. And there is no need for you to deny that you know as I can see it in your eyes."

"She and Michael decided to go see how much damage had been done to the village."

"WHAT?!" he shouted angrily.

"Calm down, Shadick! She is not alone as I mentioned before."

"She will surely get hurt! What does he know about protecting not just her but himself?! The idiot!"

"He is not an idiot Shadick and you know that very well. So I am not sure why you are being so mean-hearted."

"And why is it that you did not convince her to wait for me? Or send one of the wolves to wake me up!"

"I did try to take you with, but she said that she would only feel guilty about misusing you."

"It would have been one of the biggest pleasures to have gone with her. If she needs my help with something and really wanted it, I would not say anything about it."

"That is what I was trying to tell her, but she kept going on about how she didn't want to endanger anyone for something like this. Managwa went with her..."

"That is some comfort at least; he will protect her with his whole life. And if it comes to real danger he would come and find me. But I will not be waiting for him to come fetch me; I will leave now and run to the village."

"But what if she is already on her way back and you miss each other?"

"Amethyst you know me. And you know that is not possible," he told her before disappearing into the forest.

How was it that she still did not listen to him? It would have been no trouble for her to just wait a while longer until he was awake so that they could go together. It would be really dangerous not just inside the village, but around it as well. The Centaurs would expect her to try something like this.

He froze when he realised that he had run so fast that he was already at the edge of the village. His mother would be chastising him right about now for not paying proper attention. Yet it meant that he was closer to Alexandria and making sure that she was still alive and well.

As he looked at the destroyed village, he knew that she would have been in a state, having seen her childhood home in this condition. No one should see this happen to their home, and he should know as it had happened to him. It was then that he spotted someone crouching behind a wall and realised that it was Michael.

If the human was here, then where was Alexandria? Surely, she had not gone into the village on her own? But no, he did not spot Managwa either which could only mean that the wolf was at her side. It still did not make sense to him why Michael would be out here, hiding when he knew that this would be dangerous.

He ran towards Michael and grabbed him by his shirt collar and pinning him against a wall, growling.

"Where in the world is she?!"

"She disappeared into the village to find out what is going on!" he replied.

"And why is it that you did not follow her? Do you not realise how much danger she could be in if she gets caught?!"

"I tried stopping her! But she was there the one second and the next she was gone!"

"You could have still gone in and tried to find her. But if you will excuse me, I am going after her. Unlike you I am actually willing to help her if there is need for it," Shadick said, letting him fall to the ground and stepping over him angrily.

She was running from building to building, making sure that she could not be seen. Yet if she was being completely truthful, Managwa was running ahead of her and she was just following the wolf. His ears allowed him to listen out for danger that may be approaching as well as something that may be unseen ahead of them.

They were approaching the place that she had called home

when they ran across the first group of Centaurs. There were five in total doing what she could only assume was patrolling. She quickly ducked behind a wall before they could spot her and took a deep breath. They passed her so closely that she could hear their voices and knew who at least two of them were and she bit her lip.

"So is everything still okay around the village, Johnathan?" Balditha asked as they paused in front of her hiding spot

"Yes, sir! Justren village is secured and nothing is out of the normal. We did take a few extra precautions by stationing a few of our best guards throughout the village in case there is need for it," the Centaur replied bowing his head.

"That is good to hear! Mattson have you given the archers their orders to attack anyone that enters the borders of the village?"

"I did yes. Their answer was that if it made our leader happy then they would do it without question," Mattson replied and Balditha smirked.

"It is good to hear that they loyalties remain so strong. Have you been able to find out why Terri has been acting so peculiarly the last while?"

"I have asked him on numerous occasions as to why he was acting so strangely but all I received was an 'it is none of my business'."

"Steven, Claurent, would you please go and get a hold of Terri for me? Tell him that I wish to have a word with him."

"As you wish, sir," the two said in unison before galloping away in the opposite direction.

"If you would please excuse me for a few minutes, sire," Mattson requested.

Balditha nodded, already talking to a Centaur that had just joined them. Mattson disappeared around the corner of a building not too far away from her. For a second she considered following him, but figured that she would learn more from Balditha himself, so decided to stay where she was.

Managwa growled softly a few minutes later, but Alexandria was not paying attention to him. She felt the wolf pulling on her sleeve shirt and she tried shaking it off without success. It was as she was turning to the wolf to tell him to stop that she noticed that Mattson was standing right in front of them. She jumped up just as he threw a punch at her, hitting her hard enough that she crashed through the wall that she had been using a hiding place.

Balditha glanced at the noise and the other two Centaurs sifted uncomfortably. Managwa ran towards her and crouched in front of her growling at the Centaurs. She sat up and winched at the pounding in her head, slowly reaching for her daggers at her side.

"Are you trying to play the hero again, Alexandria?" Balditha asked walking closer.

"No, I know when I am outnumbered. And it would be stupid of me to fight when I know that I cannot win. Although I have been wondering what this specific village and its villagers did to you to warrant such destruction," she replied standing up.

"Well they are mortals... and if you ask me that is one of the worst things that you can be in this world. And seeing that the entire world will soon belong to me, I thought that I should start somewhere. Besides, I knew that this used to be your hometown and I thought that I would get rid of it for you."

"So I take it that you are still determined on your original course of action? That of taking over the world instead of making sure everyone gets along?"

"Yes, I am, because in my eyes that is the only option available. And there will be peace between the Creatures."

"And when are you expecting this peace to happen, exactly?"

"Once the world is mine, of course. They will all be my slaves and there will be a law that they either accept this... or die."

"What do you wish we do with her and the wolf, sir? Should we capture her and put her in the dungeon while the wolf becomes lunch?" Mattson asked.

"I still have plans for her so best not too harm her... too much."

Ignoring the searing pain in her head, she took their moment of distraction to start running. She dodged the arrows that flew at her but froze in place when three more Centaurs walked towards her. She had no choice than to fight as she refused to leave Managwa here on his own. It was then that she noticed the Centaur on her left look at her before pointing behind him surreptitiously.

Biting her lip, she wondered what he expected of her, but did not have much time to question it as Balditha was getting too close for comfort. So without another seconds thought she ran straight at the Centaur and was surprised when he feinted an attack before losing his balance and letting her get away.

As she ran around the corner she screamed as she ran straight into someone else. She looked up and realised that it was Shadick and not a Centaur, grabbing his hand and pulling him with her as she started running again. Knowing that Managwa was right next to them she headed straight for where Michael was still cowering behind the wall.

"Get to the horses, now!" she shouted at him, but he had frozen in place. Sighing she swerved and ran straight at him, grabbing his hand as well and propelling him towards the horses.

They seemed to sense the danger and pulled on their reigns which she quickly undid with a spell. As soon as they were clear they all jumped onto the horses backs and kicked their flanks. If they were lucky, they could get away from them without too much trouble.

"May I just inquire as to what exactly you did to the Centaurs back there that they are so mad at you, Lexie?" Shadick asked with a grin.

"If I am not entirely mistaken... it's because I am still alive and well," she replied shrugging.

"As long as you are happy with what happened back there then all is well of course. No need to worry about the mere mortal," Michael said angrily.

"Do you really think that it was enjoyable to be chased by seven Centaurs? And they all had weapons in case you didn't notice. Neither was it very nice being smacked through a wall," she muttered jumping off the horse before staggering to the stream nearby.

She bent down and started washing her hands and gingerly touching her head feeling for anything broken. Her hands came back bloody, but it did not seem that there was any other damage. Shadick got off of his horse and walked towards her still bent over, frowning when the wolf ran past him and leaned against her. He saw her shoulders sag and he knew that she had been worried.

"Are you okay, sweetie?" he asked.

"If you were to ask me, I would say that she is perfectly well!" Michael replied sarcastically.

"Would you please just go back to the Dolomite Caves? And tell Amethyst that we will be along shortly," Shadick growled, to which Michael just shrugged.

"His nerves are probably just gotten the better of him, which is why he is acting the way he is," Alexandria whispered.

"Will you please stop making excuses for him?"

Managwa suddenly stood up and growled at the spot where they had come from. They backed up slightly when a Centaur walked towards them, his hands in the air as though in surrender.

"What are you doing?" Shadick demanded angrily.

"I have come to ask you if I may join you in the fight against my kind," it replied.

"But you are a Centaur! How are we supposed to believe that you wish to fight against your own kind?"

"Shadick... wait," Alexandria said stepping closer to him. "It was you that helped me get away from Balditha and the other Centaurs, wasn't it?"

"That is correct."

"Then I owe you a very big thank you as you probably saved my life back there."

"It is only a pleasure... although I am sorry to say that I was not able to do the same for your parents."

"What... what do you know of my parents?"

"Why do you think that you can trust him, Lexie?" Shadick asked her resting his hands on her shoulders.

"He really did save me, back there. Now as I have already asked... how do you know what happened to my parents? No one could tell us anything about that day. It was eventually just assumed that they had been murdered by some kind of dark Creatures."

"They were not murdered... they were slaughtered," The Centaur said shaking his head sadly.

Alexandria gasped, putting her hand in front of her mouth. Before anyone could say anything, she fainted Shadick running forward and catching her before she could hurt herself

"Is she doing okay?"

"If you had been a little more tactful when you had told her about the slaughter of her parents, she would not have fainted in the first place!" Shadick growled putting her down softly.

"I would have thought that she would appreciate the truth for once. She deserves it after everything she has been put through."

"What is your name?"

"I go by Terri."

"Welcome back to the land of the living, honey," Shadick joked as Alexandria groaned and her eyes fluttered open.

"What happened?" she asked confused.

"You fainted... when Terri told you how brutally your parents had been killed."

"Oh... yes. I remember that now."

"Are you okay? Or are you going to have another fainting fit?"

"I promise that I will try not to faint again."

"As long as you are sure that you are okay." Shadick nodded before turning back to the Centaur "So, it was Terri?"

"That is correct."

"What is it that you are able to tell me about my parents?" she asked sitting up

"I am sorry if it came across a little coldly before. But what Balditha's father did to your parents cannot be explained with any word besides slaughter."

"Very well then, please continue with what you were saying."

"It has been fifteen years ago that this mindless act occurred. It was right after your parents were able to banish us from the forest. Diliante started a rumour that she knew would get your parents attention. And instead of sending someone else they had decided that it would be best that they travel to find out whether the rumours were true or not. As they did not want anyone to get killed.

"I will not go into the details of what happened next but I can assure you that they fought until their very last breath. Your father even tried to make your mother get out of there and to get back to you but she refused. She loved him so much that she would not allow your father to suffer alone. It was as though she knew that you would be looked after and was happy with that knowledge.

"It was on that night that they fought the Centaurs, until they were shot with arrows through their hearts. And the Centaurs being who they were, they did not stop with just one. It was as though they wanted to make sure that there would be no chance for survival.

"I was a young boy and had been taught that the warriors had done that to your parents because they were going to come after us. Unfortunately, it was a case of believing them or being killed, although I had made the decision to not turn out the way they had. Just as I thought that it was over, he gave the order to make an example of them..."

"Are you sure that you want to hear this?" Shadick asked as she paled.

"I need to hear about what happened. Please continue, Terri," she replied.

"As I said before, I will not give you all the details. After that order the guards removed what was left of your parents' bodies and got rid of it. When everyone had dispersed, I was able to slip back there and searched for anything I thought may be of importance. I was determined to salvage whatever I could and get it back to their daughter. I was able to find a necklace which I believe belonged to your father, Alexandria," Terri said handing her a necklace.

"My father never removed this necklace for anything... he considered it his most precious belonging. Besides of course myself and my mom," she whispered looking at the necklace.

"It was my hope that if I were to give it to someone they cared for this necklace would make them feel a little better. To have it as a reminder of what fantastic people they were and how they offered us some kind of deal but it was refused."

"This means a lot more to me than you can imagine. Thank you."

"May I have a look at it, Lexie?" Shadick asked.

"Of course, you can," she answered handing it to him.

"It isn't exactly the most special or expensive necklace. If you look in the centre you will see a dark blue gem, but I found it the one day when we went on one of his hunting trips. He laughed when I told him that I had found it especially for him to keep him safe when he wasn't with me.

"He thanked me for being so thoughtful. That night when we got home, he put it on a string and asked me to please put it on for him. And ever since that night he refused to remove it."

"That just means that it was special to him. I believe that he considered it a piece of your spirit that he could always carry with him," Shadick said tying it around her neck.

"Thank you for that, Shadick. It means a lot to me that you understand how much it meant to him. And thank you, Terri. For putting your own life in danger to retrieve something that did not mean anything to you."

"It is only a pleasure, Alexandria," Terri said bowing to her.

"Please... call me Alex. Alexandria seems so formal. And I will stand up for you and reassure the Creatures and humans that you are in fact on our side."

"Perhaps it is about time that we got back to the Caves, before we have a panicked Amethyst sending out a search and rescue party?" Shadick asked giving her a quick hug.

"There is no more reason for us to stay here, so yes let us return. I do believe that I will have some serious explaining to do once we get there."

They climbed back onto the horse and urged it to move,

with Terri next to them silent for now. Managwa who had been listening silently stood up ran past them and towards the Caves. Alexandria smiled a little as she watched it all happening. Perhaps there was still hope to come out of this in one piece. If more and more people joined them in the fight, surely they would be strong enough to win...

Chapter 17

Dragon Master

It was a week since she had been attacked and chased through her old village by the Centaurs, yet to her it felt like only a few hours. It had been quite an interesting task convincing the Creatures that Terri was not there to harm them. She had to stand in front of him just so that he was not attacked and killed then and there and had to almost shout the entire story to those gathered around.

They only truly relaxed when Amethyst stepped up and hugged him. Apart from a few disgruntled grumbles they accepted it and moved on with whatever they had been doing before. The evening after, Amethyst had organized a huge feast for everyone living at the Caves as a welcome to those who had joined them since they had first arrived.

Alexandria knew that her poor friend was trying her hardest to ease the tension that could be felt throughout the camp. Yet she had to admit that the Camp had grown exponentially, so some tension was to be expected. A day did not go by that Creatures and humans showed up and asked for help and swore to help in the upcoming war. Some of them had admitted that they would not be able to help with the actual fighting, but had offered their help in other fields which had come in handy.

"Once again you are lost in thought, leaving me confused as to why," Shadick told her as he sat down next to her.

"I was just looking at the camp and how it has grown since we first arrived here. We never thought that it would get as big as it has. I guess in a way we have the Centaurs to thank," she replied.

"It just goes to show that there are a lot of people out there willing to stand up to the Centaurs and not just sit back and be walked over."

"Have you realised that, while we are just sitting here, the Centaurs are taking over the world one little piece at a time? I spoke to Carla yesterday, the girl from the desert area. She said that the Centaurs had been bored when they had travelled past there and decided to entertain themselves by destroying their village. How twisted is that?"

"I promise you that we will get them for what they are doing to the whole world. We will make them sorry for going up against us and hurting all the people that they have so far."

"The inactivity has been getting me as it feels like we could be doing something."

"I have been wondering where you have gotten that strange necklace from, Alex. It has been a week and you still have not told me anything about what happened back there! All I do know is that the village does not exist anymore," Amethyst said, impatiently sitting down next to them.

"She will tell you what happened when she is ready to, Am. There is no use in forcing her into saying something when she isn't ready to," Shadick said quickly.

"But do I not have a right to know?"

"All in good time. Surely you have known her for long enough to know that she will talk to you when she is ready?"

Alexandria was absently playing with the necklace, which had not taken off ever since it had been given to her. How would she be able to tell Amethyst that it had been her father's which Terri had rescued from a bloodied field when she tried not to ever mention them?

Sure, they have spoken about them before, but it had always seemed as though she found something else to talk about instead. Amethyst huffed as she got up and walked towards a group of people that had shown up from the east and were still very nervous.

"Thank you for stepping in like that," she whispered.

"It is only a pleasure as usual. Do you want to get out of here for a bit? Perhaps go to the beach and just walk until our feet fall off?"

"Yes, I do want to get out of here. Even if it is for just a few minutes, anything would be better than the constant questions."

He stood up and held his hand out for Alexandria who took it. They walked away from the camp and all the people milling around. They were walking in no particular direction besides away from all the people.

"May I ask what happened on your mission to Sorceral Deep? Or is it still a taboo subject?"

"As I have said before... we went to King Celeriac's palace first as he wanted to meet me. He then he threw a little fit about having to go to Sorceral Deep. Which caused Starlansha to argue with her grandfather and storm out before he could say anything, really. She mentioned something about her grandparents never really cared and that they were better off without them or something. We then proceeded to Sorceral Deep and it was quiet on the way there until about halfway when the Sirens attacked us... whom I had to kill..."

"You killed someone?!" he asked surprised.

"I did yes, but it was not something I enjoyed. It felt so... wrong. It still does for that matter. Anyway, Starlansha believed that I would not be able to continue the journey, but I proved to her that I was fine."

"I am so proud of you! I never thought that you would be able to kill someone, whether you had a choice or not. Is that where you got those twin daggers from?"

"During the battle yes... I never really thought that there would be any fighting involved so I had left my weapons here. Starlansha told me to keep them as she had never felt comfortable using them."

"I do believe that they fit you perfectly. Hand me one of them, quickly. I wish to examine it," she handed the one to him and watched him inspecting it.

"So, is there anything interesting about them?"

"No, not really. Although this handle's design is most fascinating! I mean there is a swirl of genuine gold as well as Aquamarine infused in it, which is why the colour is so outstanding."

"I had not even noticed that," she said as he handed it back and looked at it closer. "Thank you for taking me on this walk; I already feel more relaxed."

"As you notice, I know what you need at times. Not always though. You can be such a closed book that I have found myself rather frustrated."

"I am so used to keeping things to myself that it has become a kind of defence mechanism. Even though Amethyst and Valencia were always there for me it always felt as though I never really had anyone to talk to about the important things. And it had always felt as though I would just be bothering them about the things I wanted to talk about. Which is when I taught myself to keep my feelings to myself and just make everyone believe that all was well."

"Well I am sure that they would have been all too happy to listen to you. But I am here for you now, and I am willing to listen to you no matter what."

"I really do appreciate that, Shadick... oh, we have already reached to the ocean!"

"So, it is not just me that thinks that didn't take all that long?"

"No, it isn't just you. When I had to come here last time, I could have sworn that it had taken longer. But perhaps it is just a spell that the Centaurs had placed on the forest to make it feel that way. I have been feeling the evil grow for a while now."

"For now we do not need to worry about them, as they aren't here. So we can just walk along the beach and relax and perhaps we could take a dip as well."

"That sounds like a fantastic idea!" she said and followed him away from the forest and the twins' cottage.

They were just getting back to the Caves when they heard the panic coming from there. Humans were screaming and they were sure that they heard clashing of weapons or something similar. She glanced at Shadick before breaking into a run towards where they would be able to see what was going on.

"It could be dangerous! And we would be of no use if we got hurt while trying to save them," Shadick said grabbing her arm.

"Surely you can hear the panic coming from everyone? They really seem to be in trouble," she replied frustrated.

"I promise that we will help them, but I refuse to just storm in there not knowing what is waiting for us."

She nodded and took a deep breath trying to calm her nerves, following Shadick as he edged closer to the panicked Creatures. Pausing just before they could walk out of the cover holding his finger over his lips in warning. He narrowed his eyes and looked at the camp, a second later he strolled out from the trees confidently, Alexandria's mouth falling open. He had just told her not to just walk out there and here he was doing exactly that.

"If it isn't my old friend Chadromida!" she heard him shouting.

"You know the Master of Dragons?" Amethyst asked rushing to his side.

"Well, well, well... When I heard that you had come to this new *anti-Centaur* camp, I never actually thought that I would find you here. I mean you can be like the wind. Here one day and gone the next!" Chadromida said jumping off of the one Dragon's back.

"You know me, Chad. I always have to be on the move otherwise I start getting irritated."

"Shadick! Would you please answer me?!" Amethyst demanded.

"Please take a deep breath and relax, Am! He is an old friend of mine."

"I am not that old, you know!" he said, feigning emotional pain.

"Oh..." Amethyst said frowning.

"I greet thee, the Queen of Faeries. And I apologize if I or any of the Dragons scared you... or any of the people in the camp. My name is Chadromida, the Master of Dragons," Chadromida said seriously as he took Amethyst's hand in his own and kissing it courteously.

"Such a gentleman! I see that chivalry is not dead, yet. And please, call me Amethyst."

"I knew that you would like him! Unfortunately, he has a flare for making an entrance as you just saw," Shadick said smiling.

Alexandria leaned around the tree glancing at where they were all standing. All the chaos seemed to have stopped now that everyone realised that they were not in any danger. Shadick seemed to be completely oblivious that she was not next to him.

"So what exactly have you been up to since I saw you last?" Chadromida asked him.

"I have been on my own little mission after my parent's death and then finding his journals. I decided that I had to find something that he had always been looking for, in his memory of course," Shadick replied.

"And are you done with that mission? Or are you just..." he started then stopped mid-sentence when Alexandria walked out from behind the trees.

Shadick turned around to see what had distracted his friend and smiled when he saw how gorgeous she was when the sun hit her.

"And who is this beauty?!" he asked walking towards her.

She froze mid-step immediately and stared at the newcomer wide-eyed; Shadick quickly ran to her side and hugged her.

"This is Alexandria. She hails from the village that used to be known as McLeod's. Lexie, please meet Chadromida. He is from Dragon Mountains."

"It is very nice to meet you," she whispered.

"I have to agree that it is indeed very nice to meet you!" he said grabbing her hand and shaking it enthusiastically.

"Let go of her, Chad," Shadick told him tersely.

"Are you telling me that you are jealous, Shadick? That she would much rather hold my hand than yours?"

"As a matter of fact, she would much rather be next to me. Holding my hand and being with me than you, any time of the day," he said as she wrestled her hand free and held onto his.

"Now that hurts! I had just thought that I had discovered her before you."

"No, unfortunately not. This is the biggest reason why I drifted from my own mission, to come help Lexie and Amethyst with the upcoming war. The Centaurs are a powerful enemy and we will need all the help that we can get to beat them."

"That is very true also the reason why I am here today. To provide not just my own but the Dragons help in whatever is needed."

"Your help is greatly appreciated, as is that of the Dragons. It means a lot that you have travelled here to come and help us. I know that some of the Dragons prefer living in their own world," Amethyst answered.

"I think that it is time to get some dinner. If you remember we have not had anything to eat since early this morning," Shadick said looking at her

"Now that you mention it, I am starving!" she replied.

"May I join you?" Chadromida asked.

Shadick nodded and they started walking to the tables. He had his arm around Alexandria's shoulders, whispering in her ear. Chadromida shook his head as he walked behind them. He had never in all the years seen his friend act like this around any girl. Yet he was happy for them if it wasn't just a relationship forged in times of danger.

They sat down to eat their meal and he swatted at what he thought was a fly frowning when it did not go away. Before his eyes a woman suddenly appeared and eyed him disdainfully before turning her attention to Alexandria.

"Amethyst has asked me to come and fetch you. She needs to talk to you about something," Brigetta said.

"I apologize that I tried to swat you!" Chadromida said quickly

"Of course, I will be there just now," Alexandria said standing up, kissing Shadick's cheek before walking to Amethyst.

"You have always had trouble with the ladies, haven't you?" Shadick asked him laughing.

"Why do you seem so nervous around Chadromida?"

Amethyst asked of her not looking up.

"It isn't as though I've known him my whole life! I just met the guy," she answered sitting down across from her friend.

"Yet, you trusted Shadick right after you met him."

"No... I actually didn't. I was very guarded when he first introduced himself to me. If I could have, I would have run in the opposite direction, I knew however that I wouldn't get very far."

"Really? Ever since I have arrived here, I have been thinking that you trust him inexplicably. And have done so since your first meeting."

"Once he explained who he was and what his purpose was for being there, I started trusting him. Not long after that I fainted because of a premonition, he did not take advantage of me or even tried to kill me. He instead helped me to the closest log so that I could sit and regain my strength."

"But was it not still the first night that you started trusting him?"

"Yes, it was... You are making it sound as though I will never trust Chadromida. It will just take a while for me to get used to him."

"Amethyst! Alexandria! Your food is ready!" Brigetta shouted from the cave entrance.

"We are on our way, Bri..." Amethysts shouted back

shaking her head.

"Now, let us go outside and be all social like," Alexandria said smiling.

"You go... I will ask Bri to bring me my food. I need to figure out some things before I can relax."

"Oh... okay then. Do you want me to ask her to bring you, your food?"

"You're an angel," she replied, still not looking up at her.

"I am worried about you, Am... I really am," she whispered as she walked out of the Cave, almost immediately walking into a big creature that was just outside of the Cave entrance.

She glanced up and swallowed as she realised that it was one of the gigantic dragons and muttered as it watched her closely.

"Oh! Uhm.. Nice dragon?"

"Lexie? Is everything okay?" Shadick asked walking towards her.

"I just got a fright when I walked into the Dragon's leg. I am not used to seeing a dragon from so close up."

"It does take a while to get used to."

"What happened? She looks as though she just saw a ghost or something," Chadromida asked as they sat down

"She ran into one of your Dragon friends, over there," Shadick told him nodding at the Dragon.

"Oh, that is just Falcons and he would not hurt anyone unless he was provoked of course."

"That's good to know... but it is still something that needs getting used to when you aren't used to it," she said frowning just as Managwa ran up to them and barked.

"Now, that... is an animal I am deadly scared of," Chadromida said whistling then shook his head as Managwa put its head in Alexandria's lap. "I am used to Dragons and fire and things like that. But when it comes to Managwa I am scared to death! And for some reason he always growls at me when I get near him. Now I have to see that he is the best of friends with your new girlfriend."

Alexandria blushed and bent lower, smiling at Managwa as he eyed Chadromida ruefully. Shadick pulled her closer to him, ignoring his friend who rolled his eyes at the wolf and took a sip of his drink.

"You see, unlike someone else I know... Lexie over here is nice to both mortals as well as animals," Shadick said seriously.

"You are trying to insult me again, aren't you? Well I will have you know that I am not falling for it. I know that you are just jealous of my abundance of women that fight over me daily."

"Do you not mean, your *lack* of women?"

"You have not seen me in a year, how do you know that has

not changed? That the women are now throwing themselves at my feet?"

"The simple fact that you still live with the Dragons in their grotto on a very permanent basis. As well as the fact that you have not been able to find someone that does not faint at the first sight of the Dragons."

"Well I am only thinking about the Dragons. They get lonely if I stay away for too long, you know."

"The Dragons are in their world most of the time, doing their own thing... all you do is sit around and doing nothing. You may go into one of their worlds when you are really bored, but that happens very rarely."

Alexandria giggled as Shadick and Chadromida argued over how the other have been living. By the time that they finally finished eating their meal, the Faeries had lit candles so that they could see. She fell asleep on Shadick's shoulder around midnight and he shifted slightly to make sure that she was still comfortable.

She barely noticed him carrying her to their spot next to the stream a few hours later, settling her on his chest while she slept, oblivious of everything around her...

Chapter 18

Fighters Surveyed

Alexandria opened her eyes slowly and flinched as the sun hit her right in the eyes. She blinked and turned her head slightly before looking up into Shadick's smiling face.

"Well good morning there, sunshine."

"Morning."

"I hope that you were able to get a good night's rest?"

"I did yes, thank you. How about you?"

"As I always do," he told her laughingly.

"If I am in your way, I can very easily move so that you can you have more freedom..."

"I do not want you to move an inch so you can stay exactly where you are."

"That is good to know, as I never wish to move... except for toilet and hunger breaks that is."

"I am sure that if we wished to stay like this that some kind of plan could be arranged to make sure that we are taken care of with the toilet and hunger problems..."

"As terrible as this sounds, we better get up. Amethyst wishes to look at the camp to see how many warriors we have as well as to see if there are any improvements that can be made to the Camp. She wants the villagers to go and get their families so that there is no more separation," she said lightly smacking his chest.

"I am sure that she is capable of doing that on her own."

"She wants to hear what we have to say about all of it. She believes that we will be able to give her new ideas because we are so young."

"That is hilarious... considering that she is the same age as you are."

"I do believe that she feels a lot older than she is, ever since becoming Queen at such a young age. You would be shocked at the changes she has undergone since her mother passed away."

"I never had the honour to have met her mother, but I do think that she has changed since the last time I saw her. Which is not as strange as one might think when you are thrown a curve ball by life. She had to adapt to something that she had probably thought would not happen for years to come."

"That is very true. From my own experiences... I know that I grew up a lot faster than I would have if my parents had still been alive. I got it into my head for some reason that I had to do things for myself and not have to depend on them."

"Certain events happen for a reason, even if we cannot always see the reasoning behind it immediately. But in the end, it makes us stronger."

There was a sudden bark from the trees and they looked up as the wolves walked towards them. This was nothing strange as they sometimes showed up in the mornings, but Managwa was growling and looking into the sky. They were suddenly bombarded by wind and as they looked up Chadromida was flying on one of the Dragons backs with a smirk on his face. She sighed and sat up.

"Did you really believe that the wolves would be able to stop me from coming to find you? Although I have to commend them for their good showing," Chadromida shouted at them as Managwa dropped next to her and looking up at him moodily.

"They just know that we prefer to be alone, which is why they stop everyone from just walking into the forest," Shadick shouted back shaking his head.

"I do hope that I am not intruding or something. If you wish I could come back in five minutes time. Although I do have to admit that I am tired of being looked at as though I am going to harm them or something."

"Or perhaps it is more a case of you sending one of the

Dragons after them."

"Did I say something wrong?" he asked frowning as Alexandria got up and walked past the both of them towards Camp, the wolves growling at him before follow her.

"No, you did not. She just wants to get back to camp so that she can talk to Amethyst. From what she was telling me before you showed up, they want to go around and have a look at all the Creatures and humans to see what we have. And to check that everyone is settling in okay. Speaking of which, we should probably get going."

"Why am I being drawn into this?"

"Amethyst wishes to make some improvements to the Camp so that it is more comfortable. The more opinions she has about what could be done differently the better. It is her plan to have all the families of the Creatures and humans already here to move so that they do not have to worry."

"Very well then, let us get going. As you have said, the more options they have the better," Chadromida said as they walked towards the Caves.

"...and as you know, they will need a lot more space," Alexandria's voice drifted to them as they arrived.

"And who exactly will need more space?" he asked putting his arms around her waist.

"I was talking about the humans. We all know that they

would prefer to be together. And some of them have quite large families and we would not want to split them."

"You have already started inspecting the Camp?"

"We were just discussing the few of the options that we have. So we have a point to start at and not just flail around like headless chickens or something," Amethyst said narrowing her eyes.

"May I join you while you do your inspection?" Chadromida asked.

"Of course, you may. It is always good to hear what someone else thinks as well. And it might mean that we come up with options and solutions faster with someone else around."

"Well I am here to help you, whenever you need me."

"Could we perhaps just get something to eat and drink before we start? We have not had a chance to have breakfast yet and I am starving," Alexandria asked.

"Your breakfast is on the tables over there; I just got distracted and forgot to tell you that. I apologise for making you wait," Amethyst said biting her lip.

"Thank you, Amethyst. It is greatly appreciated," Shadick said pulling Alexandria away. "What is with your attitude?"

"What do you mean by that?" she asked frowning.

"The way you are acting towards Chadromida. Do you not

like or trust him for some reason? Or perhaps the problem is that you like him, but just don't hope that I do not find out?"

"I have no idea what you mean..."

"This is not the time to argue over childish things! Now the both of you listen to me carefully," Amethyst suddenly burst out. "Shadick, she barely knows Chadromida and is not sure what to think about him yet which is why she is being so cold towards the man. Alexandria, you need to realise that Shadick trusts the man and for what it is worth, I trust him. There is absolutely no reason why you should be so cold towards him."

"Oh wow... uhm... I understand your point, Am. I just thought that it would be for the better to be careful about who exactly we trust," Alexandria answered her wide-eyed.

"Lexie, I have known Chadromida for most of my life and there is really no reason for you to not trust him. I would trust him with my life," Shadick said lightly lifting her chin. "and have done so more than once."

"I'm sorry if I am being stupid in not trusting him."

"There is nothing wrong with that as your father taught you to be careful. But sometimes you should go by what those around you say and think as well," Amethyst added.

"You had a very smart father," Shadick said grinning.

"He was smart man yes as well as caring. It was one of his biggest rules to not just automatically trust people that you do not know," she whispered.

"Do you still want to have breakfast and rather do the inspection later... or come with us now so that we can see what is going on?" Amethyst asked with a sigh.

"I have lost my appetite so I think that it would be for the best if we go now. If we have to look at everybody that is in camp then we should get going rather sooner than later."

"But I haven't lost my appetite!" Shadick groaned making them all laugh. Alexandria quickly grabbed two apples and handed it to him. "Yeah, right... as if that will fill this empty void that is my stomach."

"At least she gave you something to eat instead of letting you walk around with an empty stomach," Chadromida added laughing.

"Very true... but why apples? I have not seen anyone be happy with just two apples."

"Are the two of you coming or not?!" Alexandria shouted at them.

"We are on our way, Lexie!" he replied and they walked towards where the two was already talking to some of the Creatures.

Alexandria sighed as Amethyst slowed down to talk to another group of warriors that had been standing around. This was taking forever and at the rate they were moving they would never finish before the end of the day. As if that wasn't bad enough, Shadick and Chadromida were chasing each other and making jokes.

Why could they not be serious for once? The laughter kind of sounded nice, but the tension was too thick in the air and she felt as though she could not breathe. Biting her lip, she tried reminding herself that they were just trying to relieve some of their tension and that if it worked for them then it was a good thing.

She glanced around and knew that they would not even notice if she disappeared, so she stepped behind a tree and turned into an eagle and took to the skies. It had an immediate effect and she felt as though all of the stress had melted away. She looked down and noticed that Amethyst was still busy talking to the five Giants that had arrived there not too long ago. When they had showed up at the Camp everyone had been surprised as it had been assumed they would join the Centaurs.

She quickly changed direction and flew over the main area that the Trolls now called home as they had decided to rather move than have to deal with the constant meetings. The next camp was filled with fires for the Dwarves who were always busy making and improving their weapons, selling some of them to the others spread throughout. A few of the Elves had decided that they would like to be a part of this movement and had moved to an area just from within earshot of the camp, although they barely came out of their homes.

She landed on one of the trees branches and looked towards where the humans had started setting up their Camp. As she watched a bigger tent was being erected for the families that would soon be joining and knew that they would all feel better once they had their wives and children with them. She transformed back into her human form and glanced at the Camps that she was able to see from her point of view. It was her biggest wish that the Centaurs would leave the humans and other Creatures alone once they start moving to this camp, but they could never be sure of that and it was a stressful situation.

"I really hate it when she just disappears like that. All she could do is let me know what she is getting up to," she heard Shadick's voice drifting to her.

"Should I take it that she does it a lot?" Chadromida asked him jokingly.

"No, she doesn't do it a lot. But when she does it can be rather frustrating," he said while she giggled. "Hey you, Michael!"

"At least you had the courtesy of using my name this time..." Michael replied turning to Chadromida. "Nice to meet you, my name is Michael."

"And my name is Chadromida, although everyone normally just calls me Chad," Chadromida replied shaking his hand.

"Have you seen Alexandria?" Shadick demanded impatiently.

"I have not seen or spoken to her since we got back from trying to infiltrate the Centaurs new home," Michael replied calmly.

"I am sure that you are just hiding her because you do not like me or the fact that she cares about me... and not you."

"If you asked my opinion, I would rather have her safe and alive than walking around with a Wolfane. She will only get into more trouble if she hangs around you. Or even worse, for you to leave her for some stupid reason. I can assure you that she does not need any more sorrow in her life."

Shadick growled and stepped closer to Michael; Chadromida moved so that he was in between the two of them. Alexandria sighed and lightly jumped down from the tree and landed not too far away from them.

"Just when I thought that the two of you were getting along for once," she said glaring at both of them. "And with the fight not too far into the future, it would better if the two of you at least got along. Besides I am getting really tired of the bickering that keeps happening."

"But he keeps lying!" Shadick said stepping closer to her.

"How was I supposed to know that she was sitting in a tree?!" Michael asked angrily.

"She has a point... it is time for all of us to stand together and help each other. If we can't even get along how are we supposed to successfully go up against the Centaurs?" Chadromida said after glancing at Alexandria's face. "I have seen how battles like that are fought... and lost."

"Very well then. Shall we call it a truce?" Shadick asked holding his hand out towards Michael.

"Yes, I think that would be best, especially in times like these," Michael agreed and shook Shadick's hand.

"And why is it that didn't work when I was the one suggesting it?" she asked frowning.

"Because we keep disagreeing on what is best for your safety, as well that we feel the other has feelings for you" he replied frankly.

"But I've told you that there is nothing going on between us..."

"Alex, it is best that you do not question how or why they have made peace and just accept it," Chadromida said grabbing her hand and pulling her away. "Besides, I am sure that Amethyst is wondering where we have gotten to. So it is best if we got back to her."

She frowned at him as he pulled her away from the other two. Why was it, that guys always listened to each other but never when a woman got involved? And they said that women were the frustrating ones.

It was as she was about to take another step when the entire earth shook and caused her to lose her balance. Chadromida quickly wrapped his arms around her and glanced around him as the tremors slowed and the panic started to subside from around them. It had not just been them who had felt it; she could spot some of the others holding onto trees or shakily getting back to their feet

"What exactly just happened?" Chadromida asked as Shadick ran towards them.

"I have absolutely no idea, but I think it would be best that we go and find out," she replied and started running towards where she guessed the tremors had come from

As they stepped out of the forest, the alarm went off and she knew that it was time.

Chapter 19

The Confrontation

It was with steely determination that they ignored the warriors running around and gathering in front of the caves. She had known from the very beginning where the fighting would start and they were running towards that spot.

Alexandria stopped dead in her tracks as she emerged through the tree line and saw the Centaurs approaching them from the opposite hill. Their army seemed to be bigger than she ever could have guessed it would be. Her mouth dropped open slightly as they seemed to spread out and grow with every step.

"Why did you stop running?" Shadick asked her bumping into her.

"And more importantly what are you staring at?" Chadromida asked.

"What are those things behind the Centaurs?" he asked when he followed her gaze. "My eyes seemed to have gotten worse because I cannot make out what they are."

"If you are talking about the big Creatures, those would be Giants. If you are referring to the smaller things... they are called Cemlinos," she said then glanced at his confused face. "They are from the same family as Goblins and Gremlins basically. Although I have heard that they bring nothing, but bad luck to those that think to call them their allies."

"Do they look anything like their so-called cousins?" Chadromida asked her frowning.

"Well... in some ways yes."

"And what way would that be?"

"The brownish-green tinge of their skin is very much like them and they are about the same size. But that is it I am afraid..."

"What exactly do you mean by that?"

"They have razor like two-inch venomous teeth and their eyes are said to be deadly."

"Their eyes can be deadly?" Shadick asked confused.

"Not exactly deadly, but if they look at you and they use their powers, you will become paralysed for a few seconds and that is all the time they need to be able to bite you so that either the venom kills you or the rest of the pack kills you or in this case. The army they are working for."

"So basically, you need to make sure that you do not get close enough for them to be able to bite you or to be in range of their weird eye powers," Chadromida replied.

"I forgot to mention that their claws are some of their most dangerous weapon and they really do prefer using those."

"Lexie, is there something else you would like to tell us about these Creatures? Perhaps what they like to eat or do when they bored? Or is it just what you have already mentioned that we need to be careful of?" Shadick asked.

"I think the more important question would be how you even know what these Creatures are?" Chadromida added.

"My father and I accidentally stumbled into one of their nests while out hunting when I was four years old. They attacked us and we barely got away," Alexandria replied shrugging.

"You have known how to fight since you were four years old?"

"Yes, my father had taught me at a very young age how to defend myself and use different weapons. Although I disappointed him a little when I fell over while trying to hold a broadsword."

"You surprise me more and more every time, Lexie," Shadick said slightly shocked.

"When I did not see you with the rest of the Creatures and humans, I assumed that you had come here to start fighting. Instead I find you here, laughing and having a jolly old time even though the Centaurs are right there," Amethyst said as she walked up from behind them.

The three of them turned slightly and watched as all of the humans and Creatures were gathering behind them. Some looked ready to fight for their lives while others looked as though they were rather anywhere but there.

"I was just telling them that I have been taught to handle weapons from a very young age as well as explaining what Cemlinos are. For some reason the knowledge of both shocked them."

"As fantastic it is for us to know that you know how to handle all weapons, I doubt that this is the right time to discuss that. And the Cemlinos joined them?! My mother told me that they had been able to get rid of most of them a few years ago and that only a few remained that they had not been able to find."

"Unfortunately, they seemed to have been breeding ever since then as there is quite a few of them out there. They must have crawled out of whatever hole they had called home," Shadick said pulling a face.

Alexandria turned back to the army that was gathered behind her and was about to say something when she heard Balditha shouting from across the field "ATTACK!!" and watched as their army started running towards them, the

Giants lumbering closer.

"Amethyst! You need to give the order to attack!" she urged her friend but she was frozen so instead she shouted, "ATTACK!!"

In a rush the humans and other Creatures ran past them and straight towards the Centaurs whom were already past the halfway mark. There was a sudden blast as the first swords clashed. In a blur of colour, the Faeries flew right at the Cemlinos, attacking them with their magic hoping that they would be able to distract them from the main battle.

With a soft groan Alexandria noticed that some of them just dodged before going straight for the other fighters. Biting her lip, she looked next to her and realised that Amethyst, Shadick, Chadromida as well as some of the Unicorns were still right there. And from the looks of it they seemed to waiting for something specific to happen before they joined the fighting. Shaking her head, she unsheathed her twin daggers and ran into the battle barely noticing that Shadick tried to make a grab for her.

It was only then that they realised that they had to move; Shadick unsheathed his sword running at the Cemlinos and decapitating as many as he could. He rolled out of the way as a Centaur charged at him and tried to smack him with his hooves. He blocked the Centaurs sword just in time and thrusting it through its chest as soon as he found an opening, jumping out of the way as the body went crashing to the ground.

Chadromida exhaled noisily and looked at the battle already in progress. Whistling sharply and jumping into the air just as Falcons flew past, landing on the Dragon's back. The other Dragons rose up from behind the hill behind them and flew straight into the already full field. The Dragons roared in anger as the Centaurs arrows scraped against their bellies.

It circled around the battle watching closely before heading straight towards a group of Centaurs blowing a fireball at them and watching them scatter in different directions. Two Centaurs who had gotten stuck in the middle of the group were scorched and lay dead, smoke billowing from their bodies.

Amethyst shook her head and let her wings out once again and flew towards the middle of the field where the Faeries were still fighting the biggest group of Cemlinos. It was with a huge shock to see that they were trying to ambush her Faeries by having them distracted and attacking from behind. Without a thought to what might happen she sent a powerful spell at them, killing them instantly.

Alexandria looked around in frustration forcing her dagger through yet another Cemlinos stomach as it tried attacking her. Already covered in both Cemlino and Centaur blood as she had started attacking everything that was in her way. She was thankful that the Giants were concentrating more on the Dragons flying around than the humans and magical Creatures that were scattered around the entire battlefield. If they had she did not want to think what the destruction would have been and the loss of lives would have been tripled.

She ducked out of the way just in time when she heard the howl of a wolf. Managwa ran forwards and jumped onto the Centaurs back, biting into its neck. She watched as the beast reared up and the wolf lost its grip and rolled away from them. Alexandria reacted immediately and swung her daggers through its neck, slicing it off cleanly.

The wolf quickly got to its feet and ran towards Shadick who was so busy that he did not notice the Centaur sneaking up on him. She knew that the wolf would not be in time so concentrated and suddenly appeared in front of the Centaur and blocking his way. Immediately blocking the blow aimed for her head, but was surprised by this one's power and stumbled to her knees. Shadick hearing her soft scream spun around just in time to stop it from killing her, he thrust his sword through its abdomen. Alexandria stopped its angry shout by thrusting her daggers through its neck.

"Are you okay?" he asked her helping her to her feet.

"I am fine, thank you. How about you?" she asked worried.

He did not answer her, instead he pulled her into his arms and held her tightly, being forced to let go only when a group of Cemlinos and Centaurs ran straight at them. Just as they reached them there was a sudden burst of fire from above them that killed them all instantly. Chadromida quickly saluted them before urging Falcons towards a group of humans.

Shadick glanced at her questioningly and she just shrugged before running towards a group of Faeries and Unicorns who was busy fighting against the remaining group of Cemlinos.

Managwa growled and ran in the direction of the twins who had shown up a few minutes before and was already facing off against three Centaurs, but was being overpowered. Shadick ran after the wolf and helped them.

Mattson was busy fighting a group of Skeletons that had been bewitched. He was having a lot of success as he was able to just knock off their heads or breaking their bones with his hands. It hardly seemed fair, but he would not complain and kept fighting.

Alexandria killed the last of the Cemlinos and paused to glance around the battlefield. The entire field was covered with dead bodies, from both good and bad side. She really wished that she had been able to save them from death, but knew that there had not been much of a choice. And knew that not fighting wasn't an option either.

Some of the Faeries had transformed back into their human forms and was standing with some of the Unicorns watching the battle. It was at that moment when Alexandria spotted Balditha, Justren and Diliante standing away from all the fighting. They had not joined in on the fighting even though it had been their idea for them all to fight. Glaring at the small group of unmoved Centaurs.

"My son! My son has gone missing!" someone shouted from behind them, giving her a fright.

"What happened, madam?" she asked the panicked woman.

"My son ran after his father onto the battlefield! I tried stopping him, but with all the chaos he was able to lose me in the bushes! Please, I have to find him as I can't lose him!"

"I promise that we will find him, madam..." she started but froze when Ashley screamed and pointed at the battlefield.

She spun in the direction and barely heard the woman's shocked gasp as she saw the little boy in the middle of the field. There were Centaurs approaching him with a hungry look in their eyes, as though they were ready to kill for meat.

She instinctively knew that she would never reach the boy in time if she was to run towards them and, from what she had seen last, Shadick and Chadromida was nowhere close to being able to help. Taking a deep breath and before any of them could stop her she ran forwards and changed into an eagle and flew straight towards the trembling child.

She was right above them when one of the Centaurs swung his sword towards the helpless child. Alexandria dove sharply, transforming back into her human form and slashing the Centaurs neck and successfully severing its head. The other two Centaurs were shocked and paused watching her and she took this distraction as a good thing. She quickly transformed into a wolf saying a quick thank you for being able to do it successfully. She quickly grabbed the boy by the shirt and threw him onto her back; he instinctively grabbed onto her fur and held on tightly.

She ran away from the Centaurs before they could move and headed straight towards where the Faeries were trying to revive the mother whom had fainted. There was no time for her to pause and look at what was happening on the battlefield. Running past Shadick who glanced down at the new wolf in shock before realizing that it was her, a second later noticing the two Centaurs that were hot on her tail.

He quickly stepped into their path and slashed at their front legs and successfully stopping them from going anywhere else. Using the momentum of his swords to swing at their necks, cleanly severing the ones head. The blade being stopped halfway through the others neck.

Alexandria finally reached the group just as Amethyst got there and picked the child up and she was able to transform back into her human form breathing heavily. The mother groaned as she slowly came to and her son wrapped his arms around her neck.

"There is no way how I can thank you enough for saving my child's life. I am forever indebted to you," she whispered softly holding him tightly.

"Do not worry about it. Please just make sure that you get back to camp as quickly as possible... and stay there," Alexandria replied with a smile.

They watched as they boy and his mother disappeared back towards the camp before turning back to the battlefield. She sighed and ran forward ready to fight once again. Unsheathing her daggers just as she got next to Shadick, attacking one of the Centaurs that had just reached him while he took the other. She jumped over the Centaurs head thrusting the one dagger through its right eye, landing on its back pulling it through its skull. It screamed in pain and fell to the floor and she lightly jumped off before it could fall on her.

Shadick attacked the other one at the same time, sliding underneath it and slashing open its stomach from one side to another, jumping up on the other side and kicking it so that it fell over dead.

"Did you perhaps notice that the three that started all of this has not even moved an inch since the fighting started?" she asked him wiping her forehead.

"I have yes and I have been wondering if I shouldn't perhaps just run over there and attack them. They should be fighting along with their warriors but instead they are just standing there," Shadick replied glancing at them.

"Let us rather not tempt faith. Maybe it is for the best that they are not fighting right now. Who knows whether they made the Sea witch put a protective spell on them or not. But if they start fighting, I say we head straight for them and make sure that they know what they have gotten themselves into."

"I know that we shouldn't, but it is so frustrating to seem them just standing there."

"In case you had not noticed, this is not the time to just stand around and chit-chat! There is a battle going on around you and your friends would be very grateful for any help that you can give them," Amethyst said as she landed next to them.

"Oh, yes of course!" Alexandria muttered, going red.

Shadick ran towards a group of fighters, a small smile on his face. He quickly relieved the Unicorns of the Centaur they were fighting with a quick swipe at its legs. It changed the direction of its attack, thrusting its sword at Shadick who merely stepped out of his reach. He jumped up slightly and landing on its sword making it collapse from the sudden weight, taking advantage and thrusting his sword through the beast's heart.

Amethyst took to the sky and flew toward the Faeries that were quickly being overpowered by a small group of Centaurs. She sent spells in their direction and grinned as they hit their mark. Alexandria ran forward and attacked the rest of the Centaurs, quickly spinning in a circle and bringing her daggers down a Centaurs back and scarring it deeply.

She was just getting ready to swing her daggers at him again when an awful alarm or wail went off all over the battlefield. All the warriors stopped fighting and looked at each other confused. They all tried locating where the noise was coming from. The Centaurs lowered their weapons and without hesitation or second thought ran back to Balditha. Alexandria glanced at the group of Centaurs just as Falcons landed behind her and Chadromida jumped down. Shadick joining them a few seconds later frowning.

"What do you think made that noise? More importantly where you do you think the Centaurs are disappearing to?" he asked.

"When I was still in the air and fighting, I noticed Balditha blowing on some kind of horn. Which is when the Centaurs started running back to him," Chadromida replied

"Why in the world would they do that if there is still a battle going on? Especially if they want to try and win and take over the world," Alexandria said sheathing her daggers.

Before any of them could say anything, Balditha's voice echoed across the field...

Chapter 20

Ephemeral Cease Fire

"You want to surrender?! But we are so close to victory that you cannot possible be serious!" Justren said shocked.

"Do not assume that you have the right to tell me what I can or cannot do! And as I have told you before, it is not surrender. We are giving them some time to cure those of the warriors that they are able to. And then just as they believe that they are free to live their lives we will strike. More importantly we can strengthen our army even more and secure our victory," Balditha replied.

"Your father has a point. Some of our best warriors are hurt and in serious need of care. And some of the fools from the other side might realise what a big mistake they had made and join our side," Diliante said, putting a hand on her sons arm.

"But we are clearly outnumbering them and could easily kill them! It would be dim-witted to just let them go," Justren replied before running towards the battlefield.

"Let him go, Diliante. All he needs is a way for him to get rid of some of his impatience and anger. But I assure you that he will not get hurt or do anything stupid for that matter. Now come on, we have a message to deliver to the 'good' people that have been laying their lives down so... bravely," Balditha said and they walked to a group of Centaurs who was standing around a cage, holding a Unicorn that they had captured earlier in the day.. "So tell me Markus... will you help us or not?"

"Whatever they are gathering around seems to be rather big. Any guesses as to what it is?" Chadromida asked staring at the Centaurs.

"I would say Justren or Balditha, but I wouldn't put my hopes on it. But there is no way to be absolutely sure," Alexandria sighed.

Shadick nodded glancing up and down the group of Centaurs. While some of them had gathered around something that had been brought there, a line had spread out from there to protect their leader. Justren had broken away from the main group a few minutes earlier and they were hoping that he would not be causing any trouble.

"So what do you suggest we do, Amethyst?" Chadromida asked turning to her.

"I think that it would be best to wait and see what they do

next," she answered and smiled slightly at their incredulous looks. "As you have just observed there is no way that we could figure out what they are busy doing. And I refuse to send someone over there as it would just end up with them dead."

"I have to agree with Amethyst on this one. No one, would be able to get close enough to see what is going on. They would not pause to kill someone if they thought they might cause them any trouble," Shadick said.

"We have had enough losses already to risk another out of curiosity," Alexandria agreed.

"Do not get too comfortable with this temporary break in fighting," Balditha's voice was suddenly from all around them making them flinch. "And do not assume that we are giving up the fight as that would be very foolish. We are simply giving you the chance to try and strengthen your forces. This... Ephemeral Seize Fire, oh yes, I do like that. It will not last forever. For all you know it could last a few hours, a few days, a month, a year or a decade. This war will continue you will just not know when."

"As if I could really relax knowing that you and all of your little minions are still on the loose and causing trouble," Alexandria muttered under her breath.

"Take this as a chance to heal your hurt and strengthen you forces. If that could even be possible at all."

"They are so uncouth!" Ashley whispered angrily.

"And what is it you expected from the Centaurs, Ash? But I have to say that in all my years that I have never seen them this uncooperative and mean-hearted," Amethyst said shaking her head.

"I hope that you are clever enough to realise that a surprise attack on our Camp would be extremely foolish. It would only lead to death for any of those found accountable," Diliante added.

The Dragons roared and moved their wings restlessly looking as though they were about to take to the skies. Chadromida said something in another language and they all settled down once again.

"They are getting very impatient with all of this sitting around. They are not used to only listening to idiots trying to give orders," he told them seriously. "I'm not sure if they will listen to me much longer if this continues."

"We now give you an opportunity of sorts, to make a decision that will affect the rest of your lives. You can attack us and the murdering will continue or you can agree to this Seize Fire. You have two hours to make your decision. And then the wretched little witch can come give me your answer."

"Wretched?! Does he really believe that he scares me with his vulgar remarks?" Alexandria asked crossing her arms.

"He is trying to aggravate you, Sweetie," Shadick said unfolding her arms and taking her hands in his.

"So what do you think we should do?" Amethyst asked looking everywhere but at them.

"What do you mean 'what should we do'?" she asked shocked.

"You heard him, Alex! He put the power in our hands to end all of these unnecessary deaths if we surrendered!"

"So you want to just give up? Do you think that they would actually keep their word? Or do you believe that they will actually go away and just leave us in peace if we were to surrender? If your mother was here, she would have seen that this is all just a gigantic trap! They are *waiting* for you to show some sign of weakness so that they can go through with their plan with grins on their faces!

"And the moment they are sure that the world is under their control they will kill every single Creature who had ever *dared* to stand up to them. And guess what, Amethyst! That would be every single magical Creature and all of the humans that are on this earth. Do you really think that they would just give any of us a chance to live if we gave up right now? Well you have to rethink that because they won't!"

"Honey... calm down. I am sure that Amethyst is really just considering all of the options there are," Shadick said holding her hands tighter.

"You are wrong, Shadick. I have known Amethyst my entire life and I have seen her act like this once before. And that was when her mother was teaching us how to fight and she was backed into a corner and she could see no way out. She gave up without even trying. But what she does not realise is, is that her friends are always here to help her. No matter how dire the situation might seem."

"Is what Alexandria is saying true, Amethyst?" Chadromida asked.

"Is it such a sin to try and do the right thing? What if it is the right decision but it just doesn't seem that way in that moment?" Amethyst asked fighting tears.

"No, it is not a sin to try and do the right thing. But what you are suggesting is the worst thing we can do at any time," Shadick answered.

"And what makes you so sure that they wouldn't just keep their word? I mean... for once in their lives they can decide to make the right decision! They could just let us go and both groups could live in peace!"

"And when have you ever seen a Centaur backing down from *anything*? Especially if it is something they want as badly as they want this forest!"

"Perhaps we could just talk to them and try to work out

some kind of plan that will suit everyone."

"You know as well as I do, that will never happen. Not in a hundred years or even a gazillion. And if you really think that I am just going to give up the forest at all then you have completely lost your mind. It is the only reminder I have of my parents as they burned down their home. What I did not tell you about my trip to McLeod's... before I was chased by the Centaurs, I was able to catch a glimpse of the Cottage. And there was nothing but dust left."

"They... they destroyed your parents' cottage?!" Amethyst gasped.

"Yes, they destroyed it," she replied before walking away from them.

Shadick quickly ran after and grabbed her shoulders so that she would stop walking. He turned her around and took her into his arms, hugging her tightly. She did not move at first, just stood there stiffly, but after a minute she relaxed and laid her head against his chest sighing softly.

"I am so sorry that you had to see that. Your parents' home was an important part for you," he murmured into her hair.

"It is not as though I expected less from the Centaurs. But it was still a shock to see the place I had called home in such a sad state."

"We will make them pay for destroying your home."

"If I have to, I will make sure of that myself if I have to. I just don't understand why Amethyst would want to surrender, just because she wishes to see the best in them. Have they not shown multiple times that they do not care about anything or anyone?"

"I think that the stress from all of the fighting is getting to her. In that moment it probably seemed like the most logical thing to do. Although I do not believe that she would have actually surrendered."

"I guess that I was a bit hard on her."

"Hey, lovebirds! This is not really the time or the place for that matter to kiss each other senseless," Chadromida called to them.

"May I ask that the two of you come back here? We really need to discuss the matter at hand. And before you say anything, we are not surrendering," Amethyst said quickly.

Shadick grabbed Alexandria's hand and led her back to Amethyst and Chadromida who were surrounded by some of the Faeries and Unicorns. They decided not to interject the Unicorns as they seemed to be trying to relieve some of the tension by telling jokes.

"So, what is our plan exactly?" Alexandria finally asked squeezing Shadick's hand.

"Well they gave us two hours to make the decision and then

we have to send you to them with our answer. Not sure as to why they said that you should go," Amethyst said shaking her head.

"I know exactly why they want me to go across the field to give them our decision," she replied glancing at Shadick.

"They are planning on killing Lexie. Or at least that is what they told us the night we found out about Justren. Although I was thinking they needed to wait for something more specific," Shadick answered.

"Why did you not tell me about this, Alexandria?! This is one of those things I really think that I should know!" Amethyst said as the colour drained from her face.

"It kind of just slipped my mind until now... and truthfully they haven't tried killing me yet so I thought that they had changed their minds about it," Alexandria said shrugging.

"They are probably waiting for the right moment to do it! You of all people know that you can never tell what is going on in their heads."

"You have not called me Alexandria since your mother took me in when I was six years old!" Alexandria said bursting into laughter.

"Really? I never even realised. I got so used to calling you Alex that I forgot that I used to only call you by your first name."

"Yes, when you still believed that I was some kind of threat."

"You probably were a threat back then... then again, if you think about it. You still are a threat," Shadick said grinning.

"I was only six years old! What kind of threat am I supposed to be at such a young age? And your statement about me being a threat will not be commented on."

"It seems that you never know when I am joking. I was just pulling your leg, honey."

"Oh... right!"

"Back then I seriously believed that you were going to take my mother away from me or something," Amethyst laughed.

"Do you remember the night you kicked me out of your room? Which of course was conveniently for you situated next to the steepest part of the waterfall..."

"I was just teaching you a quick way to transform into an animal. It was not as though I intentionally pushed you off the ledge. Mother was complaining that you were not picking up the transformations as quickly as she would have liked and I thought that I would help."

"Well... I didn't transform into the right animal at the time and almost *drowned*!"

"If I am not mistaken... you turned into a cat!"

"You almost drowned?!" Shadick asked at the same time.

"I was only eight years old and had not learned how to swim yet. My mother had always insisted that my father didn't teach me how to swim because she had never learned. She thought that it would be inappropriate for her daughter to know something that she didn't know how to do," Alexandria said smiling.

"It was in that moment that mother decided that you needed to learn how to swim as soon as possible. And of course, had a very serious talk to me about manners and how I should learn to show respect," Amethyst said.

"I am sorry to interrupt your reminiscing, but the two hours are almost up!" Ashley said anxiously.

"Times has passed so swiftly?"

"YES!!" she shouted making everyone stare.

"Ashley, I have said this before... you really need to learn how to calm down," Alexandria said squinting at the Centaurs.

"Calm... calm?!" she started just as Balditha's voice echoed across the field once again.

"Your time is up... I await the witch and your answer in five minutes."

"He really thinks too much of himself," Alexandria muttered.

"We shall go with you," Shadick said, indicating himself and Chadromida.

"You really do not trust him, do you?" Amethyst asked.

"Only as far as I can throw him."

"I guess that I should get going then, there is no use just standing around here," Alexandria said taking a deep breath. "They might just send a Giant over here to come get the answer."

Nodding to Amethyst she started walking across the field. Her hands shaking and just starting to think that she was alone when she felt Shadick's hand in her own. Glancing to her right she saw Chadromida right there and she smiled a little. The Centaurs seeming to sense some kind of trouble, lifted their bows ready to attack at the first sign of deception. She glanced up at the row of Centaurs to where Balditha was standing grinning arrogantly. Glancing at her up and down in contempt before looking at first Shadick and then Chadromida.

"Did I not tell you that you were to come alone, witch?" he sneered.

"And I made the decision that it is unfair of you to ask that. I mean you have all of your Centaurs as well as the Giants to make sure that you do not get attacked and there I would be, all on my own. I just did not like those odds."

"So you are scared that I will give the order to have you killed?"

"No, we are just making sure that if you decide to kill her

that we will at least take a few of you with us," Shadick said arrogantly.

"Very well then, is that your answer? Did you decide that you will surrender and stop the fighting for good... or did you decide that you are going to take this Ephemeral Seize Fire we offered and start fighting whenever we want?"

"How arrogant do you have to be to believe that we would just surrender to you? Our decision was made even before you offered us a chance to surrender. Our choice had been in fact been made even before this war was started!" Alexandria shouted.

"Well the choice was yours and you have certainly made up your mind. Just know that there is absolutely no going back," Diliante said from beside her husband.

"We have no reason to change our minds about the decision we made," Chadromida said and they turned their backs on the Centaurs.

"You will come to regret your decision!" Balditha shouted at their retreating backs.

It was only when they were about halfway across the field when she started relaxing a little. They had not killed her like they had thought they would. Perhaps they had realised that it would not have helped them if they had and she was thankful for that.

"You did great back there, Lexie. I would not have been able to do it any better," Shadick said lifting their linked hands and kissing it.

"That is very true, Shadick. You would never be able to pull off the egotistical look as well as she just did," Chadromida joked.

"I did not look egotistical!" she replied. "I was just exuding a lot of confidence."

"That is just a very nice way of admitting that you had been very egotistical," Shadick told her grinning.

"You lot seem to be very happy about something," Amethyst said as they got to them.

"Well... for one thing, Alex just told the Centaurs what she thinks of their proposal to surrender," Chadromida told them.

"From the looks of things, their whole army is retreating. We can give the order for our own soldiers to start moving back to Camp so the healing can start happening," Alexandria observed as she watched the Centaurs.

Amethyst nodded, lifting her hand into the air and indicating that the army should move back to camp. A lot of the humans ran to help those that had been injured. Chadromida whistled and jumped onto Falcons back as the rest of the Dragons headed for the Caves. Alexandria was keeping back, walking slowly Ashley at her side.

"You did really well, Amethyst," Shadick complimented her.

"I did well? I almost surrendered to the Centaurs!" she replied sadly.

"You were stressed and thought that you were doing the right thing, just like you said earlier."

"We should catch up to them before they send a search party out to look for us."

"Sounds like a good plan," Shadick said smiling and started walking away.

"It would be an excellent idea to actually make sure that the enemy is completely gone *before* letting your guard down," a voice said from behind them.

Shadick turned around just as Justren got to him; he was unable to do anything as he had sheathed his sword. Amethyst was frozen in fear and could not say a spell quick enough to stop the attack. Justren ran closer and thrust his sword into Shadick's abdomen, the point breaking through the skin at the back.

"And now I will follow my family and celebrate the murder of the Wolfane," Justren sneered as he turned his back on them and disappearing over the hill where his family had been only a few minutes ago...

Chapter 21

Fusion of the Stones

"Shadick!!!" Amethyst shouted as she searched for Alexandria, quickly ordering the Faeries to catch him before he fell.

Why was it her friend had just been there, but now seemed to be nowhere to be seen? She watched as Shadick's body lit up as the Faeries spun around him and gently putting him down.

"Go find Alex! The girl needs to be here."

"Do no... do not call her," Shadick said coughing up blood. "I do not want... her to see me... like this."

"But she may be able to help you!"

"It will only... hurt her more... to see me like... this... she will also... blame herself... for this and that... she was unable... to stop it... from happening."

"Well I am blaming myself for not being able to stop the attack! If only I had the ability to heal you I would do it in a heartbeat!"

"You worry too much, Am... I will be fine and will go back to Camp," he said and tried sitting up, the Faeries flying around him and trying to force him back down.

"Shadick, in case you did not notice... the sword went right through and if you were to move it would do more damage than good right now," she whispered, putting her hand on his shoulder before listening to a faeries whispers. "Thank you for letting me know. Alex is on her way back. She does not know what has happened and it will more than likely be a huge shock for her. Oh, what am I supposed to do?!"

"You were... the one that... wanted to call her here... in the first place," Shadick told her smiling weakly.

"Alex is like my sister and I hate to see her hurt! Oh, why was I not able to sense that Centaurian idiot? We all saw him running away from the group, but thought nothing of it! And to make matters worse, it was Justren!"

"Why is it that everyone has stopped moving back to camp? The Centaurs and all their helpers have already gone so there is no need for us to still be here," Alexandria said confused.

"Now, Alex... there is no need to worry... too much... everything is okay... or rather everything will be okay. There was just a little misfortune that happened after you left," Amethyst said standing up and blocking her view of Shadick.

"Am, what in the world are you talking about? What

misfortune are you talking about? And of course, every..." she started then faltered as Amethyst moved to the side and revealed the ashen Shadick. "SHADICK!! No... no... this cannot be happening."

"Please do not shout honey... I will be fine. It is just a small wound and nothing... nothing to worry about... promise," he whispered before coughing again.

"Just a small wound? You call that a small wound?" she asked falling next to him.

"Okay fine... maybe not... that small... but it is not life threatening."

"Not life threatening? Shadick, in case you did not notice... you have a gaping hole where your stomach used to be. How can you say that it is not life threatening?"

"Alex, calm down! He will be fine as soon as you use your powers to heal him. We will them be able to go back to camp and know that everything is fine."

"But, Am... I have never had healing powers!"

"Oh... I forgot about that! But what are we going to do now?! My mother could heal and not you!"

"I do not want to lose you, Shadick. What can I do to make it better?"

"I promise you that I will be fine, sweetie... all we have to do is get back to... camp and find an elf... who specializes in healing," Shadick said weakly grabbing her hand. "And I promise you... you will never lose me."

"We need a Troll who can carry him! We need to get back to Camp as soon as possible so that he can be healed!" Amethyst said glancing around panicked.

"You know that they... would not be able to carry me... with the sword still right there... it would hurt me more... than I already am," he said seriously before looking at Alexandria. "Honey, you will need... to remove the sword."

"I can't! I will hurt you more than if someone else does it," she said shaking her head.

"But you must..."

"Look at my hands! I am shaking like a leaf. With my luck it would slip out of my hands and stab you somewhere else!"

"Please... do it for me, Lexie... I can assure... you... it will only make it worse if it stays."

"But..." she started but looked in his eyes and knew that she had no other choice. Nodding she stood up and wrapped her hands around the hilt of the sword.

"I trust you, Lexie," he whispered closing his eyes.

"Oh, that makes me feel so much better," she whispered meekly.

"Just do it, Alex! The sooner you do it the sooner it will be done," Amethyst said stepping out of the way.

She nodded again and took a deep breath. Biting her lip and hoping that she would do it right, she pulled on the hilt firmly and felt it slowly give way. She closed her eyes without realizing it and pulled harder, hearing the squelch as the blade came free from Shadick's stomach. A soft groan of pain escaping from his lips.

Slowly opening her one eye and then the other looking down at the sword she now held in her hands. One would not think that this sword had just been in his stomach if it had not been for the blooding dripping down the blade. It was then that she glanced at Shadick and saw that he was not moving and his eyes were closed.

"Oh no, oh no... this isn't happening!"

"He is still breathing, Alexandria. He just passed out from the pain and should be fine," a Dwarf told her bending next to Shadick.

Amethyst indicated that the Troll pick him up and Alexandria relaxed a little. As she looked up, she noticed that the Creatures and humans had made a pathway for them and was saluting them with their weapons held high. A tear rolling down her cheek slowly as she watched the procession.

"You did really well, Alex. You may have really saved his life by removing that sword," Amethyst said standing next to her.

"But he is still in so much danger and I am not sure at all whether the Elves would be able to heal him," she replied.

"The only way we can be sure of that is to ask them. If they cannot heal him, I am sure that they will know someone. All is not lost."

"What if I lose him, Am? I know that I have not known him for that long, but I do not think that I would survive if he died."

"I promise you that you will not lose him, Alex," Amethyst said hugging her.

"But..."

"There is no need for buts. He will make it through this alive and well. And *if* something happens and I am not saying that anything is going to happen. But if something does happen to him, I will be there to help you get through it."

"I really do hope that nothing happens to him."

"I can tell that your feelings for him have changed, haven't they? I have noticed it before, but did not say anything."

"You have really been able to tell that?"

"Yes, I have been feeling the power emanating from the two whenever you are next to each other. Love is a very powerful emotion and has moved through the ages. There is no stop to it and it can be felt from miles away."

"My feelings for Shadick has been growing stronger and stronger, from the very first moment we met. And something may have happened between us the night before you arrived at the Caves."

"I knew it! I have felt the vibes between you since the very first minute I arrived," Amethyst said smiling.

"Then why if you felt those vibes between us, did you separate us?"

"I would have been able to cut the tension between the two of you with that bloody sword in your hands. I thought that it would be for the best to give you some time apart so that you both could sort through the feelings. Unfortunately, I was not able to see that your time together would be so limited once you did return from the quests. I now realise my fault in that and I apologise. I could easily have sent some of the other warriors on the quests, but went against my own thoughts."

"There is no reason to worry about it, Am. You only did what you thought was right and I can ensure you that I would have done exactly the same. I think in some strange way you strengthened what is between us."

"You are a wonderful person and from what I have seen Shadick realises that. Besides who wouldn't want to get closer to you?"

"We should probably get back to camp and find an Elf to help him."

"I am sure that one of the Faeries have already gone

through the Camp in search of someone capable of healing so there is no need for us to worry. But yes, let us get back."

Alexandria started walking away from the battlefield still carrying the sword although not realising it. About halfway up the hill she realised that Amethyst was still on the same spot and frowned.

"Is everything okay, Am? I thought that we were going back to camp?"

"I just thought that I felt some kind of power stir in the air."

"I'm not feeling anything... are you sure? Although I'm sure that you would more readily be able to tell."

"You are stronger than I am and you know that. As for if I am sure... yes I am. But perhaps it was just some residue energy after the battle," she commented and started walking towards her pausing when she reached Alexandria. "What is that in your hair, Alex?"

"The three stones that Shadick and I retrieved... I thought that it would be a safe enough place to keep them as we never knew when we might need them," she replied touching the stones.

"The colour of the Stones seems to be more intense than before, but perhaps it is just the exhaustion talking. Shall we go?

"Yes please, I need to make sure that Shadick is doing

better."

They walked to the Camp quickly and split up when the whole place seemed to have come to life. Amethyst walked off to find one of the Faeries and find out what had been happening and what they had been able to have gathered. Alexandria wandered around looking for Shadick, wondering where they might have taken him. She would not be able to relax unless she was able to find him and assure herself that he was okay.

"Excuse me," she called to one of the Dwarves. "Could you perhaps tell me where they have taken Shadick?"

He just shook his head after a few seconds and continued shuffling to wherever he was planning to go. She stopped what she thought was some kind of Tiger warrior, but it just growled at her and continued on its way. Exasperated she continued walking between the tents hoping to see anything that might be able to show her the right way.

"Miss Alexandria!" someone called her and she realised that it was the Dwarf from the battlefield. "Mister Shadick is just through that tent over there. We put him on one of the beds for recuperation."

"Thank you so much! Sorry... I did not catch your name?"

"The name is Lagonith, Miss Alexandria."

"You may call me Alex, Lagonith," she told him but he

ignored her and kept walking.

She shook her head and walked towards the medical tent that he had indicated. It was as she was walking that the true extent of damage hit her. Those who had not been injured were taking care of their fallen comrades and she was shocked at how badly some of them had been injured. As she entered the tent, she noticed a lot of nurses bustling around trying to get to all of the people that were on the cots. She bit her lip when she noticed that a lot of the nurses seemed to be gathered around his bed.

"Is he okay?" she asked approaching his bed.

"He sure is a tough one, that one," the one nurse answered her.

She walked around the nurse and straight to the bed he was on although he still seemed to be unconscious and unmoving. A small gasp escaped her lips when she got to his side and noticed how pale he was. Taking a deep breath, she glanced lowered and saw the stab wound. She put her hand over her mouth trying not to scream and to try and control the shaking. A nurse touched her shoulder causing her to jump in fright.

"Is everything well, my dear? It looks as though a ghost has just walked over your tomb."

"I am doing fine, thank you for the concern. But more importantly how is he doing?"

"I am sorry to say that if he does not get some proper medical treatment soon that he will not be with us for long. His health has been deteriorating ever since he was brought here."

"No! He has to get better. I can't lose him when I only found him not too long ago," Alexandria said sinking to her knees next to his bed.

A sudden flurry of lights from the entrance announced Amethyst's arrival. The Faeries flying straight at Alexandria pulling her to her feet and soft hands wiping at the tears running down her face.

"You have to keep strong, Alex. He needs not just his own strength but yours as well," Amethyst whispered wrapping her arms around her friend.

"I am trying, Am. But it isn't easy to stay strong when he is just lying there hurt and I can do nothing."

"I know, but you have to try your best."

They were suddenly pushed away from the bed as the nurses ran to him, his body shaking uncontrollably. She gasped and hid her face in Amethysts shoulder crying. It was too difficult to just watch it happening and know that she was not able to help. The nurses as one suddenly moved away from the bed and she heard him calling her softly.

As she reached the bed, Shadick tried lifting his hand to touch her face, but was too weak. She grabbed his hand and held it against her tightly.

"Save your strength..." she whispered.

"It is too late for me, my love," he replied weakly.

"No! I know that you will make it. I will not let you die, because I will not survive then."

"Lexie, you need to fight for what you know is right. Stop the Centaurs from taking over the land. Stop them from killing anymore of the Creatures."

"I can't do this alone... I will only keep fighting with your help."

"I know that you think... you are not strong enough for this... but you are, Lexie."

"You promised me that I would not lose you... you promised me!"

"I apologise that this... is the one promise... that I am unable to keep."

"No... I cannot lose you Shadick!"

"We will be able to get you help, Shadick. There are a couple of healers in the South that work wonders with stab wounds," Amethyst said.

"It... it is too late... for that, Am," he whispered before starting to cough. Blood splattering over the sheets that had been placed over him the nurses flinching as they could not help him in anyway.

"No... no! Shadick please do not leave me," she whispered desperately.

"It is... too late..." he whispered before going completely still.

"I love you... Shadick."

"I am sorry to inform you that he has gone from this world," one of the nurses said as she covered him with a sheet. "He does not know pain anymore which is better for him."

"NO!! He cannot be gone; it is not possible. He promised me that he will never leave me."

"Alex, it is too late! Let us go and get something for you to calm your nerves. And we can have you rest."

"But... but, Am. I love him."

"I know you do, my sister. But we cannot do anything about it anymore. He... he has passed into the other world. A better world," she replied choking back tears of her own.

Alexandria looked down at Shadick's lifeless body and thought about how much she loved him. No, how much she had loved him. She corrected herself mentally. The dam of tears that she had been holding back suddenly burst and she shook from all the tears.

"Your majesty we need to prepare his body for burial," the nurse said desperately.

"I know that it is hard to hear, but we cannot stay here.

And... Alex, what is happening to the Stones in your hair?!" Amethyst asked as the Stones started glowing.

Alexandria was deaf to what was going on around her, the glow from the Stones growing bigger. The pale blue light extended slowly from her own body to Shadick's. But it was soon filling the entire tent before stretching further and enveloping the entire Camp.

The Stones lifted from her hair of their own accord and started circling around Alexandria. The air seemed to get lighter and darker at the same time and Amethyst frowned. There seemed to be a miniature storm to be happening within the circle of stones, although Alexandria seemed to be untouched.

She tried moving, but was unable to and felt herself start panicking as the stones got closer to her friend. How was she supposed to with something she did not even understand? In front of her eyes she watched the stones become one.

There was no more Aquadious, Trilate Amethyst or Septer Quartz but something completely new and unheard of. It was the colour of the sky and was in the shape of heart. The light finally dimmed around the camp just as the stone seemed to fuse with Alexandria, herself.

"Alex, is everything okay? I am not sure what just happened but it was powerful," Amethyst asked glancing around.

"It is called the Nornien Stone... and it has one true heir and it stays with that one person until the day they die," Starlansha said as she walked into the tent.

"I have heard of it, which is why I sent them on the quests. But when I tried combining them, nothing happened."

"That is because it was never meant for you. It only happens with its one true heir; before then the stones will be just that. It is only when the possessor of stones has real need of it that they will be able to increase their power ten-fold and they will be more powerful than anyone would have been able to imagine."

"I thought that the fusion was done?! What is happening this time?" Amethyst asked panicked.

"I do believe that she is calling forth the power of the Stone," Starlansha told her as Alexandria placed her hands over Shadick's wound and it started healing.

She then moved her hands towards his heart. Without warning Shadick suddenly sat up coughing for air as though he had been drowning. Tears were still running down her cheeks as she healed him, although she seemed to not notice what she was doing.

"What just happened?" he asked and grabbed Alexandria as the power seemed to leave her and she dropped. "Lexie, is everything okay?"

"Shadick?" she asked lightly touching his face.

"As far as I can tell, I am still me. Although very confused."

"Shadick is alive!!" a nurse shouted out of the tent.

"The patients have made a full recovery! We have no explanation as to why!" another said before collapsing

"Are you sure that you are feeling okay, Shadick?" Amethyst asked walking closer as a nurse rushed to her friends side

"I am feeling a lot better than just okay. But as I said I am not sure what is going on... the last thing I remember was dying," he answered grimacing.

"Alex was able to heal you."

"Honey, are you feeling okay?"

"Are you really alive or am I just having a really screwed up dream?" she asked.

"I can assure you that I am more alive than before. And I love you too."

She threw her arms around his neck and hugged him tightly and not letting him go even though the nurses reprimanded her. They tried pulling her away from him, but she refused to let go and Amethyst shooed them away.

"You see, I kept my promise... with your help, of course," he told her laughing softly and holding her tightly.

"Never, ever leave me again. I beg you."

"I promise that I will not leave you, as much as that is possible," he said then stood up with her in his arms. "I thought you said that she was not able to use healing abilities?"

"It is not one of her natural abilities, but the Nornien Stone has given her a lot of new powers," Starlansha commented.

"The Nornien Stone? What is this thing you are talking about?"

"It is the Stones from the myth of the Norns, which are the three Faerie sisters of Fate. Amethyst tried and failed to fuse the stones as only the rightful holder has that ability. And as we have noticed a few minutes ago, Alexandria is the true holder."

"I think that my brain is still recovering from dying because that makes me even more confused."

"The Stones that you and Alexandria retrieved during your quests. As well as the Aquadious Stone that my Grandfather gave her fused together to form the Nornien Stone."

"Does this Stone give the true holder the ability to heal?"

"Not just the ability to heal apparently. But it is supposed to strengthen the holder ten-fold," Amethyst said hugging Shadick carefully.

"Then I am very happy that she had been able to release the power of the stones. Otherwise I would not be here right now. I really do owe my life to you, Lexie."

"No, you don't... although I am very happy that I was able

to save you," she whispered looking up at him.

"So am I, my love."

"Do you feel okay, Alexandria?" Starlansha asked stepping closer.

"Why do you ask Star? I feel absolutely fine actually."

"I expected you to feel tired or drained after receiving that amount of power."

"I feel great now that I think about it. Better than I have the last while."

"Could we perhaps go and get some food? Personally, it feels as though days have passed in the last couple of hours." Amethyst asked smiling.

"I have to vote for food as well, honestly. Dying and being brought back makes a man hungry," Shadick joked.

They nodded to the astounded nurses and walked out of the tent and towards the smell of food. Amethyst saw that it had not just healed Shadick, but that the entire camp was truly sitting up and they all seemed to be in good spirits.

"You were really able to heal the entire Camp, Alex!" she said glancing behind her, smiling when she noticed that Shadick and Alexandria were walking together hand in hand.

For the moment there was no need for them to have to worry and she could see that it made them happy...

Chapter 22

The Farewell

That night he sat next to Alexandria as they gathered around the fire to listen to the stories the warriors were telling. Some of the stories were quite outlandish and made them laugh while others were not believable at all and he shook his head. He laughed at one of the jokes about an old war story that someone was telling them, but he was not truly paying attention to him.

His thoughts were with what he had to do next. It was important that he got back to his own mission, but he was not sure whether he would be able to leave Alexandria behind. He had grown very fond of her since all of this had started. From the very beginning he had known that it would be dangerous for him to fall for someone which is why he had been trying to avoid people. Yet Alexandria had crept into his heart and he knew that she would not be going anywhere.

She seemed to be at peace as she sat next to him, completely relaxed and holding a warm drink in her hands. It was as though she was living herself into some of the stories and it made him smile. Deciding that it was time that he told her about his plans, he lightly grabbed her hand as he stood up and pulled her up after him. She smiled and waved at the Creatures and humans sitting around the fire, holding his hand tighter.

He quickly paused next to Amethyst and assured her that they would not be going too far before continuing their walk away from all of the people gathered there. Alexandria glanced around her and noticed Roslata standing away from the fire. She seemed very mad and was looking at her with contempt as though she knew that she would not be able to get Shadick to herself. Starlansha was trying to talk to her sister, but she was being given the cold shoulder.

"And where exactly is it that you are taking me?" she finally asked smiling.

He did not reply, but squeezed her hand and kept walking. After a few minutes of quiet walking she heard the stream and her heart fluttered happily. This place had become like a second home to them and she knew that she did not have to worry about being bothered.

Not long after, she spotted the stream where they had lain a few nights before. Truthfully it felt as though they had not been here for years with everything that had happened the last while. When they reached the stream, he took her into his arms and started kissing her passionately. Reaching up and wrapping her arms around his neck, deepening the kiss even more.

"Lexie, we really need to talk about something," he whispered with his mouth on the nape of her neck.

"Does that really have to happen right now, Shadick? Could we not just talk later?" she asked lightly putting her hands on the inside of his shirt.

"Very well then, we will talk later," he said biting her lip lightly before taking her top off and letting it drop to the floor...

"What exactly did you want to talk about?" Alexandria asked lazily a few hours later still in his arms.

"Hmm... give me a minute to think about that... you made me forget what I wanted to talk about," he said then laughed when she lightly slapped his chest.

"Do not give me the lies about not remembering what you wanted to say. I can see in your eyes that you just wish to avoid it."

"Very well then, but I warn you that you will not be happy with what I have to say."

"Oh dear, I already do not like the tone in your voice... but please, tell me what you need to."

"Do you remember the first night we met and I told you

about the mission I was on and that as soon as I could I would get back to it?"

"Yes, I do remember the conversation that we had. But it is not as though the war against the Centaurs is over..."

"I know that, sweetie. And I also know that the Centaurs will not call an end to the Ephemeral Seize Fire until their armies are stronger. And that would take years to achieve."

"Are you trying to tell me that you are leaving, Shadick?"

"Something like that, yes..."

She quickly sat up and grabbed one of the shirts laying on the ground, randomly noticing that it was Shadick's as she pulled it on. She jumped up and paced away from him a few steps frowning and crossing her arms.

"So you want to leave me, again? Even after I just saved your life? And please do not pretend that it is not exactly what you are planning."

"So now you are holding bringing me back to life over my head?! Even though I have told you numerous of times that I appreciate it? And yes, I am planning on leaving to continue my mission as soon as possible."

"Of course, I am not holding it over your head! I would do it again in the blink of an eye."

"It sure seems as though that is what you are doing."

"Well, I'm not!" she shouted at him and turned her back on

him biting her lip to stop the tears.

He pulled his pants back on and walked towards her until he was just behind her. "Lexie, I just have to finish my mission. And it is not as though it will take that long to finish, I promise."

"I'm not sure whether I will be able to control my new powers if you were to leave... I'm worried."

"Even if I am not here, you would be able to control your powers. You are a strong woman, capable of a lot more than you think."

"But am I truly strong enough to control these new powers I have been given?"

"Yes, you are strong enough to control them. You being able to control them or not has nothing to do with me being here or not."

"I have been a lot stronger ever since you showed up in my life and that is the truth."

"I just helped it along, Lexie. I was just able to show you that you are capable of a lot more than you thought you were. It will not go away if I were to leave. Besides, you will be busy with training and you will be even more powerful than ever before."

"The training seems to be very difficult and I am unsure whether I will be successful."

"You will be able to do the training quite easily, honey," he told her putting his hands on her shoulders.

"And what if I am not able to do the training? What if something goes really badly while I'm training?"

"I promise you that nothing will go wrong as you will have a lot people around you to help you. They will be able to teach you the things you need to know."

"Then do as you will," she told him shrugging off his hands and grabbing her clothes. Quickly disappearing behind a tree, emerging a minute later fully clothed. Dropping his shirt and running back to Camp dodging the trees.

"Lexie! Come back here please. We really need to discuss this," he shouted after her and shaking his head.

She ran blindly through the forest, not noticing where she was going. Without warning she ran into something really hard and fell on the floor. She looked up at the trees sighing softly and trying to get the strength to move. Exclaiming softly when she was suddenly pulled up off the floor and placed on her feet.

"I really thought that I had gotten away from you this time. But I guess I should have known better than that," she said despondently.

"And you should really pay more attention to where you are going. It could have been anything you ran into," he told her seriously.

"I did not run into you! You were the one that decided to

stand in front of me, even though you saw that I was heading in your direction."

"Let us not fight about something as impractical as this."

"Yes, seeing that we are already fighting about you leaving to go on some mission of yours."

"We are not fighting about it."

"Oh yes I forget. You have already made up your mind about the decision, now didn't you? You just decided that you should inform me of your plans the night *before* you leave."

"It really is for the best, sweetie. If I am successful, I will come back to you stronger than ever!"

"And if the Centaurs call off this Seize Fire while you are away?"

"Then you can send me a message by one of the Wolves to inform me of what is happening and I will return as soon as I am able to."

"I cannot believe this! I... I tell you that I... I love you and I know that I did not hear wrong when you said it back and now you just want to up and leave?"

"I did mean it, Lexie. I still do! But I need to finish my own mission so that I can get stronger for you. Then I promise that I will be back."

Exasperatedly she threw her arms in the air, screaming softly as a thunder bolt hit right in front of her.

"Do you see why you need to go into training? So that you can actually control your powers! Otherwise something like that might happen and hurt someone that is next to you!" he said grabbing her shoulders. "And I know that you do not want to harm anyone."

"I understand that, but it would have been so awesome if I could have trained with you. As I am sure that you could teach me a lot. It is not as though I don't accept that my powers have gotten stronger since I got the Nornien Stone. As well as ever since you have come into my life and okay, I admit that they will not disappear when you do."

"I am sorry to say that he would not be able to help you with your training, Alexandria. You will be going to the deepest parts of the Ocean to do your training and he cannot breathe underwater," Starlansha said stepping away from a tree.

"How long have you been standing there exactly?" she asked surprised.

"Not that long at all... I noticed the thunderbolt and knew that it had been you. I knew that it was important for us to get started on your training as soon as possible."

"But that was nothing!"

"She is right, honey. And my mission is up north near the Icy Caverns," Shadick said.

"And what are you going to be doing there? I've heard a lot

of stories about how treacherous the roads are not to mention the Creatures that live there!"

"For now, I cannot tell you what my mission involves. It will stay secret until I have successfully finished my mission. And you do not need to worry as I know that it is dangerous there, which is why I am going there by myself."

"Alexandria, you have to get training so that you can use your powers to its maximum potential. It is especially important in these troubled times that are lying ahead," Starlansha added seriously.

She looked between the two of them at a loss for words. How could she explain to them how she felt Shadick when it felt as though it was obvious? Yes, she had told him that she loves him and he had replied. Yet she was unsure whether he had taken it seriously or not.

"Lexie, I need to leave at first light," Shadick said suddenly.

"Then I think that should be the time that she leaves for her training as well. Perhaps it will help her not think of you too much, as I know she will."

"How dare you think that my life can be organised right in front of me as though it does not mean anything to me? I would appreciate it if I were to give my own opinion on what I will be doing next," Alexandria replied angrily.

"I apologise as that was not my intention, Alexandria. I just thought that it would be for the best that you get started with your training as soon as possible."

"You are right of course; the faster I learn how to control my new powers the sooner we can end this war. And the sooner that is the less fatalities there will be when the Seize Fire is cancelled," she said taking a deep breath and shaking her head.

"That is exactly what I meant! Besides you will not be alone while you are training as I will accompany you."

"No, I shall be going on my own. Who knows what could go wrong the first few times I unleash my powers? I wouldn't want to hurt you."

"I shall leave the two of you so that I can go prepare for our departure," Starlansha said walking away.

"I know that you will be able to do the training, Lexie. I have faith in you and your abilities. I believe in you and I know that you believe in yourself as well. The day you finish your training I will be there, waiting for you. I will be the very first one to greet you. And that is a promise I will most undoubtedly be keeping. Even if it turns out to be the very last promise I make to anyone," Shadick told her walking towards her.

"You have not disappointed me thus far so I know that you will keep your promise," she said then laughed softly. "Except of course when you died, even though you had promised me that you would never leave me."

"You see, there is light at the end. I was able to see your smile once again and I will carry it with me during my mission. I will let it strengthen me when things feel as though they get too much."

"Then I better be positive then... who knows what you would do to me if I wasn't happy. Perhaps set one of your Wolf friends loose on me!"

"You know that I would never do anything to hurt you. And I would give my own life to keep you safe if it came down to it."

"I know you would and I appreciate that," she whispered as she turned around and kissed him passionately.

"You better appreciate it," he growled softly before bringing his mouth down to hers and returning the kiss fervently.

Standing next to Amethyst the next morning was one of the hardest things that she had ever been asked to do. Shadick has asked her very nicely to stay there, knowing that it would only make it harder to say goodbye if she was next to him. He was standing with some of the other warriors discussing details of the area he was going to. The previous evening they had made love one last time before they had to return to camp. They needed to make sure that he had everything that he might possibly need while on his mission.

"Surely you know that everything will work out for the best, Alex?" Amethyst asked her.

"Yes, I do know that. It just feels a little strange for him to leave so soon after the battle," Alexandria replied hugging herself.

"He will return before you know it. Besides... you will be so busy with your own training that you will hardly notice his absence."

"I know that I will be busy with training. But there is no doubt in my mind that I will notice his absence."

"And how can you know that? You will most likely be so tired that you will hardly remember to have dinner!" Amethyst joked then sighed when her friend lightly touched her chest. "You will survive! It is not the end of the world... yet."

"Not if I have anything to say about it," a voice said from behind them.

"Roslata, why do you even bother trying to get attention? Especially when you know that Shadick doesn't feel anything for you?" Alexandria asked not turning towards the other girl.

"Because unlike you... I have known him for much longer. So I know that little girls cannot possibly keep him happy for long."

"I was wondering why Shadick was ignoring you! Thank you for clearing that up for me."

Amethyst giggled then tried to control herself when she realised that some of the Dwarves were staring at her and pointing.

"I was actually talking about you. This mission of his? How do you know that he isn't just lying to you just to get away from you? An excuse because he is trying to be gentlemanly or whatever it is."

"Because unlike you, he does not lie. And he would not lie about something that is this important to him. And the simple fact that he mentioned this mission to me since the first time we met."

"You are being such a naive child! You think that you can trust everyone, just because you are so pure of heart and innocent."

Alexandria's temper flared and with it the wind started blowing around them

"And not everyone is as bad as you seem to think they are."

"Alex, please just calm down!" Amethyst said panicked, glancing to where Shadick was still standing with the Trolls and Dwarves.

"Oh, so you mean like Justin and how much you trusted him? Oh wait! I forgot that his name is in actual fact Justren. The one guy you thought was so pure of heart but then turned into the one responsible for the death of *how* many magical

Creatures?"

"Roslata, will you just keep your mouth shut?!"

"Please do not let met even start with you. The one who thinks she knows everything about everyone and everything just because she is the Queen. Also, the one who believes for even a second that she can be a better leader than her mother."

"Do not start with my friends, Roslata. You can have a go at me all you like, but my friends are to be kept out of this," Alexandria said as the wind speed picked up even more.

"I will have a go at whomever I choose and you have no right telling me what to do. I am an independent woman who does as she pleases."

"Oh yes and throwing insults at the one person who was willing to take you in if you had wanted to is what you think is the *right thing to do*? Or in fact any pleasant to those people around you?"

"I can talk to her as I see fit. It was not her who gave us the option and I am disappointed to see how badly things have gone since she took over."

"I, on the other hand think that you should stop back chatting everyone and actually be nice to Amethyst," Shadick said finally, appearing next to them and putting his hand on Alexandria's arm. "Calm down, sweetheart."

"And now she needs to be rescued by you? Well who would

have guessed that *she* needs rescuing?!"

"You know very well that your attitude does not impress me at all and I am shocked to see that nothing much has changed since the last time I saw you."

"And you do realise that the last time you saw me, you were on top of me?"

"No, I was not in your bed Roslata. I have never been in your *bed*."

"Whatever makes you sleep better at night, Shadick," she said walking away from them.

"I am telling you this in full honesty... we kind of had a thing going a few years ago, but I ended it when I found out that she was sleeping with Chadromida behind my back. I have not touched her ever since."

"I trust you and I know that you have been with other people before me," Alexandria answered him.

"I appreciate your trust, thank you. I should get going... the sooner I start the faster I can finish with my mission and get back to you."

"Oh... right... I guess you have a point," she whispered smiling sadly.

"I will send you a message by Wolf or Eagle as soon it is possible. Please do the same if you need any help at all," he told her hugging her tightly and kissing the top of her head.

"I will do so and will await your messages with bated breath."

"Work hard during your training and I will see you when we are both done with what is needed of us."

"Good luck with your trip and dream of me every night," she whispered.

He nodded then walked to the warriors to say goodbye to them all, it seemed as though they all moved as one to greet him. Alexandria stood to the side watching Shadick's receding back, fighting the urge to run after him or to even cry.

It was difficult to watch him walk away, but she knew that in the end it would be for the best and she couldn't wait for that day when he would return...

www.ingramcontent.com/pod-product-compliance
Lightning Source LLC
Chambersburg PA
CBHW030542260626
47157CB00006B/2160